Praise for PERRY and CLOSER B

"Perry Chafe's *Closer by Sea*, is a coming-of-age story full of friendship, love of the ocean, cod tongues, bullies, boyhood crushes, mysteries, and monstrously beautiful icebergs—fast one-liners and sharp wit. Chafe writes about what it means to belong and to be cast out. About the end of a kind of life in outport Newfoundland and the end of childhood. About moving on. All of this with a pacing that clips along at a thousand knots a minute. Chafe shows how ninety percent of a human being is below the surface, and how we have to dive deep to know each other. These characters are rich, multifaceted, and unforgettable. And this novel has all the makings of a beloved, classic bildungsroman, as tender as tender can be."

LISA MOORE, bestselling author of
Caught and *This Is How We Love*

"Chafe's teen mystery is salt-stained Newfoundland mixed with West Irish legend and the classic adventure of *Goonies* and *Stand by Me*. Equal parts haunting, heartbreaking, and hilarious the reader is drawn into the tragic 1990s Grand Banks cod decline, foreboding paternal absence, and growing up an uncertain Islander amid great social change. Sure to be loved on our shores and beyond."

JESSE THISTLE, #1 bestselling author of *From the Ashes*

"Tiny, isolated fishing towns are postcard cute and perfectly wholesome. Until they are not. Where there's the charm of kids cutting cod tongues, there's also the tragedy of men lost at sea and the horror of a missing teen while suspicions and rumors are whispered on the wharf and altar alike. In *Closer by Sea*, my lifelong friend and Petty Harbour native Perry Chafe has seamlessly woven the innocence and underbelly of Perigo Island in a who-done-it dance that will keep you guessing till the final page."

ALAN DOYLE, musician and bestselling author of *Where I Belong*

"*Closer by Sea* will have you on the edge of your seat with each page turned. Filled with dialogue that will stay with you long after you're finished and characters that will stay with you for the rest of your life. An astonishing debut by someone sure to be your new favorite author. He's mine."

MARK CRITCH, comedian, bestselling author and cocreator of hit TV show *Son of a Critch*

"At the center of Perry Chafe's endearing novel *Closer by Sea* is a deeply emotional exploration of the important ties that bind us to the people and places we love. It's also a fine coming-of-age story compellingly grounded in adventure, intrigue, best friends, and the struggle to find a way through all the awkwardness of adolescence. Set in the unique landscape of an isolated island off the coast of Newfoundland, Chafe's novel brims with seafaring charm and the marvelous details of a fishing village on the verge of economic collapse. *Closer by Sea* is a bittersweet, lovingly told tale that's sure to win your heart."

WILLIAM KENT KRUEGER, *New York Times* bestselling author of *This Tender Land*

"Set in an ancient Newfoundland community on the cusp of momentous change, *Closer by Sea* is an evocative, tender novel with a haunting beauty that lingers long after you finish the last page."

ELIZA REID, author of *Secrets of the Sprakkar*

"A memorable coming-of-age tale in the spirit of Ray Bradbury and Stephen King. There is mystery and danger, shadowy figures who are not quite who they seem, and a wistfulness for that strange and beautiful time bridging our younger and older selves—but Perry Chafe's story is uniquely his own, uniquely of his place and of its people. With *Closer by Sea*, Chafe stakes his place in Newfoundland's writerly pantheon."

CRAIG DAVIDSON, bestselling author of *Cataract City* and *Precious Cargo*

"Perry Chafe writes in the best tradition of the Hardy Boys books I read as a young fellow. He makes the smallest of places as big as the world. Outport Newfoundland here is filled with mystery and adventure, as it always was for us as kids. Perry Chafe hasn't forgotten the wonder of Newfoundland; it's there on every page. I loved reading this book."

SEAMUS O'REGAN, Member of Parliament

"A standout novel and story from a singular, unique voice. Perry Chafe manages to grab our hearts and doesn't let go until the final page. Told through the eyes of a young man named Pierce, we experience firsthand the struggles, heartbreak, and repercussions of losing someone close to us, too soon. At first glance *Closer by Sea* is a thrilling mystery, but as you delve deeper, it's truly the story of loss, innocence, mourning, and friendship. I cannot recommend this book enough. Bravo!"

ALLAN HAWCO, award-winning actor, writer, and producer

CLOSER BY SEA

A NOVEL

PERRY CHAFE

PUBLISHED BY SCRIBNER CANADA

New York   London   Toronto   Sydney   New Delhi

SCRIBNER
CANADA

Scribner Canada
An Imprint of Simon & Schuster, Inc.
166 King Street East, Suite 300
Toronto, Ontario M5A 1J3

This Scribner Canada edition May 2023

SCRIBNER CANADA and colophon are trademarks
of Simon & Schuster, Inc.

For information about special discounts for bulk purchases, please contact Simon & Schuster Special Sales at 1-800-268-3216 or CustomerService@simonandschuster.ca.

Manufactured in the United States of America

3   5   7   9   10   8   6   4

Library and Archives Canada Cataloguing in Publication

Title: Closer by sea / Perry Chafe.
Names: Chafe, Perry, author.
Description: Simon & Schuster Canada edition.
Identifiers: Canadiana (print) 2022043199X | Canadiana (ebook) 20220432058 | ISBN 9781982185251 (softcover) | ISBN 9781982185268 (EPUB)
Classification: LCC PS8605.H3275 C56 2023 | DDC C813/.6—dc23

ISBN 978-1-9821-8525-1
ISBN 978-1-9821-8526-8 (ebook)

For my sister, Diane Kieley,
who was with me in spirit on this journey

PROLOGUE

People really can vanish without a trace. I was only nine years old when I learned that my father, Luke Jacobs, would never be coming home again. It was the summer of 1988. My uncle found his thirty-foot trap skiff drifting a couple of miles out from Perigo Island—our island—just off the northeast coast of Newfoundland. He was not on board.

Many believed that my father disappeared on a fishing ground known as the Saddle, where the depth of the ocean would suddenly plummet hundreds of feet. It was a tricky fishing berth to navigate. Nestled between two large groupings of rocks, it was an area notorious for rogue waves, the result of ocean swell interacting with fast-moving currents. Such waves had been known to sink ships.

A search was conducted by the coast guard with just about every single boat on the island joining in to help, but after two days, it was called off. Forty-eight hours of searching for a life. His body was never recovered. It's a tragic story, all too familiar amongst those who make a living at sea. The cold North Atlantic had claimed another soul.

For the longest time, I couldn't believe my father was gone. He was an experienced fisherman from a long line of fishermen and there was no storm or even rough weather that day. And the boat, which came to rest in our back garden, showed no signs of damage. Even though the wooden vessel had been riding the waves some ten years before Dad bought it, it was extremely well built, a testament to the centuries-old boat builders' tradition on the island. Unfortunately, due to a combination of outward migration and waning interest in the ways of the past, these skills were not being handed down to future generations like they once were. Some years later, a professor of mine would refer to these artisans as the last of a kind, meaning when they left this world, they would take all that knowledge with them.

My father's boat was constructed out of spruce and juniper trees, and was designed so that heavy cod traps could be pulled aboard in such a way that the side of the boat almost touched the top of the water. It had a large single-cylinder engine mounted in a small motor house with the propeller running to the stern. And though it was meant to haul traps with three or four men aboard, my father was a hand-liner, which meant he caught fish using lines and hooks baited with capelin in early summer and squid later in the season. It also meant he could fish alone.

Though the official search ended after just two days, my uncle Donny and a few other fishermen continued to search for another two days. But their efforts were in vain, and a service was held shortly thereafter at our church to commemorate the life of a husband and a father. It was standing-room only in the small timber-built structure as the community paid its respects. There would be no interment to follow since there was no body to be laid to rest. Instead, my mother placed a small, flat headstone in the family plot. At the time, I didn't understand why she would do this because to me a missing body didn't mean a dead one. Maybe my father made it to one of the smaller islands nearby or even to that grouping of rocks where murres, gannets, and puffins nested.

After the service, I decided to take matters into my own hands. It was a Sunday; no boats would be leaving the harbor. I packed a lunch of assorted cookies, casseroles, and sandwiches that folks had dropped off over the past week. People always took to the kitchen in times like these. Food expressed condolence.

I waited until the last visiting family left and my mother succumbed to exhaustion. Then I grabbed my knapsack and headed out the door.

The late afternoon sun poked through the billowing clouds overhead as I walked along the shoulder of the winding road toward the harbor. I kept tight to the guardrail that served as a buffer between me and the jagged coastline. It was a narrow road and drivers needed every inch of it to safely navigate their way along. A cool breeze blew in off the water and filled my lungs with salt air as it had done since I took my very first breath. It was eerily quiet and I encountered no one on my journey. Even the gulls had soared farther out to sea since there were no free meals to be had at the idle fish plant.

I turned down the steep gravel lane that led to the wharf and made my way around to the fishing stage at the south side of the harbor where my mother's brother, Uncle Donny, tied up his small fiberglass speedboat. I had been out with him and my father a few times for a quick spin in the bay. I'd watched my father and him fire up the engine before navigating the boat through the narrows. They even let me take the tiller on a couple of occasions. I figured I could do the same again without them. Once outside the mouth of the harbor, I'd head northeast, following the small brass compass suspended in a wooden box that my uncle kept in the cuddy, which was a covered storage space in the boat.

I threw my knapsack into the stern and began to climb down the makeshift wooden ladder. But just a few rungs into the journey, I stopped. I found myself paralyzed with fear. Though it must have been only a few minutes that I was frozen in that spot, it felt like an eternity.

"You coming or going?" a female voice called down from above.

I looked up to see her standing there. She stepped closer, blocking the glare from the sun. Anna Tessier. Twelve years old to my nine.

"I don't know what I'm doing," I replied.

"You don't know if you're coming or going?" She chuckled. "Boys."

"I might go. Or I might stay," I said, my knuckles white from gripping the rungs so tightly.

Anna knelt down and extended her hand to me.

"Come back up. You can decide the rest later."

I released one hand from the ladder and grabbed hers. It was warm and surprisingly strong. On her wrist was a wide silver cuff bracelet that reflected light into my eyes, causing me to squint a little. With her help, I began my ascent. At the top of the ladder, I stopped. I was face-to-face with her, with Anna. Her deep blue eyes studied me carefully under the brilliant sun until a smile formed on her full lips. I smiled back, until my foot slipped off the final rung.

"Easy now," Anna said as she held me fast, her slender frame much stronger than mine. "You don't want to go swimming in that."

We peered down to the dark, churning water. Back then, undesired parts of the fish, the guts and organs, found their way into the harbor as the fishermen processed their catch. You could see pieces rotting away in the water. If the gulls or rats didn't consume the flesh, the maggots would make short work of it all. There was also a layer of sludge from some of the boats' diesel engines. It gave the water a slick, ominous hue. Needless to say, it was not a place anyone would want to fall in. I felt relieved when Anna held on to my arm as I climbed back up to the wharf.

Of course, I knew who she was and she kind of knew who I was. But being three years older meant that she went to the school in a larger town across the way on the main island of Newfoundland, or the mainland as we called it, so we'd never spoken before.

"Pierce, right?" she asked as she brushed back her jet-black hair from her lightly freckled face. "Sorry about your dad."

"They didn't find him," I said, looking down at my feet. "They gave up."

"So you were going to go look for him yourself?" she asked. Her face tightened, causing her high cheekbones to become even more pronounced.

I didn't respond.

"I get it," she said as she adjusted her sky-blue hiking backpack that had an oversized spiral notebook sticking out the top. "I'd probably do the same if it was my dad." She pointed to the fluffy, cumulus clouds above the horizon. "Oh my. Dark clouds. There's a storm coming."

"It looks pretty clear to me," I replied. I knew what storm clouds looked like. Everyone living here did, including Anna.

"Those clouds are definitely gray," she said, doubling down on the lie. "You might wanna wait a couple of days."

"Probably a good idea," I replied, relieved.

She caught me staring at the small yellow button on her jacket. At first glance, it looked like one of those happy-face images I'd seen on T-shirts. But this one was different. It had the same two black dots for eyes, but it sported a frown instead of a smile. I'd never seen one like it before.

Anna climbed down the ladder into the boat, retrieved my backpack, and shot back up as quickly as she went down.

"Don't forget this," she said, handing me my bag. Then she turned and started walking away. But after a few steps she turned again and walked back toward me.

She took off the frowny-face button from her coat and pinned it to my blue windbreaker. "Here," she said. "Hold on to this for me."

She turned once more and really did walk away.

I began to wonder what she was doing at the wharf on that quiet Sunday afternoon. I would find out the next time we crossed paths. I would see Anna twice more before she too would go missing.

ONE

From the sloping incline behind my house, I would watch the boats steam through the narrows atop my dad's grounded, overturned thirty-foot trap skiff. It was the early summer of 1991, and the boat had been lying in our back garden for three years. The white paint covering the overlapping spruce planks that ran the length of his boat was peeling badly and some rot was settling in. The vessel had braved the extreme weather conditions that came with life on and around an island in the cold North Atlantic, but it was no longer getting the attention needed to ensure its continued survival. Even my name, which I had etched into the planks with my knife, was beginning to disappear. PIERCE. It was my great-grandfather's name too, an old name for a now twelve-year-old boy.

"It has character," my mother said. "You'll grow into it. One day."

The truth is, I liked being the only Pierce on our small island. And somehow, being the only one gave me a reprieve from the often unflattering nicknames given to distinguish those with the same first names.

The boat took up a good deal of space in our garden. Before it was parked there, we grew potatoes, carrots, cabbage, and turnips, or whatever the soil would allow. But we hadn't planted anything in a long while, a combination of waning interest and declining necessity since it was just the two of us now, me and my mother, in our small two-story, saltbox-style clapboard house. It was my grandfather's house. And his father's before him. We could trace our family back some two hundred years, like most families on Perigo Island. And we were all tethered to the fishery.

Looking through the scratched lenses of a worn pair of binoculars, I would check the horizon every few minutes. During the summer months, the boats would leave our harbor early in the morning, just before sunrise, and would return hours later, hopefully with a load of fish. Cod to be precise. Though only twelve, I had become very good at being able to guess how much fish a boat was carrying given how it was riding on the ocean. You wanted to see a boat riding low, with the water almost up to the gunwale near the top edge of the boat. That translated into at least a couple of thousand pounds of fish. A fine day's catch. On the contrary, a boat riding high on the waves usually meant a few hundred pounds; sometimes it meant no fish at all. We were currently on a string of days without anyone landing a good haul.

In our world, cod was king. Though it was a relatively short season, running from June to September, this fishery guaranteed our very survival. For us, it was a family-based industry with everyone involved one way or the other, either catching the fish with lines and nets or processing the haul in our local plant. In school, we were told that Newfoundland cod was exported all over the world, to markets in the United States, Japan, the United Kingdom, Brazil, and Puerto Rico. It was funny to think that fish taken from our waters would end up in places we could only ever dream of visiting.

Since my father's disappearance, I had developed a strong dislike of the ocean, an affliction that often proved problematic, considering I spent most of my childhood surrounded by it. During particularly bad storms, I would lie awake and listen to the pounding waves crash into the shoreline not far from my bedroom window. The salt spray would coat not only our front door but also every car, bike, or piece of metal we owned, reducing everything to piles of rust. Salt also weathered the paint on our clapboard house and made it difficult to grow any root vegetables in the front garden. But such was life in the cold North Atlantic on a small island only sixteen miles long and half as wide. It was named by Portuguese fishermen and means "danger," perhaps a reference to the difficulty that fishermen had navigating the currents around it. Perigo was only a thirty-minute ferry ride to the larger island of Newfoundland, but it might as well have been a million miles away.

Through the lens, I could see the corner of our small school. It was there that we first learned that the very ground we were standing on was composed of limestone, granite, and volcanic rock, some of the oldest on the planet. These lessons conjured images of molten lava spewing up from the depths, which did little to alleviate my distrust of the ocean. We were also told that we had subarctic terrain, which explained the bogs and barrens that were a prominent feature of Perigo's landscape. There was only one wooded area left on the island, a small stand of spruce and fir trees, the rest having been cut down over generations for lumber and firewood. All this meant was that it was easy to get around on our trikes. These three-wheeled, all-terrain fun machines skipped across the land with ease, their only limitation being the jagged cliffs that fenced the island in.

From the top of my dad's boat, I could also see the heavily tarred flat roof of our fish plant, which processed thousands of pounds of fish a day, impressive for a community of under 1,500 residents, most of whom either worked the plant or fished cod for a living. The rest braved the ferry run, day in and day out, for work across the way. After unloading their catch on the north side, the boats would steam across the way and tie up at either the south side or at the very end of the harbor. A small breakwater protected the entrance to the harbor from large waves. This man-made barrier ran from the north to the south side with a wide enough opening in the middle to allow boats to safely pass through but too wide to jump across, as proven by Billy Maddox in the summer of '85. His failed attempt earned him a nickname he would carry with him for the rest of his life: Just Short.

The breakwater and adjoining fish plant were always a beehive of activity during the summer months. There was even money to be made for a bunch of twelve-year-olds with sharp knives.

As I swept back over the horizon, adjusting the large focusing knob, I spotted what I'd been waiting for—boats steaming toward the harbor. They were riding fairly low in the water. They had fish. I slipped on my rubber boots, picked up my white plastic pail, and ran my thumb across the blade of my knife, checking the sharpness before inserting it in the sheath that hung from a loop on my belt. My dad had given me the knife, which I had promptly inscribed with my name on the wooden handle.

I ran down the gravel lane of my house, took a hard right, and headed up toward the fish plant. As I neared my destination, I could hear the unmistakable *put-put* of a single-cylinder make-and-break engine. The name was in reference to the motor's ignition system, which made a spark before breaking once a certain speed was reached. One fisherman, however, said the name had more to do with the fact that you could make something to fix those engines whenever they broke down. Before their invention, people like my great-grandfather had to row to the fishing grounds. "Back then, the men around here had arms like legs," my father used to say. The image always made me smile.

I rounded a bend in the road that took me within fifty feet of the ocean and found myself running parallel to one of the boats that was about to cross through the breakwater and into the harbor. Jacob Maloney, a man who knew the fishing grounds like the cracks in his leathery hands, was at the rudder, while his son, Bobby, was up at the bow, uncoiling rope in preparation for docking. They were now within earshot.

"Can I have your tongues?" I shouted at Jacob.

Jacob looked across at me. We were almost eye level now; I was on land and they were on the water. He nodded yes.

The deal was done. Just like that.

I made my way past dozens of kids of varying ages, also armed with knives and buckets, waiting since sunup for a chance to make some money. The cod tongue, which was actually a muscle on the neck of the fish, was considered a delicacy, and as such, a kid could make a good dollar selling them. Ross Coles and his cronies, whom we unaffectionately referred to as the Arseholes, were also waiting on the wharf. Ross Coles and the Arseholes. It had a nice, rhythmic ring to it, reminiscent of the bands on the covers of my dad's old records. I'd sometimes catch him and my mother waltzing to a song in the kitchen on a Saturday evening after supper. He'd pretend to tip an imaginary hat to me as he dipped my mom in my direction.

Ross was tall with blond, stringy hair and an athletic build. He was also two years older, though just one grade ahead. He and his friends were a constant source of aggravation. But Ross stood out from all the other bullies. He was not only the ringleader but the very worst person I knew.

I arrived at the wharf just as Jacob and Bobby were tying up their boat. As fishermen began to unload their catch, forklift drivers from the plant dropped off large polyurethane fish coolers, or fish boxes as we called them, next to the splitting tables used to gut and clean the fish. The fishermen would drop the gutted fish into these boxes four feet high by four feet wide, which would be brought into the plant. Once inside, plant workers like my mother would clean, fillet, and trim the fish by removing scales and scrap parts before boxing and bagging them for shipment off the island.

A familiar voice lofted past my ears. "I guess you're better than the rest of us."

I turned around to find my longtime friend and associate, Thomas Dwyer, sitting on his overturned bucket, sharpening his knife on a small rectangular stone.

"Work smarter, not harder," I fired back.

Thomas smiled. His wiry red hair was a perfect match for the color of his face. Hence his nickname, Riblet, in reference to a pork rib cured in brine, which gives it a pinkish-red hue. Salt pork and beef were a staple for all of us on the island, part of the Sunday meal known as a Jiggs dinner, which also included boiled potatoes, turnips, carrots, and cabbage. The meat came in four-pound white plastic tubs that, when empty, were ideal for our work on the wharf.

"Where's Bennie?" I asked as I surveyed the area. He was the third associate in our cod tongue enterprise.

"Not a clue. All I know is it's your turn," Thomas said as he motioned to Jacob's boat. This was all part of the quid pro quo of getting cod tongues. Some fishermen would let you have them, but you had to earn each and every one by helping unload the fish from their boat.

"You think it's *my* turn?" I said, looking down at the load below us.

"Bennie's not here and I unloaded yesterday." Thomas handed me the fish prong—a long wooden pole with a metal hook fashioned to the end.

I always hesitated at this part. It's not that I was lazy; I just didn't like being in a boat on the ocean, even if it was tied to the dock. Just being on the wharf made me queasy. It's why I watched for the boats from my backyard every morning, so I didn't have to sit on the wharf. Of course, I would never tell Thomas any of this, so I began my one-handed descent down the ladder, using my other hand to grasp the prong, which was at least a foot longer than I was.

At the bottom, I got myself to the middle of the boat and removed the gangboards covering the midship room, or fishing room as we called it, where the day's catch was stored. Jacob and his son climbed out and made their way to the splitting tables with knives in hand. I was spot on, it was half-full, roughly eight hundred pounds of fish. Some were twenty pounders, which added a degree of difficulty to the work.

"You gonna throw them up here or are you gonna give 'em all a goodbye kiss first? Hurry up already!" Thomas shouted.

"Arse!" I shouted back.

I started the tedious task of pronging up the fish. I was taller than my friends, possessing what Thomas called "arms that were way too long for my body." He wasn't wrong in his observation, but his delivery could have been a tad softer. I stuck the metal hook at the end of the long shaft into the head of a fish. It always made an eerie popping sound. We were careful not to stick it into the body, as we'd been told by Wes Bartlett, the plant's foreman, in no uncertain terms that it damaged the fillet and would affect the quality and thus the price.

"If I sees one of yee crowd driving a prong into anything but the fish's head, I'll boot you in the hole and send you home out of it," Wes would often say, glaring down at us with a cigarette dangling from the corner of his sixty-year-old mouth.

Once I had the fish on the end of the prong, I'd catapult them overhead with one sweeping motion. As soon as the fish hit the concrete above, Thomas would remove the tongue by turning the fish over, grasping it by the head with one hand, and cutting slits along the sides of the exposed neck with the other. He'd then stick his finger underneath the tongue and make cuts to the back and the front. It took just a few seconds to perform the task. They would fetch a good price, a dollar a pound, a decent wage for three twelve-year-olds in 1991. Later, we would figure out it was even more profitable to sell them by the dozen, which worked out to be less than a pound. "Economies of scale," Bennie called it. Thomas referred to it as "more money for less tongue."

As I continued to prong up the fish, another boat out in the harbor caught my eye. Steaming past on a twenty-foot fiberglass boat was Solomon Vickers. Solomon had lived in our community for only six months, having arrived early in the New Year. When we first saw him head through the narrows, Solomon was aboard a smaller inflatable boat. It looked like it was made of black rubber. We'd never seen one in our waters before. One of the fishermen called it a Zodiac. We knew very little about the stern-looking man who kept to himself on the far end of the island. The little we did know we deduced from observation. Solomon was in his mid-sixties, tall with a full head of silver hair that was long enough for a small ponytail, but we never saw him indulge in such a style. We also knew that he lived alone, with no wife or children to speak of. As they tend to do, rumors filled in the missing pieces. Some heard he was on the lam, hiding out from the law. Others said he was some kind of artist who liked to paint fish and smoke dope, ideas likely born from his long hair and hand-rolled cigarettes.

His boat came within a few feet of the one I was standing in. Just in front of him on the gangboards was a matte black tarp held down at each corner by a large stone. A gust of wind lifted a corner, exposing something that caught my eye. Small bones, laid out in rows. Solomon caught my gaze. His dead eyes were cold like the fish at the bottom of the boat. He sailed past the plant and headed to the end of the harbor where some of the fishing stages were located. Like most fishermen on the island, Solomon stored his fishing gear in this shedlike structure built at the water's edge.

I finished unloading the boat and carefully climbed the ladder. Once on dry land, I thought about telling Thomas what I'd just seen. What was old Solomon doing with bones in his boat, and what kind of bones were they? I took out my knife and joined Thomas, who was on one knee in the middle of the pile of cod covered in what we called the gurry or the sludge of fish guts. Cutting out tongues is a messy business, but Thomas had a way of making it even messier.

"Not bad, not great either, but not bad," Thomas proclaimed. It had been a rough summer for the fishermen on our island. Rumor had it that it was rough everywhere else too.

"It'll pick up. It always does," I said.

Off in the distance, Bennie Nayak barreled down the steep road to the fish plant, bucket and knife in hand, zigzagging between kids and small mounds of fish. Finally, he jumped over a pile of netting and stuck the landing right in front of us like an Olympic gymnast.

"Sorry, me and Mom were late getting back from the ferry," Bennie said as he ran his hand through his thick black hair before starting in on the fish.

"Unacceptable." Thomas shook his fiery red head in disapproval.

"Like I can't catch up with you two." And he could do so easily. Bennie was the smallest of us but by far the fastest. He was like a surgeon with that knife, which was no surprise given his father was a doctor. A steady hand ran in the family.

"In your dreams you're faster than us. And speaking of dreams, I had that one again last night about your sister," Thomas quipped.

"So you're even dreaming about rejection now." Bennie's fast comebacks were one of the things he was known for.

"That's no way to talk to your future brother-in-law," Thomas said.

All three of us got into the rhythm with our knives, making short work of the remaining fish.

"Hey, there was a cop car on the ferry," Bennie said. All of our knives went still. He had our attention.

"Someone robbing crab apples out of old Gerard O'Byrne's trees again?" Thomas asked.

"That was you," I said. I knew because I had stripped the old man's tree of the fruit with him.

Bennie shook his head. "Nothing to do with that. I heard Mom talking with the officer. A girl's gone missing on the south side."

"Missing? Who?" I asked.

"Anna Tessier."

The name landed heavily. "I know her," I said.

"Everyone knows her," Thomas replied. "There's not a soul on this island we don't know."

"Think she ran away?" Bennie asked.

"She did once before. No one disappears around here," Thomas said, and then saw the look on my face. "Sorry, you know what I mean."

Thomas was looking out at a new boat coming in when something hit him in the back of the neck, sending him face-first to the ground and knocking over his bucket of tongues.

"What the hell was that?" Thomas asked as Bennie and I helped him to his feet, crushing some of the tongues in the process.

Lying on the ground next to our buckets was a sculpin, a spiny, prehistoric-looking fish. A bottom feeder.

"You're bleeding," Bennie said.

Thomas felt the back of his neck, his fingers coming up red. Its sharp spines had pierced his skin.

It was then that we heard the laughter. We turned to see Ross being congratulated on his marksmanship by two other boys. Pete "Rounder" Parsons and Jody Buckle. Rounder, who was almost as wide as he was tall, had earned the nickname when he stood too close to a globe one day in geography class, which led to someone remarking that Pete was rounder than the blue orb. Jody Buckle, in contrast, was tall and skinny. He was speed incarnate with a knife. He was fast, some say as fast as Bennie, which would be a showdown for the ages, like the quick draws from the Wild West.

"Ugly attracts ugly, Riblet!" Ross shouted from thirty feet away. He waited for a response, something saucy enough to warrant throwing Thomas over the wharf, but Thomas remained mute. Ross and the Arseholes soon tired and walked off toward the incoming boats.

"You okay, Thomas?" I asked once they were far enough away. I rarely said his name, but it felt necessary this time.

"I hate those guys."

We gathered up our tongues and threw the ones we stepped on into the ocean, where the gulls fought over them. They too had a pecking order, the larger ones bullying the smaller ones. We spent the rest of the morning and afternoon collecting tongues from other boats. Eventually, Thomas came around to his old self, and was laughing and joking as usual.

I, however, remained quiet. I couldn't stop thinking about Anna Tessier.

TWO

Later that day, I came home to a quiet, empty house. It was something that I had grown accustomed to during the fishing season. My mother, Diane Jacobs, worked long shifts at the fish plant, which seemed even longer now that there was just the two of us. It was a comfortable home with a simple layout. A small kitchen greeted me as soon as I entered through the porch door, and just beyond it was a modest living room with thick orange carpet and brown paneling on the walls. A narrow staircase led to three small bedrooms and a bathroom, all with faded wallpaper and linoleum flooring in an orange and green floral pattern.

Being first home meant that I was the designated cook. I was no culinary wizard, but I knew my way around a bag of crinkle-cut fries and a tin of meatballs and gravy. As I stirred a pot on our old harvest-gold-colored stove, my mind drifted off to Anna Tessier and her family. Anna's parents had broken up a few years back—a big deal, on a small island. Her dad moved to the other side of the country while her mom, Doris, worked with my mother at the fish plant. Anna's new stepdad, Jimmy, came into their world a couple of years back. He worked on the council and I'd often see him driving the garbage truck or repairing potholes around the island.

Anna had a younger brother and sister who went to my school. For some reason, I thought about them the most.

The front door swung open and my mother entered the kitchen sporting her work gear—white smock, rubber boots, and a warm smile that contradicted the exhaustion in her eyes.

"It smells great." A white lie she sold well as she scrubbed her hands with a bar of Sunlight soap under the kitchen faucet.

"Thanks," I said.

I placed a plate of food on each end of our chrome kitchen table.

"And how was your day?" my mother asked, putting some much-needed ketchup on the fries that were either burned or undercooked depending on their placement underneath the busted heating element in our oven. I usually turned them over to ensure even cooking, but I was distracted by my own thoughts.

"I heard Anna Tessier is missing," I blurted.

"Yes, I know," she replied, calmly. "Doris wasn't at work today, but her cousin Phyllis mentioned it."

"How long has it been?" I asked, pushing my food aside. I had no appetite.

"Phyllis said it's been a couple of days now," my mother replied, pushing my plate back in front of me. "But I don't want you to worry. That girl has run away before. You're probably too young to remember."

But I did remember. Anna and I had talked about it. That's why I was worried. She'd promised she would never do it again.

"The police are involved. They'll find her or she'll come home like last time," my mother said as she handed me my fork.

Usually, I took comfort in my mother's words, but not this time.

After supper, we washed the dishes in the white enamel sink

that Dad had salvaged years ago from an abandoned house on Clayton's Island, which had been resettled. As she passed me the last saucer to dry, she said, "You know, Joe Blackmore asked about it again." She looked through the kitchen window to where my father's . . . my boat—lay on the ground, overturned.

"It's not for sale," I said quickly.

"It's just going to rot out there. We could use the money." I couldn't argue with her about that. Money was tight since Dad's disappearance. And fewer fish landing on the wharf meant fewer that were processed at the plant. Everyone on our island was feeling the pinch one way or another. Some, like my uncle Donny, had already left to find work elsewhere and more were considering it.

"It's mine now. We agreed."

My mother had perfected her stare-down. I would usually cave in after a few seconds, but this time was different and she knew it.

The unmistakable sound of an ATV horn broke the tension.

"I'm going out," I said.

"Are you now?" she shot back.

I paused at the door and waited for her permission. She nodded.

Outside, Thomas was sitting on his old three-wheel ATV. His jeans were tucked into a black pair of rubber boots. And around his waist he wore a gray, nylon fanny pack in which he kept a tire repair kit, a few wrenches, and some other small tools. The trike didn't have an original part left on it. When parts broke down, Thomas replaced them with whatever he could get his hands on or simply made do without them. It came to him naturally, the ability to fix things. His father and oldest brother ran the only service station on the island. Though it wasn't pretty, his ATV ran well.

"Not bad, wha'?" Thomas said as he got off his trike and did a double-finger point at it.

The plastic shell, steel frame, and gas tank were no longer a faded hue but a bright crimson red.

"Did you paint it with a broom?" I asked as I ran my hand over the red splatter on the tires.

"Roller mostly."

"Yeah, you can hardly tell."

"I can do yours next," Thomas offered, motioning to my yellow trike, which was parked at the corner of the house.

"Naw, I'm good," I said as I walked down the steps and past the front garden where we used to grow root vegetables but now was overtaken by dandelions and other weeds. I hopped on my trike, which I always parked next to a large tree stump that we used as a chopping block. I'd split many a log on it with my father's long-handled axe that was propped up next to it.

I turned the key and pressed the start button on the grip with my thumb. The engine roared to life. The handlebars sent vibrations up my arms. I always loved that feeling, the power the machine possessed.

"Race ya," Thomas said for the thousandth time as he fired up his trike.

"Don't," I replied. "You'll pelt the house with rocks."

But Thomas ignored my warning and peeled down the lane, his wheels sending gravel flying toward the house as I predicted. I took off after him before my mother could get to the door to see what all the commotion was about.

At the end of the lane, we headed up an old power-line path that circumnavigated the harbor. Near the top of the hill, we came upon Bennie's house. It was hard to miss, being the largest one on the island. And, unlike most of the other homes, it was a modern two-story with deep-blue vinyl siding, double-paned windows, and an attached garage. We got off our trikes and were walking toward the house when something caught Thomas's eye. Glass, shattered on the ground from a side door that led into the garage.

"Something's up," Thomas said as he grabbed me and pulled me to the side of the house. "It's a break-in."

A red liquid stained some of the shards.

"Blood," he said.

"What? No way." I bent down to examine the glass.

Our island was a safe place to live. Everybody knew one another so no one ever locked their doors. But something was obviously wrong here. And these were different times. Anna Tessier was proof of that.

Thomas and I looked at each other. Someone had to go inside and check it out.

"I think it's your turn," Thomas whispered.

"Right, you went first the last break-in," I said sarcastically.

Reluctantly, I crept up to the busted window and was about to look in when the door swung open, sending me flying to the ground and causing Thomas to release a high pitched squeal. When I looked up, I saw a tall girl with sandy-colored hair. Her right hand was bandaged.

"What are you doing?" she asked as someone exited behind her, someone we knew well. It was Bennie, with a broom and dust-pan in hand.

"I see you met my cousin, Emily," Bennie said as he started to clean up the glass. "She and my aunt Sandra are staying with us awhile."

"Cousin?" Thomas asked. Emily held a hand out to me and helped me to my feet. I smiled at her as I remembered fondly the only other time a girl had done that for me.

"I'm Pierce. He's Thomas," I said. "We thought you broke in."

"If I broke in, why is the glass on the outside of the house?" Emily asked.

"I was moving kayaks and stuff to make room for suitcases," Bennie said. "Hit the window by accident." He finished cleaning up the mess.

"Kayaks?!" Thomas said. "Man, you got some pile of money."

Bennie gave him a look. He was a little embarrassed that his parents were well off, by small-island standards, anyway. Bennie was the richest kid anyone knew.

"That's a nasty cut," I said, pointing to the blood beginning to soak through the bandage on Emily's hand.

Emily smiled. "That's what I get for trying to help clean up."

"You don't look like him." Thomas nodded toward Bennie. Bennie's father was South Asian, originally from India, and met his mom while attending university in St. John's.

"Emily's mom and my mom are sisters," Bennie explained.

"Where are you from?" I asked.

"The East Village."

"Like out near the mall in St. John's?" Thomas asked, nodding toward the mainland where our capital city lay some six hours' drive from where we stood.

"No. In Manhattan."

We stared at her blankly.

"New York City," Bennie said.

"Oh, that Manhattan. Great spot," I said, trying to sound cooler than I was.

"You've been there?" Emily asked.

Thomas and Bennie started laughing.

"Oh yeah, world traveler, that one," Thomas said.

"I mean, on the TV. I saw *Home Alone*. New York looks cool."

"Let's get down to business," Thomas said. After all, that's why we'd come over—to settle accounts.

We followed Bennie into the garage.

"How much we got?" Thomas asked.

Bennie removed a piece of the gyprock from the wall, reached his hand in, and pulled out a large coffee can.

"I counted it last night," Bennie said as he opened the lid and revealed a rolled-up wad of bills. "Five hundred and forty-five dollars."

"Not bad for a slow year at the tongues," Thomas said.

"This is two summers of work!" I replied. "We're running out of time."

"What do you guys need the money for?" Emily asked.

"To fix up Pierce's boat. Well, his dad's boat. It needs some work and maybe a new motor," Bennie said.

"Then we're taking it out fishing," Thomas added.

Emily looked confused. "In the ocean? You're not old enough, are you?"

"Not now, but we will be," Thomas explained. "Rodney Mullins was only sixteen when he started fishing on his own."

It was common for kids to fish with their fathers and uncles at an early age, and some would eventually go off and get their own boats. We had a simple plan. Finish high school, then go fishing for a living. There would be no need to leave the island to find work. We'd make our own way. Like my father and his before him and so on down the family tree.

"My boat will be rotted away if we don't earn faster," I said as I took the money from Bennie and put it back in the can. Bennie immediately hid it in the wall, replacing the drywall so you couldn't tell it was there.

"Why don't you just buy a new boat when you're old enough?" Emily asked.

"We have to fix mine," I said, my voice sharp.

"Whoa, okay. Whatever," Emily said, turning away from me.

"The fish will come back, they always do," Bennie said.

Emily walked outside, and not knowing what else to do, we all followed. We had never really hung out with a girl outside of school. Thomas and I didn't have a sister. Bennie did but she was much older than we were, so little could be safely deduced of girls' ways from her, other than that they really didn't want you in their room.

"So, are you guys gonna show me around the place?" she asked. "Or do I just go off by myself and die of boredom?"

"No time for that," Thomas said.

Bennie pulled us aside. "Mom said I have to take her around. And she's not that bad, for a girl."

Emily looked over at me, her eyebrows drawn down, closer together. It was the same look my mother would give me when she suspected I was up to no good. No doubt, Emily knew we were discussing her. We were as subtle about it as the bell at recess.

Thomas and I walked back to our trikes. Bennie jumped on the back of Thomas's three-wheeler and I got on mine. Emily stood to one side, arms crossed.

"Well?" she said.

"Well what?" I asked.

"She wants to get on your trike," Thomas shouted over his revving engine. "Make room, ya dope."

"Oh." I moved up on my seat. Never in my life had a girl ridden on the back of my trike. It was as strange and improbable as the ocean parting and creating a landbridge to the mainland.

"You may want to hold on to me," I yelled over the motor. "Or hold on to the back of the seat. You know, whatever you do in New York."

It was a stupid thing to say. I'm pretty sure there weren't too many three-wheeled ATVs tearing up the streets of Manhattan. Still, Emily wrapped her arms around my waist, and we followed Thomas and Bennie south to the ferry docks, where commuters were returning from work on the main island. We traveled past salt-box houses painted red, yellow, and green with clotheslines held up by long birch sticks in the backyards. Gannets and kittiwakes soared overhead. It was perfect, like a tourism commercial come to life just for us. As Emily tightened her arms around me, I realized two things: that this was the most physical contact I had ever had with a girl. And that I liked it.

We continued on to the north of the island, where Emily spotted something she'd never seen before.

"Stop here!" she shouted in my ear.

I pulled off the trail. Emily leapt off the trike and walked to the edge of the cliff.

"Careful!" I said. The cliffs were tricky to navigate even for those who grew up clinging to them. To outsiders, they were fatal. But Emily wasn't listening. She was completely transfixed by the huge iceberg just off the coast, bright white with faint blue streaks, towering some fifteen stories above the water.

"I've never seen anything like it," Emily said.

"You've never seen an iceberg before?" It was as normal to me as seeing the clouds overhead. Each spring, hundreds of these glacial giants traveled down the Labrador current to the waters off our coast. You could always see a number of them from the shore.

"Not many in New York," she said.

"Ninety percent of it is still underwater. What you're seeing is only the top."

"Wow. It's as tall as a skyscraper. Where did it come from?"

"Greenland. Chunks break off the glaciers and drift down here," I replied. "And some, like this one, hit bottom and stay till they break apart or melt away. We call the breakaways growlers." I pointed to the bobbing ice that feathered out from the base and drifted close to shore.

Every spring and summer, tourists would flock to the icebergs with cameras in hand. I never understood it. To us, the ice was a nuisance, damaging fishing nets and making treks to the fishing grounds and ferry crossings more challenging.

"You know a lot about them," Emily noted.

"A friend of mine is really into them," I said. And then it spilled out of me. "Her name was Anna."

"The girl who ran away?" Emily asked.

Just then, Thomas's trike came barreling toward us, loud and furious. He hit the brakes and almost sent Bennie arse over head.

"Cops! They're right behind us!" Thomas shouted.

The police frowned upon twelve-year-olds riding around on three-wheeled machines, so we had to move fast or else we'd be finishing off Emily's island tour in the back of a cruiser. I hopped on my trike and soon felt Emily's arms around me again. I started it up and followed Thomas and Bennie away from the edge of the cliff.

We drove into the bog just below the road and held our breaths as the police car approached. Fortunately, the cruiser drove past us and continued heading east.

"That was close," Bennie said.

"Where are they going?" Thomas asked.

A police car on the island was always newsworthy.

"So, this is a thing? There's a cop on every block back home," Emily said to a bunch of blank stares. "Fair enough, let's follow them."

We all looked at Emily and then at one another.

"You heard my cousin," Bennie said. "But let's not go tearing down the road after them like a big redheaded idiot, all right, Thomas?"

"I only got one speed: flat-out," Thomas replied.

Thomas and Bennie took off down the road. I was about to do the same when Emily grabbed my shoulder.

"Mind if I give it a try?"

I was caught off guard.

"I guess so," I said. "It can be a little tricky with the three wheels and all."

"I'll figure it out," she said. She hopped off the trike and pushed me to the back. When she was in the driver's seat, she revved the engine and hammered the throttle like a pro.

"You've done this before?" I shouted above the noise of the engine.

"It's similar to a dirt bike, just an extra wheel."

Dirt bike? Who was this girl? I wondered.

She drove with me on the back, right to the most easterly part of the island. I wasn't about to wrap my hands around her waist, so I held on to the sides of the trike, hoping to hell I wouldn't be thrown off.

When we caught up to Thomas and Bennie, they had pulled off to the side of the road. The police car was parked at Solomon Vickers's place, the old hermit who had given me the stare-down earlier that day. The cop car was blocking Solomon's red pickup with a missing antenna. The sprawling, bungalow-like structure was in a sad state of disrepair, with weathered narrow clapboard and boarded-up windows. Any white paint left on the place was peeling badly, and over half the shingles were missing from its hipped roof. It also had a partial second story with large dormers covered by sheets of plywood.

"What are they doing at Solomon's place?" Bennie asked.

"Strange fella. Who knows what he's up to," Thomas replied.

We watched in silence. After about ten minutes, two uniformed officers, a male and a female in their thirties, emerged from his house, got in their car, and drove back toward the ferry. Once they were gone, Solomon came out and stood on his dilapidated stoop.

"What would the police want to talk to that old man about?" Emily asked.

"Anna Tessier," I replied.

THREE

Thomas and I were sitting on our overturned buckets waiting for the boats. We were surrounded by other kids playing the same waiting game. The midmorning sun amplified the smell of rotting fish that emanated from the large gray offal shoot, where unwanted parts of cod and discarded bycatch were kept until disposal. The waters outside the breakwater were calm, which made it easier to spot incoming vessels. The boats were coming through the narrows with fewer and fewer fish. It was happening in many other coastal communities, not just ours. Less fish meant less cod tongues, which meant less money for us kids.

It also meant tensions were high everywhere in our tiny community. Some of the adults were in foul moods most of the time, and we kids seemed to be in their way no matter where we were. People got upset at the smallest things, like someone getting an extra shift at the plant over someone else. I even noticed more beer bottles than usual strewn around the harbor. Competition on the wharf became fierce and we acted accordingly. We were careful to keep a safe distance from Ross Coles and the older kids. One sculpin to the head per season was enough. As for me, I was still wrestling with what we had witnessed the day before—police officers at Solomon's place.

"I'm getting too old for this racket," Thomas said as he unwrapped a stick of gum and stuffed it in his mouth.

"Yeah, it's a young man's game," I said, mocking him.

I stared at the yellow frowny-face button pinned to my jean jacket, the button that Anna had given to me. I'd been wearing it for three years, moving it from coat to coat as I outgrew them, but I never outgrew that button.

"Did you hear anything about Anna?" I asked. It was a foolish question. News traveled at the speed of light on the island, and if Thomas knew anything, he'd have said.

"Nope," he replied as he sharpened his knife on his pocket stone. "You think Solomon knows something about it?"

"Maybe," I said.

"I feel kind of ridiculous." It was a girl's voice, coming from behind us.

Thomas and I turned. Emily stood with her hands on her hips. She was wearing a long, red checkered shirt over a blue top, and a pair of yellow rubber boots. The shirt was unbuttoned, which made the tail billow in the wind like a cape. She looked like some strange superhero, there to save the day. A green-handled knife tucked into a sheath on her belt completed the ensemble. Bennie stood next to her, looking like a proud coach.

"You look great," I said a little too eagerly.

"I can't believe this is the only thing to do on this island," Emily said as she surveyed the wharf.

"It's not the only thing. It's just the only thing to do right now," I explained. From the time school ended in late June till we returned in early September, the wharf was all we knew.

Thomas was strangely silent throughout the exchange. Eventually, he got off his bucket. "This work is serious. This isn't some trainee program."

"Come off it, Thomas," I said. "There's not much to cutting out tongues."

"If you can do it, literally anyone can," Bennie added.

"It's a goddamn art form passed down through the generations," Thomas said.

"Your parents own a garage," I fired back. "They never fished in their lives."

"My cousins on Mom's side all fish. And besides, she's a . . ." He paused.

"Girl? You can say it," Emily said. "I'm well aware."

Men caught the fish and it was mostly women who processed them in the plant. That's the way it was on our island.

Our conversation was interrupted by the distinctive *put-put* sound of a single-cylinder gasoline engine. We turned to watch a boat sailing through the narrows. Katherine Boyer was at the rudder, the only female fisherperson on our island. She knew the fishing grounds as well as anyone and she had a full load of fish to prove it. Ross made a beeline for the boat. Following behind were the rest of us—some fifteen kids eager for cod tongues.

"No chance. Ross is Katherine's nephew," Thomas said. He was addressing Emily, who was rushing to the dock.

As Katherine tied her boat up to the rusty cast-iron cleat, she spotted the unfamiliar face in the crowd. Emily stood, tall and still, bucket and knife in hand, cape flying in the wind. She nodded at Katherine and Katherine nodded back.

The deal was done.

The rest of the kids, including a disgruntled Ross, walked away. She waved us over.

The four of us got to work. Thomas pronged the fish from the boat while Bennie, Emily, and I took care of them as they hit the dock. For a first-timer, Emily was fearless. Her hand was steady as she pressed her thumb inward and made the triangular cuts to extract the cod tongues.

"Not too shabby," I said.

"Way easier than cutting out human tongues," Emily remarked with a straight face as she eyed Thomas. Then she laughed.

"You're sick. I like it," Thomas said, smiling.

Together, we made short work of the pile of fish around us. I found myself staring at the girl in our midst, who was covered head to toe in fish offal like the rest of us.

Emily caught me staring at her.

"Has she come home yet? Anna?" she asked.

"Not yet," I said.

"They'll find her. She's run away a bunch of times," Thomas said.

"Twice. And she was younger then," I said.

"I heard someone saw her on the ferry three nights ago when she first went missing," Bennie said.

"I don't believe that," I fired back.

I knew her better than my friends did. And rumors here were like a dense fog that rolled in from the ocean, making it difficult to see clearly.

"What do you believe?" Emily asked.

I had a lot to say on the subject, but not in front of my friends.

"Tourists!" Thomas shouted. He pointed to a family of three walking back to their car at the top of the road that led down to the plant.

There were a couple of ways you could make money selling cod tongues, but by far the best was to ply unsuspecting tourists.

"Let's go make a sale!" Thomas said as he gathered up his things.

"Wait, let's send Emily in," Bennie suggested. "After all, they're her tongues."

"Plus, she has a way nicer face," I added. Emily looked at me and I quickly avoided her gaze.

"Depends on who you ask, but whatever," Thomas said. He handed the bucket and some plastic baggies to Emily. "Go on then, ask if they want your tongues."

"Don't be too aggressive, but don't be afraid to push a little," Bennie added.

"Tourists are rich, so start at a dollar-fifty a dozen. But don't go any lower than one twenty-five," I said.

"Guys, I'm from New York. I know how to haggle," Emily said.

"Hurry, they're almost at their car," Thomas said.

Emily shot off like a rocket, her superhero cape blowing in the wind. "Tongues! Lots of tongues!" she shouted as she ran up the hill.

She stopped the couple and their young son just as they were about to get into their minivan. The husband and wife were wide-eyed and speechless as this girl covered in fish offal and blood careened toward them with a bucket in one hand and a knife in the other.

"Tongues! Big juicy ones!" Emily called out.

The husband frantically searched for his keys, dropping the ice cream cone he was holding, while his wife screamed at him to hurry up. Their son just stood and stared at Emily. Finally, the husband found his keys, unlocked the doors, and the family jumped in. All on board, they started the van and peeled away, leaving Emily in a cloud of dust.

Emily turned and walked back to where we were standing. "They must not have heard me," she said.

"Oh, they heard you," Bennie replied. "People on the other side of the island heard you."

"Maybe less knife waving next time," I suggested.

Emily looked down at herself and started to laugh. Soon we were all laughing hysterically.

We were interrupted by an all-too-familiar voice. "Those are mine."

We turned to find Ross walking with purpose toward us with a half-empty bucket. He wasn't alone. The Arseholes, Jody Buckle and Rounder, were with him. They looked at us the way Thomas's five-year-old beagle would when it got close to his feeding time.

"That was our boat," Ross said, eyeing Emily's bucket full of cod tongues.

"Katherine gave it to Emily," I countered.

"Emily, is it? You're the girl who just chased the tourists away? You'd make a fine dog."

Ross's stooges laughed on cue. Emily stepped forward and the laughter stopped.

"I earned these, so they're mine," she said.

"Not from around here, I see. No little girl is gonna take money from our pockets," Ross said.

He nodded at Rounder, who made a move to grab the bucket in Emily's hand. But Emily was too quick.

"Last chance before I rip that bucket from your hand," Ross warned.

"Make your move, hotshot," Emily said.

Ross's jaw tightened and his eyes bulged as he glared at Emily. Then he broke into a nefarious grin but just on the left side of his face. I remembered seeing that look before, when I was seven. Though I wasn't supposed to, I had wandered down to the wharf by myself and saw an older boy fishing with a rod and reel at the end of the breakwater. I walked slowly up to him and saw that it was the older kid at school whom everyone avoided, a then nine-year-old boy named Ross Coles. He had caught a conner, a small shallow-water fish with an oblong body and a pointed snout. But instead of either killing it or throwing it back in the water, he had somehow run a fishing line through its back, to which he attached a large piece of cork float from a nearby fishing net. Then he threw the fish back into the ocean. I watched as that piece of brown cork circled round and round inside the mouth of the harbor, bobbing up and down as the fish desperately tried to return to the bottom of the sea to no avail. Ross, somehow sensing my presence, turned and smiled at me with that same evil half-grin. I turned and ran all the way home. I never told anyone about what I'd seen that day. I hadn't thought about it until I now saw that same look appear on Ross's face.

Thomas grabbed the bucket from Emily's hand and with one fluid motion flung it over the guardrail and into the ocean.

"What are you doing?" Bennie shouted.

"No one gets them now," Thomas said, folding his arms across his chest.

Ross and the older kids looked on in disbelief. But before they could react, we heard the voices of some of the plant workers. Revenge would have to wait.

"Nice one, Riblet. Now you dicksmacks owe us the money for those," Ross said, and then motioned to Rounder and Jody to head back to the wharf.

We all let out a sigh of relief. All of us except for Emily.

"Why did you do that?" Emily asked Thomas. "They were mine."

"I just saved your hole and everyone else's. So you're welcome."

"He was full of shit. He wasn't going to do anything," Emily said.

"He might have. He's different since he started going to school off the island," I said.

Our school went as far as grade six, after that you were bussed off to a bigger one on the mainland across the way. Since Ross, Rounder, and Jody started going to that school, they'd become even more belligerent and aggressive. It was like something over there was making them angry and they were taking it out on us. I wondered what it could be and whether the same thing would happen to me, Thomas, and Bennie.

We walked to the guardrail and watched the white plastic bucket bobbing on the waves.

"What's a riblet?" Emily asked.

Bennie discreetly shook his head at Emily. This was not a topic open for discussion.

It was then that we saw him. Solomon Vickers. But he wasn't steaming into the harbor, he was leaving it. This was odd. Fishermen left early, just before sunrise, to secure a prime fishing berth and be back in time to have their catch processed in the plant. Solomon was heading out late in the day.

"Where's he off to now?" I wondered out loud, remembering the small bones I'd seen on his boat.

"Who cares?" Thomas replied. "He's just some weird old man off doing some weird old-man stuff."

"Why were the police at his house?" Emily asked. "What's with that guy?"

I looked at Emily, eyes wide.

"I saw something in his boat," I blurted out. "Yesterday, when he passed by the wharf."

"Let me guess, was it fish?" Bennie asked.

Emily shot him a look of disapproval. "What did you see?" she asked.

"Bones," I said, which immediately got the boys' attention. "Thin ones, all different shapes and sizes."

"Bones? From what?" Thomas asked. He was now fully engaged. Thomas loved a good, scary story as long as there were others around to hear it with him.

"I'm not sure." I suddenly felt self-conscious, unsure of what I had seen.

"We need to look into this," Emily said.

Thomas looked at Emily and then at me, and groaned. This new girl was already becoming a thorn in his side.

"If you think he's really up to something, why don't you run a stakeout at his place?" Thomas said.

"Great idea. I'm in," Emily replied.

Thomas shook his head. "That was a joke," he said. "This isn't friggin' New York City, you know. Not everything is some big detective crime show."

"Guys, look at the facts," Emily began. "This Solomon guy lives in a creepy house and keeps to himself. Then we all witnessed the police at his place. Pierce saw bones in his boat. Oh, and there's a girl missing. Don't you think that's all kind of suspicious?"

I couldn't help but be impressed at her assessment of the situation. She presented the case better than I ever could.

"You're right, we should check it out. I'm in," Bennie said, succumbing to logic. "Come on, Thomas, there's shag all else to be at."

"Shag all sounds good to me," Thomas grumbled.

But Bennie wasn't giving up. Like a seasoned fisherman, he'd reset his line and try again.

"We need your muscle in case things get messy. You know you're stronger than all of us," Bennie responded.

Thomas thought on this for a second. He looked Emily up and down. He didn't trust girls. Most of his misguided information on them came from his four older brothers, who were largely ignored by the opposite sex.

"I suppose so," Thomas said slowly.

"Pierce?" Emily asked.

"Yeah. But we need to move fast," I said as we watched Solomon sail out past the narrows and disappear into the deeps. "We'll go tonight."

FOUR

It was late Saturday afternoon by the time we packed up our camping gear, which was stored in Bennie's garage, and strapped it to the rear rack on our trikes. Tomorrow would be Sunday so there would be no fishing, which meant we had the day off. We told the adults we were going to camp out in the field just behind Thomas's house because Emily had never seen stars in a clear night sky. Some truth mixed in with a white lie. And we promised to make it back in time for church the next morning. This was a different time and place, where kids could camp out overnight without fear and, especially in Thomas's case, give parents a much-needed break.

After that, we had a plan—get as close to Solomon's as possible without being spotted. We decided that we would park our ATVs at the bottom of Watch Hill and hike the path to the top. The hill, which boasted the only trees left standing on the island, overlooked Solomon's place but was also a safe distance away. Not all of us were thrilled with this plan. The hill was fairly steep and slippery in places due to a constant stream of spring water running down it.

"This is a bad idea," Thomas said for the fifth time at about the halfway mark of our ascent. "We could turn around and camp closer to his place."

"Solomon would spot us. This is the only way," I said as I took a swig of water from an old army canteen that my dad had picked up at a yard sale.

"We're not kids anymore, Thomas. This place shouldn't scare you," Bennie said.

"That's got nothing to do with it," Thomas fired back.

"To do with what?" Emily asked.

"Why do you think they call this place Watch Hill?" Thomas said.

"It's where people would watch for ships," I replied, remembering when I'd asked my father that very question.

"Not watching for ships. For fairies," Thomas explained.

"Fairies? Like elves?" Emily tried to contain a laugh.

"That's right. And they must be avoided at all costs," Thomas said. "They don't want anyone up here. Fairies can entrance you and make you lose all sense of direction."

Fairy lore is a tradition the Irish settlers brought over from the old country. These creatures are notorious tricksters who can assume the form of a child, animal, or even a glowing light. Adults told stories about the fairies to their children to keep them from wandering off. *Don't go near the water or the fairies will get you.* This warning was heeded by all youngsters on our island.

"Have you ever seen one?" Emily asked, trying to maintain a straight face.

"Not me, personally, but my cousin's buddy's friend was walking up this very hill when he saw a bunch of them," Thomas said. "They were only two feet tall, but they were hideous, all deformed with big bug eyes and nasty teeth, dancing around a fire. The creatures tried to put him in a trance to do god knows what to him, but he got away."

"Your cousin's buddy's friend was clearly drunk," I said.

Thomas began removing his beige hoodie, turned it inside out, and put it back on again.

"Is he okay?" Emily whispered to me.

"Wearing your clothes inside out confuses the fairies," I explained.

Emily looked back at Thomas. Then she took off her sweater, turned it inside out, and put it back on. Bennie and I exchanged a look and then did the same.

Things got quiet for a spell. It was humid, which made it harder to breathe let alone talk, so we chose instead to concentrate on our footing, especially since the soles of our sneakers were worn smooth. We wouldn't get new ones until the fall when school started again, though I suspected Bennie had a new pair at home but chose not to wear them to avoid Thomas's gibes, which usually started with "must be nice." The last half of the trail was the most difficult. The path got narrower just as the incline became steeper. But after emerging through some alder bushes, we found ourselves at the top of the hill. We continued on a rocky footpath through some spruce trees until we got to a clearing that overlooked the entire island. From there, we could see the colorful houses that dotted the rocky terrain, and the roads and paths that zigzagged the landscape.

Emily walked up to the edge of the cliff and gazed out at the ocean. She laid eyes on the iceberg that had captivated her on her very first day here. Larger pieces were breaking off now and drifting in closer to shore. And just below us was the farthest dwelling on the island, the house of Solomon Vickers.

I took out my binoculars and scanned Solomon's house. "A perfect view."

From this new vantage point, we could see both the side of the oversized dwelling and its backyard. The structure itself was bigger than a house but smaller than our school. And like the front, the rest of Solomon's place was also in a state of extreme disrepair, with missing or rotting pieces of clapboard and more boarded-up windows. The backyard was devoid of grass and enclosed by a crosshatch fence made from birch trees. But it wasn't the state of the yard that caught my eye—it was more what was in it. Four large, black, steel barrels were piled near the fence and a number of glass jars of varying sizes sat on a large metal table. And right smack in the middle of the yard was a huge rectangular object covered in a light-blue tarp.

"What is that?" I asked.

Thomas grabbed my binoculars and scanned the yard. "That big blue thing?"

Bennie took his turn looking through the lenses. "Gotta be at least seven feet long, maybe two or three feet wide."

Emily grabbed the binoculars next. "It's flat on the top and sides, like a box."

"It's a coffin!" Thomas said.

This was out there even by Thomas's standards.

"I think you got your brain turned inside out," Bennie said. "But I'll play along. Who do you think is in there?"

"Who do *you* think?" Thomas replied.

"Anna?" Emily asked. We shared a somber look.

"Guys, we have no idea what's under there. Let's not jump to conclusions," I said with an air of adult clarity.

"You're right," Bennie said. "And I don't see Solomon or his truck, so why don't we just keep a lookout while we set up camp for the night."

Bennie took out the vinyl bag that contained our old patched-up tent. It was a hand-me-down that we called the Stink Dome due to the musky aroma that lingered while we slept. But as Bennie unfolded it, we quickly realized that it wasn't the Stink Dome at all but a brand-new eight-foot domed tent.

"Lady, gentleman, and Thomas, the Stink Dome is no more," Bennie proudly declared.

"You must have some pile of money, Bennie," Thomas remarked, poking at a nerve. "I bet if you put it all in your back pocket, you wouldn't be able to sit down."

"It's a gift from my folks for getting straight As on my report card again this year. It's their money, not mine. Plus, I earned it," Bennie shot back.

"Must be nice," Thomas ribbed. "I never got anything for my report card."

"That's because yours had letters on it that were much farther down the alphabet," I said.

"I'm just happy I'm not sleeping in something called the Stink Dome," Emily said. "Bad enough that I have to sleep with you guys."

We set up the tent in the clearing, which took no time at all since, unlike the Stink Dome, it had all its original parts. After, Bennie and Thomas made a firepit with jagged granite stones while Emily and I collected some firewood from fallen trees. The whole time, we took turns with the binoculars, keeping an eye on Solomon's place, hoping he'd return and uncover his secret in the backyard.

As night approached, we decided it was no longer feasible to stand watch since we could no longer see our target. We settled in around the crackling fire and dined on bologna sandwiches made with my mother's homemade bread. Thomas tore off some crust and put it in his back pocket. Emily looked on with confusion.

"Bread wards off the fairies," I said.

"Easy now, we shouldn't even be talking about them up here," Thomas warned as he looked around. "They could play a trick and lead us right off the cliff or worse."

"What could be worse than certain death?" Emily asked while finishing the last of her sandwich.

"Oh, not much, just a fairy blast," Thomas replied sarcastically. "That's when a fairy hits you and your wound gets all infected and turns into a big boil." Thomas leaned into the fire as he spoke. His red face looked contorted and devilish through the flames. "But that's just the beginning. After a while, it bursts open and some nasty stuff comes out, like nails, sticks, and even fish bones."

"No way, that never happened to anyone ever," Emily said.

"Oh, it did. Pierce's dad told us it happened to someone he knew," Thomas said defensively. My father had told Thomas that story to keep him from getting too close to a fire we had started on the beach. "Mind yourself, young fella," my father had warned him. "Any closer and the fairies could give you those nasty boils." It kept us all a safe distance away.

"Shut up, Thomas." Bennie looked at me.

"What?" Thomas said, then stopped short when his eyes fell on me. "Sorry, Pierce. I didn't mean anything. And you shut up, Bennie." He took a marshmallow he was roasting over the fire and threw it at Bennie. It struck him square in the forehead, sending us into a fit of laughter.

"Bellhead!" Bennie shouted as he jumped up and tore the hot pile of goo from his forehead. The soot had left a mark that looked like the kind we received on Ash Wednesday.

Things got quiet. The only sound was the rhythmic waves of the ocean. I thought about the time my father had taken me and the boys out in the boat. We were eight years old. It was a treat for Thomas and Bennie, whose fathers didn't fish for a living so they didn't get out on the water much. The ocean was as smooth as a pond that day. Dad put on the radio and we took turns jigging fish, which entailed dropping a treble hook attached to a stainless-steel sinker and monofilament line into the water, then yanking it back and forth in the hopes of catching a codfish. Soon after, we saw some humpbacks and watched with wonder as one swam underneath us. "You see, boys," my father began. "The ocean is full of surprises." Thomas began crying, and Dad gently reassured him. "Don't worry, Thomas, they're not here to hurt us," he said, putting a hand on his shoulder. "They're gentle giants who are just curious about the little fella staring back at them, is all." My father winked at Thomas, who stopped crying and gazed down at the majestic beasts, just a few fathoms below us. One breached a few feet away, spraying water into the air that rained down on us as a gentle mist. "Well, that's a wet hello," my father said, eliciting a laugh out of us all.

We cooked up our lunch surrounded by whales and soaring seabirds as Dad told us stories about other whales in our waters, like minke, fin, and potheads. But his favorite was always the humpback because they're the most playful. "They sing underwater and dance above it." He also told us that whales were once hunted for their meat and oil, some species almost to extinction. "We know better, so we should do better," he said.

As we steamed back toward the harbor, my father let me steer the boat. I remember the beaming smile on his face. It was a day I will never forget.

"Are you okay?" Emily asked.

I nodded. "I'm fine."

"Bennie told me. About your dad. I know it's not the same, but my dad kinda disappeared too," she said. "My folks are separated. I don't see him anymore. Just me and Mom now, so I guess you and I have some things in common." Emily tossed the balled-up paper bag that once held our sandwiches into the fire. It was quickly engulfed in flames, burning bright for a brief second before being reduced to ash.

"You never told me that before," Bennie said with hurt in his voice.

"I thought you would have put it together by now," Emily replied. She turned to me. "And you're not scared about going out in your dad's boat someday?"

"We're going to be with him, so there's nothing to be afraid of," Thomas said as he threw another log onto the fire. Sparks danced around his face.

"You mean there's nothing to be afraid of other than Ross Coles and the Arseholes," Bennie said, changing the subject. "We're gonna be in the same school with him and the other tools next year."

"Aren't you in the same school now?" asked Emily.

"Our school only goes to grade six. We go to the big one on the mainland in the fall," Bennie explained.

"As long as we stick together, we'll be fine," Thomas said. But his eyes told a different story.

"I know big schools," Emily said. She pierced a marshmallow with her stick and placed it over the open fire. "They can be scary at first. But you get used to it. Eventually."

Thomas, Bennie, and I had been in the same class since kindergarten. It was frightening to think that we'd be going it alone in a place full of Ross Coles.

As we sat around the fire, Emily talked about her home in New York. We heard about the busy subway lines that ran underground and how she and her mom took them to get around the city. She spoke about buildings so high they touched the clouds, skyscrapers with more people living in them than we had on our entire island. She told us about massive sports arenas, fancy art galleries, all the theaters on Broadway, and about the Statue of Liberty and Central Park, which attracted millions of visitors each year, numbers we couldn't possibly comprehend. It all seemed so wondrous, almost fantastical, even though we knew it was real.

It was getting close to midnight. It was time to turn in. We'd get up at the crack of dawn to resume our stakeout of Solomon's place. The new tent came equipped with a room divider, which meant Emily could have her own space. Still, she preferred to sleep with us since she was part of the team now, but Thomas insisted on using the divider because she was a girl.

The night air was warm and blew a sweet scent of the summer marsh through the mesh windows.

"It's so quiet," Emily said. "I can't get used to it."

"Don't worry, it won't be quiet for long," I replied. "Thomas's snoring will take care of that."

"I'd be more concerned about what comes out the other end of him," Bennie added, which filled the tent with giggles.

"Right, like you all smell like roses," Thomas countered as he zipped up his sleeping bag.

After exchanging a few good nights, we all drifted off.

A little after two, I woke to a rustling sound just outside our tent. I looked over and saw the dark forms of both Bennie and

Thomas fast asleep. Then I heard the noise again. Whatever it was, it was getting closer.

Footsteps.

An exhaled breath.

There weren't a lot of animals on the island, and the ones we did have didn't make that kind of noise. I poked Bennie and then Thomas, because fear can always use a little company. They were groggy and crooked as sin, but at least they were awake.

"I don't hear anything," Thomas grumbled as he turned over.

Then we all heard something else, a clanging sound, like metal hitting stone.

"It's probably Emily messing with us," Bennie said as he peeked outside the mesh window.

"Nope. I'm right here," Emily answered, unzipping the nylon dividing wall.

"Quiet," I said.

I carefully unzipped the mesh door. All four of us peered out. Hunched over the burning embers of the fire was a dark form. My hand shook as I held up my aluminum flashlight and flicked it on. A beam of light struck the figure's back. It turned and faced us.

It was a man. He was tall and lanky, dressed in dark clothes, and had brilliant white hair and a two-day-old beard. The flashlight reflected off the silver blade of the round point shovel in his hand.

It was Solomon Vickers.

All four of us let out a bloodcurdling scream.

Solomon jumped back. "Smarten up!" he said. "You have to put out the fire before you turn in." He dug his shovel into the earth beside our firepit and threw a scoop of dirt onto the embers. "Do you want to burn in your sleep?"

No one said a word. Solomon didn't need to shine a light back on us to see us shaking. He knew we were scared. After staring at us for a while, he turned and walked out of my flashlight beam and down the path toward his house.

We were frozen in place, our heads still peeking out of the tent, our eyes scanning the darkness for movement. It was Emily who broke the silence.

"How long was he out there?" she asked in a hushed tone.

"I . . . I don't know," I whispered back, fearful he was still out there, listening to us. Watching us.

"He just walks around in the middle of the night with a shovel?" Thomas asked. It was the quietest I'd ever heard him speak.

"Hard to believe he came all the way up here to put out a tiny fire," Bennie whispered. "Could he even see it from his place?"

"He asked if we wanted to burn in our sleep. That was a threat," Thomas added.

"Was it?" I asked, looking at the firepit.

"I don't know. He just walked away," Emily said.

There was much discussion after that, our voices low. Should we leave, or should we try to sleep and decide what to do next at first light? I pushed for us to stay put given the dangers of a night descent. Emily and Bennie both agreed that it was sound logic. I got Thomas, the only holdout, on board by subtly referencing the possibility of a fairy ambush on the way down. For better or for worse, we weren't going anywhere.

We purposely neglected to put Emily's partition back up. This was no time to be separated, even if it was by just a thin vinyl wall. It didn't matter anyway; none of us slept that night.

As the sun rose, we emerged from the tent together. Placing the binoculars to my eyes, I scanned the perimeter of Solomon's house. A look of confusion fell across my face.

"What's wrong?" Emily asked, grabbing the binoculars from my hands. Thomas and Bennie joined us at the edge of the cliff.

"It's gone," I said.

We took turns scanning Solomon's place, but none of us could find it. There was no sign of the blue tarp or the large rectangular object underneath it. Overnight, it had all disappeared.

FIVE

I was the first to arrive at church that morning. We had left Watch Hill just after sunrise, giving us lots of time to go home and make ourselves presentable, or at least passable, for mass. I saved room in the pew for the others. Being older now, we didn't sit with our families. Instead, we sat on our own, halfway up the left-hand side of the church, the closest seats to the center aisle.

The building itself sat on an incline at the end of a narrow path just up the road from the fish plant. My great-grandfather and other members of the community had built the timber-framed structure, using repurposed sections of an old schooner that had run aground to construct the steep gable roof and the frames around the arched stained glass windows and doors. They crafted everything by hand, from the pews and kneelers to the fluted wooden columns, using chisels, hand planes, and pitted saws, the same tools employed to build houses on land and boats on the water. It was a beautiful building, a testament to the ingenuity and craftsmanship of a people who for generations had clung to this rock out in the middle of nowhere. Though I never really felt spiritual inside it, I did feel something that I'd later come to know as a sense of pride. When he was alive, my father helped maintain the church. He never really expressed his religious views verbally so it was his way of showing his devotion, through hammer and nail, keeping the place in good order from the foundation up. On occasion, I would be the official tool getter. "Grab me that block plane, son," he'd said when he was making the new door for the front entrance of the church. He also took the time to show me how it worked. "Just hold it at a slight angle, quick and even strokes, putting more pressure on the front," he'd instructed. He'd guided my hands and together we'd shaved down the bottom of the vestibule door. Like most fishermen on the island, Dad was handy, a self-described jack-of-all-trades but master of none. His father had shown him, like his father's father had shown before him. But the chain was broken now. I would never be able to continue the tradition.

My mother was absent that morning. In fact, she had not darkened the church's doors since my father's death. My presence was still compulsory, however.

"After your confirmation, your attendance is your decision," Mom decreed, which I found illogical. Shouldn't I commit before confirming? But I didn't mind my mother's edict because I felt a powerful connection to the building itself.

My thoughts were interrupted when Thomas and his family arrived for mass. His parents sat in their usual berth, three-quarters of the way up the aisle, while his older brothers dispersed to various other locations. Thomas slipped in next to me with the grace of a bull moose. To make matters worse, he was emitting a rather pungent aroma.

"What the hell is that smell?" I asked, holding my nose when he sat down.

"My brother's cologne." He leaned in close, which caused my eyes to water.

"Why are you wearing cologne to mass?"

"To cover up the smoke smell from last night," Thomas said, offended by the sheer stupidity of the question.

His eyes traveled to Emily, who had just entered with her mom, Sandra Picco. She had the same eyes and sandy-brown hair as her daughter, but it was cut much shorter at the back and sides, with longer bangs in the front. I heard my mother refer to a similar style she saw on TV as a pixie cut. Parishioners watched as she made her way up the center aisle, drawn to her like the moths to our porch light. In addition to the unique hairstyle, she was dressed differently from anyone else, sporting a long, light-brown blazer and pleated white pants. It was clear that even though she was born here, she was what we called a CFA, a Come From Away.

Close behind them were Bennie, his mom, and his older sister. Bennie's mother was Catholic, while his father was Hindu. Dr. Nayak was a compassionate man who respected other religions, so he was okay with his family attending church. But he also passed along teachings of Hinduism to Bennie and his sister at home. Bennie liked having "dual religionship," as he called it. "It doubles my odds at the afterlife lottery."

Emily and Bennie joined us in our pew. It didn't take long for them to pick up on Thomas's scent.

"I think there's a dead mouse in here again," Bennie said, checking under the pew.

Emily sniffed at Thomas's neck. "It's him."

"It's called English Log. What do you think?" Thomas leaned into Emily.

"I think you need to move to the other side of Pierce," Emily suggested, waving him away.

Thomas stood up, allowing me to slide over next to Emily, and then plopped back down in a huff. I was not disappointed by the change in seating arrangement. It was nice being close to Emily. And she smelled way better than Thomas.

My excitement faded the moment I saw them walking up the center aisle of the church—Anna's mother and stepdad, with her younger sister and brother in tow. All eyes followed them as they walked slowly up the center aisle to a pew at the very front of the church.

"We gotta go to the police, tell them what we saw," Thomas whispered. We had developed a method of whisper-talking while avoiding eye contact so as not to draw attention to ourselves at church. The older parishioners were always looking for a reason to hush us young ones.

"What would we tell the police?" Bennie asked. "That there was a coffin in Solomon's backyard but now it's gone?"

"We don't know what was under that tarp," Emily said. "And why are we whispering? The show hasn't started yet."

"The show?" Thomas said, snorting. "You mean mass?"

"Yeah, that," Emily said.

"We can't tell anyone anything because we don't know anything about nothing," Bennie said.

"What about the human bones Pierce saw in Solomon's boat?" Thomas asked.

"I didn't say they were human," I replied.

Familiar music began to play, signifying the start of the mass. An eerie feeling always washed over me when the sustained notes emanated from the old pump organ. As mass was about to begin, one last patron made his way to a pew directly across from us on the other side of the aisle. He was tall and lanky, with brilliant white hair, sporting the same two-day-old beard we had seen before.

Solomon Vickers.

True fear is the kind that can take hold even when you're surrounded by family and friends. My heart began beating so fast that it drowned out the music.

"What's he doing here?" Bennie whispered.

"I take it he doesn't show every week," Emily said.

"Nope," Thomas confirmed. "Never."

My focus was on Solomon, who sat quietly across from us. He turned his head and gazed at us for a moment, then looked back toward the front of the church.

When the organ music stopped, Father Jerome took his place at the altar and delivered the week's sermon on the dangers of pretty much everything. He was a bald, short man with a rotund middle, the result of the many home-cooked dinners he enjoyed in the kitchens of his parishioners over the years. Given his advanced age, his mass was helped along by Sister Ida, a schoolteacher who kept Father Jerome from rambling by giving him a look. She also used the same look to keep the altar boys in line and the parishioners generous when the collection plate was passed around.

During the mass, we snuck glances at Solomon Vickers. He remained singularly focused on the wooden cross suspended above the altar. And when it was time for communion, he remained seated while the rest of the congregation lined up to receive the host.

"I'm telling you, Solomon knows that we know that he knows that we know," Thomas whispered behind me as we returned to our seats.

"Maybe we can make an anonymous call to the police," Bennie said.

"Right, like they're gonna believe a kid," Thomas said far too loudly, causing Bennie to shush him before anyone else did.

"Or maybe they have it figured out," Emily said, nodding toward the back doors, where two police officers stood. They were the very same ones we saw at Solomon's place.

"What are they doing here?" Emily asked.

"They're going to arrest him," I replied, looking over at Solomon. Seeing a few turned heads, Solomon looked back at the officers for a brief second before turning around again. His face was void of any emotion.

The mass concluded without the standard announcements of bake sales and community bingo. Instead, the two police officers made their way up the aisle. This was it. They were going to arrest Solomon for his involvement in the disappearance of Anna Tessier. But they walked right by the old man and continued on to the front of the church.

"What are they doing?" I asked, confused. "He's right there!"

The female officer said something to Sister Ida and Father Jerome, who both nodded to her in agreement. The officer removed her cap, revealing dark black hair in a bun underneath. She introduced herself to the congregation as Sergeant Trang and her partner as Constable Munro.

"We're sorry to interrupt. We just wanted you all to know that we are following some leads," she began, capturing everyone's attention in a way that Father Jerome could only dream of. "But as I've told the Tessier family, we have no updates to share at this time. I do want you to know that everyone is doing their best to find Anna."

I'd heard those words before, when my father failed to return to the safety of our harbor.

"I'm here because we could use some volunteers to help search the island," Sergeant Trang continued, looking around the church. Her eyes fell on Anna's mother, who pulled Anna's younger siblings close while Anna's stepfather stared straight ahead at the wooden crucifix.

"And if anyone here knows anything that might help our investigation, don't hesitate to contact us. And we look forward to meeting some of you as volunteers."

Sergeant Trang thanked everyone, stepped off to the side, and gave the floor back to Father Jerome. My friends and I looked at each other, then at Solomon, but we said nothing.

Sister Ida whispered a reminder to Father Jerome, who asked everyone to bow their heads in one last prayer for Anna's safe return.

I broke with protocol and lifted my head before the silent prayer had ended. Anna's mom was now standing with Father Jerome at the foot of the altar. Her face held such great sadness. I looked over at Solomon, whose face was still void of any emotion.

My friends were right, we had to do something. I had to do something. The police were right there. I stood up from the pew.

"What are you doing?" Thomas said, yanking at my jacket. "Sit down."

All eyes fell on me, including those of Anna's mother.

I wanted to tell her, the police, everyone, about Solomon and what we saw in his yard, but I could feel Solomon's eyes on me, turning me to stone. I don't know how long I stood like that, but eventually, Emily jumped up and grabbed my hand. It felt warm against mine, and brought me back to life. She coaxed me back to a seated position in the pew. I avoided eye contact with my friends and the other parishioners by keeping my head down for the rest of the prayer, which seemed to go on for an eternity. When Father Jerome finally lifted his head and finished the mass, telling us all to go in peace, Emily quickly pulled me up to my feet and took me through the side door of the church.

Once outside, she led me down the narrow concrete steps to the gravel parking lot. I felt like I was floating, tethered only to her. If she'd let my hand go, I would have drifted up and away like a balloon.

"It's okay," she said, squeezing my cold hand tighter.

"They need to know about Solomon," I said. "Anna's mom needs to know."

"We don't have any proof. You can't just get someone's hopes up only to have them crash back down," Emily said.

Her words resonated with me. I knew all too well the fleeting comfort of false hope. All those people in that church who'd told my mother and me that they would find my father and bring him home. But they never did.

A few seconds later, Thomas and Bennie came running down the steps.

"You should have seen the way Sister Ida was glaring at you. If she had a ruler in her hand, she would have thrown it at you," Thomas said. He looked down at our hands. His smile instantly disappeared and Emily let go of my hand.

People began filing out of the church. We watched Anna's family walk slowly down the steps toward their small silver pickup. Anna's younger brother and sister climbed in the back and sat on the folding jump seats. It was a tight fit. I couldn't help but think that Anna, being older, must have had to ride in the back of the truck since there was no room in the cab.

"So, what are we gonna do?" Bennie asked.

"We have to get in there," I said as I watched Anna's mom climb into their truck.

"Get in where?" Thomas asked.

"Solomon's place," Emily said, finishing my thought.

"Are you crazy?" Bennie asked.

"Anna's still on this island. I know it," I said.

"How do you know that?" Emily asked. I didn't respond.

"It doesn't matter what you or anyone else thinks," Thomas said. "Watching Solomon's place from the top of a hill is one thing. Breaking into it is another."

"Solomon's onto us," Bennie said, his eyes wide.

"I don't care. We have to act fast." I gave Emily a pleading look.

"Pierce is right," Emily said. "She's been missing for four days now. Time's running out."

"Mom gets the ferry every Monday to get a few groceries on the mainland," Thomas said. "And she says that Solomon's been on that boat every time too. She sometimes sees him on the return trip a couple of hours later."

We all looked at one another. Today was Sunday. Tomorrow was Monday. If we were going to do something, tomorrow was the day.

SIX

A year after my father's death, I crossed paths with Anna Tessier for the second time. I was ten years old. It had been a difficult twelve months without him. So many firsts. First Christmas without him. First Father's Day without him. Those first birthdays and anniversaries. What was once considered cause for celebrations became somber commemorations. No matter the occasion, for the rest of our lives it would always seem like something . . . someone was missing. There would always be a void in my life as deep as the ocean that took him.

Other burdens entered our lives. In order to make up for the lost income, my mother took on extra shifts at the fish plant and picked up some part-time work at the video store on the mainland. I helped out more around the house with the cooking and cleaning, as well as keeping the front lawn well groomed. The back garden was no longer an issue since Dad's boat took up most of the yard. It too had been there a full year.

But it was during this transitional period that Thomas, Bennie, and I first hatched the plan to fix up Dad's boat and take it out fishing when we were old enough to do so.

It was the beginning of summer holidays. I was riding my trike on the north side of the island. Thomas and I had just repaired the suspension on my ATV, and I wanted to test it out on some rougher terrain.

That's when I saw it. A large iceberg had run aground about five hundred feet offshore. But this one was different from any I'd seen before. I'd seen many, including some with varying colors throughout them. But this one was a brilliant blue, almost electric. I drove up to get a better look and found I wasn't alone. Someone else was captivated by its beauty. Anna. She was sitting on a rock with a sketchbook in her hand, the same kind I'd seen sticking out of her knapsack the first time we met.

She turned when she heard my bike.

"You've got to work on your sneaking-up-on-people skills," she said, stuffing a pencil into the front pocket of her oversized black denim jacket before retrieving the one next to it. She had rolled up her sleeves, exposing the wide silver cuff bracelet on her left wrist.

"I wasn't sneaking," I replied as I shut off my trike and jumped off. I realized she was joking only after the words left my mouth.

"I've never seen one like that," she said, nodding at the majestic iceberg. "You?"

"No," I said. "Not that color. Never."

We were seeing something for the first time, witnessing it together.

"It has something to do with the air bubbles and the minerals and tiny microorganisms trapped in the ice. Or something like that," Anna said. "And, of course, how the light reflects off it."

"Yeah, I read that somewhere," I lied.

I walked up to her and looked over her shoulder. She was putting the final touches on a drawing of the iceberg. The sketch showed the brilliant color and angular lines above the water, but it also revealed everything below the waterline, the magnitude of the glacial giant in the hidden depths.

"Are they really that much bigger under the water?" I asked.

"Yup," she said. "Kind of like people."

I went silent for a long while. I had no idea what she meant.

"You're really good," I said eventually. "At drawing."

"Think so?" she asked, handing me her book, then patting the space next to her. I sat down beside her.

I flipped through the large pad and saw Anna's drawings of the boats, stages, and the rocky shorelines. I liked the way she used curvy lines within the images themselves, as if there was movement, life in everything she drew. Anna's initials were on the bottom right corner of each sketch. I came upon one sketch that was different from the rest. It was a portrait of a girl roughly Anna's age. The girl was looking slightly off to the side, as if she was having a conversation with someone just off the page.

"Who's that?" I asked.

"A new friend I met this year. It's from the last day of school."

Anna had been going to the bigger school on the main island all year.

"What was your first year like?" I asked. By then, I'd heard all the rumors about the tough kids at the big school who would rather punch you in the face than talk to you. At that time, my friends and I were only a couple of grades away from having to make that crossing. It was becoming a more frequent topic of conversation between us. I wasn't afraid so much as curious. But details about how it was over there were scanty. Anna seemed like a reliable source of information.

"Way more kids, which means you'll find new friends you'll have lots in common with," Anna said.

This eased my worries a little.

"So, you think she'll like it?" Anna asked, taking the sketch-book from my hands.

"Like what?" I asked.

"The sketch. Do you think my new friend will like it?"

"Yeah, it's really good."

"Cool. I'm going to go see her tomorrow." Her eyes met mine. "She lives close to the school."

"But we're on summer holidays now," I said.

"I don't need the school bus to get there," she said. "But don't tell anyone."

I nodded slowly, but I didn't really understand.

"Why shouldn't I tell anyone?" I asked.

"Because it's a secret. I'm going alone. Last time I did something like that, my folks were pissed. But I'll make the ferry back before dark this time."

This was no easy task. Without the school bus, Anna would have to take the ferry on her own and then make her way to her friend's house once she was on the other side, probably by hitching a ride.

"Be careful," I said. Even I could hear it, how I sounded like an adult and not a child.

Anna smiled.

"You're still wearing it!" she said, touching the small frowny-face button she'd given me the first time we spoke.

"You want it back?" I asked.

"No, I don't need it yet," she replied, pulling her hand away from my jacket. "You still think about your dad?"

I could feel myself welling up inside. I wanted to tell her just how much I missed him and how I would have given anything to have him back.

"Yeah," I mumbled, forcing a smile.

"Good. But you don't have to put on a face for anyone," she replied, gently tapping my lips with the end of her pencil. My smile was now legit.

"Do you want a ride back to your house?" I asked.

"Nah, I'm not done here." She got to her feet and started to walk down the incline. "I'm going to sketch it from a different angle."

"Right, of course," I said as if I understood.

I got back on my trike and drove off without saying goodbye.

This was the second to last encounter I'd have with Anna before she disappeared from our little island forever.

SEVEN

The next day, I got up early and began making scrambled eggs and toast. The toaster only browned the bread on one side, but Mom said it was okay, that it was very British and many people would pay extra for such a feature.

We sat in our designated places at the kitchen table and ate in silence. The events of the past few days were racing in my mind. My fork seemed to mimic my thoughts; I was shoveling the food into my mouth as if I hadn't eaten in days, something not lost on my mother. When I reached for some homemade blueberry jam, I finally noticed her staring at me.

"No one's going to steal your food," she said, putting her outstretched hand around mine on the mason jar

"Just hungry, is all," I replied, knowing my answer wasn't going to cut it. She knew what was on my mind.

"There's a lot of good people looking for her here," she said, gently squeezing my hand. Many of those very same people had gone looking for my father, but to no avail.

"And the police are following leads on the mainland," she continued.

"They're not going to find her over there," I replied, pulling my hand out from under hers. "They're wasting time. Everyone should be looking for her right here." Anna had been missing for five days now. Mom and I knew that five days was a lifetime when searching for a loved one.

"Pierce, I know this must be tough. Maybe it's bringing up some memories for you—"

"I'm fine," I said defiantly. "Really, I'm okay."

Mom took a piece of toast from my plate and spread some of her homemade blueberry jam on it with a butter knife, then placed it next to my scrambled eggs.

"No one is ever prepared for something like this. When your dad went missing, we held out hope for as long as we could, even after the search had ended. We did everything possible to find his b—to find him. You know that, right?" she asked, her eyes staring deep into mine.

"I do," I replied. The last couple of years had brought perspective; I knew this was true, or close to true. I knew this was what she needed to hear from me.

"But like your grandmother's handmade patch quilt, we try and sew the pieces back together the best we can, to make something out of what's left, even though, when you lose someone, you miss them all the world. Work keeps our minds occupied, but the loneliness is always waiting."

I didn't want to talk about it anymore. It was more than I could handle. "Speaking of work," I said, nodding to our digital clock radio on the shelf above the stove, "you'd better get going."

"You're right," she said, grabbing her car keys and the rest of her things.

She walked to work most days, but this wouldn't be one of

them. I didn't need to ask why. She was tired and her concern for me was robbing the last of her energy.

I followed my mother to the porch but was startled when she stopped suddenly. She turned and smiled, then rubbed my cheek with her hand. As I got older, she'd often pretend to wipe away a little grime as justification for touching the face of her son who had outgrown such physical signs of affection from his mom. Then she turned back and rushed out the door.

I watched her through the window as she made her way to the car. She threw her smock and knife in the back seat before opening the driver's-side door. The trunk of the now ten-year-old light-brown sedan was completely rusted out and could no longer be trusted to carry even the lightest of loads. The driver's-side door squeaked as my mother opened it and hopped in. The engine struggled but finally came to life after the third twist of the key. She backed down the lane and headed up the road toward the plant.

As she disappeared out of sight, a feeling of regret came over me. I should have listened, given her time to finish her thoughts. Maybe I could have said some things that needed saying too, about my father, about her, about this life he left behind.

I put the eggs back in the fridge and made quick work of the dishes, leaving them to dry in the yellow plastic-coated dish rack. I grabbed my coat and walked outside, pausing for a brief moment as I considered locking the door behind me for the first time ever. We had never done it before, but things felt different now. I always felt safe on the island, but a missing girl and a strange old man was beginning to change that. It was a moot point anyway because the keys had long disappeared, from lack of use.

I walked down the steps and jumped on my trike. I started it up, drove down the lane, and headed off in the direction of the ferry terminal.

Some fifteen minutes later, I arrived at the small clearing overlooking the dock. The others were already there, waiting for me. Thomas drove his poorly painted trike, while Bennie and Emily made the trek on foot.

"There he is!" Thomas announced as if I was the guest of honor. "The boy who stood up in church. Great speech by the way. Oh wait, you froze up like our bathroom pipes in February."

"Don't be at it," I warned. I was in no mood to be picked on.

"Maybe you should hold his hand again to calm him down," Thomas fired at Emily.

I moved toward Thomas. "You want a punch in your big fat face?"

"Try it, lover boy," Thomas responded.

Lover boy? The insult stopped me in my tracks.

"Enough," Emily shouted, getting in between us. I unclenched my fists and let the blood circulate back into my fingers.

"What were you thinking anyway, standing up in church like that?" Bennie asked.

Emily and I shared a look. She knew why, but I didn't want to explain it to Thomas and Bennie.

"He was thinking it was time to get out of there," she jumped in. "Talk about a real downer. I get it, we're all going to hell, thanks for the heads-up, Father Sunshine."

Bennie and Thomas chuckled. We were all good again.

A familiar old red pickup with a missing antenna drove up to the ferry ramp. It made a rumbling sound.

"Buddy there got a hole in his muffler," Thomas remarked.

I scanned the vehicle with my binoculars. Solomon. The back

of the truck was loaded down with black metal barrels and gray plastic totes.

"That's him," I said.

Emily took the binoculars from me. "What do you think he's carrying back there?"

"Don't know, but it's not the thing we saw in his backyard," I said.

"Okay. We have exactly two hours before the boat returns." Bennie clicked a button on his digital watch.

"Some fancy watch," Thomas said. "Must be nice having new things all the time."

"Shut your face," Bennie snapped.

"Boys," Emily said. "Enough."

"Let's go," I said as I fired up my trike. Emily hopped on the back, her arms tight around my waist.

Bennie jumped on Thomas's trike, and the four of us rode toward the most easterly part of the island, to Solomon's place.

EIGHT

We stood and stared at Solomon Vickers's crumbling dwelling. Rough lumber stairs that looked like they could give way at any moment led to the large wooden double doors. There was a thick layer of rust on both the knobs and hinges. There was nothing inviting about the place.

It took us some thirty minutes to get there, which, according to the Monday ferry schedule, left us just an hour and a half before Solomon would return.

We parked our trikes in the barrens, about a quarter of a mile down the road. We couldn't chance some passerby seeing them in front of his place.

"It's so run-down," Emily remarked.

"Mom said it was built after the Great War," Thomas said.

"It was a cottage hospital," Bennie added. "But it closed down when our parents were kids, back in the sixties. My dad said it was taken over by the university on the mainland, but then they left after a while too. One of Dad's old profs worked there years ago. He said it was used as a sanatorium."

"A whatatorium?" Thomas asked.

"A place to quarantine tuberculosis patients," Bennie elaborated. "People actually died in there."

"And that's why it's haunted," Thomas concluded.

"It's not haunted . . . much," I replied.

But there were countless ghost stories about the place, which usually involved seeing lights inside the building at night. Some even say they saw little creatures in and around that area, which added to the fairy lore of the island. Like most kids, we always stayed far away from the place, until now.

"We don't have much time. If we're going to do this, we have to do it now," I said.

We walked with determination through the space where a gate once stood, through the yard full of crabgrass and dandelions, and up the dilapidated stairs with the missing handrail to the double wooden doors. After a deep breath, I tried to turn the doorknob, to no avail. This was weird, since most people on the island kept their doors unlocked.

"Now what?" Bennie asked.

"Plan B," Thomas replied, opening up his fanny pack and taking out a small, rusted crowbar. "We bust it open, old school."

"He can't know we were ever here," Emily said, grabbing the crowbar from Thomas. Her conviction didn't leave room for debate.

We followed her to the side of the building, pulling on the boards that covered the unglazed windows until she found what she was looking for. A loose plank.

"This is as good as any," she said, sticking the hooked end of the crowbar in between the boards and the window frame.

Once she pried a board so far, the rest of us grabbed it with our hands and pulled it off the house until we had an opening.

Thomas shone his flashlight into the house. "Looks like a four-foot drop to the floor," he said. "Who wants to go first?"

"I'll go," I heard myself say as I peered into the darkness. It had to be me. This was my idea and though I had no idea what awaited us on the other side, I had to be the first to find out. I instinctively looked at Emily, who nodded her approval.

I climbed into the square opening feetfirst. Thomas and Bennie held on to my arms as my legs searched for the floor. Once I found my footing, I took out my flashlight and looked around. I was in a small storage room with a number of oversized jars on the shelf, similar to the ones we saw in the back garden during our stakeout. There were also a couple of large black metal drums stacked in the corner.

"All good in there?" Emily asked.

"Yeah, come on in."

Emily came down next. I went to help her, but she was too fast and stuck the landing like a pro. Bennie followed with similar success. Thomas was much less graceful and came crashing to the floor, knocking us all down in the process.

"Get off me," Bennie yelled.

"Not my fault, I had no help like the rest of you," Thomas snapped.

We all got to our feet and looked around. Emily picked up an oversized jar on a shelf.

"Jars," Emily said. "All empty."

"Mom uses jars for homemade jams," Thomas said.

"Look at the size of it. Even you couldn't eat that much rhubarb jam," Bennie noted.

"Hazardous material," Emily said, reading the labels on the drums. "What's in there?"

"Let's just keep moving." I carefully opened the door, giving us full access to Solomon's world.

We shone our flashlights down a large hallway with doors on each side. Emily found a switch on the wall and flipped it. Nothing.

"Must be on a generator," I said. "No power lines this far out."

"Where do we start?" Bennie asked. He shone a beam of light behind us, illuminating an L-shaped staircase.

"How about up there?" I suggested.

"I think we should split up," Emily said. "Me and Pierce will take the upstairs and you two start down here."

Thomas and Bennie shared a look.

"Let's stick together," Bennie said.

"Good idea," Thomas immediately agreed.

We ascended the staircase. When we got to the top, we found ourselves in an open loft with exposed beams that ran the length of the ceiling. There was a small mattress on a brass bedframe and next to it was a handmade dresser that had been painted many times over. A couple of heavy wool sweaters and a red flannel checkered shirt hung on four-inch nails on the wall.

"Solomon's bedroom," Thomas said.

"Yeah, this is probably taking it too far," Emily said slowly. "Let's go back downstairs."

But something caught my eye. The old floorboards creaked as I walked toward a large midcentury oak desk pushed against the side wall. A nautical chart of the waters off our island took up most of the working space. A framed corkboard was suspended on the wall above it. It was covered with photos, newspaper clippings, and other printed materials all pertaining to the ocean and marine life. Next to the corkboard were three large bookcases filled to capacity.

Thomas pulled an oversized book from the lower shelf. "*Pre-*

serving Specimens," he said, reading the title on the dust jacket. "Creepy."

"He has a thing for the ocean," Emily remarked, pointing to an article on the declining cod fishery that was pinned to the corkboard.

I shone my flashlight across the board. The beam landed on a sketch of a weathered old man. It was him. Solomon. Except his eyes seemed softer in the sketch than in real life. I'd seen this style before, the curvy lines that helped fill out the image. My suspicions were confirmed when I spotted the initials on the bottom right-hand corner: A.T.

I carefully removed the sketch from the board and ran my shaking fingers over the initials.

Bennie appeared at my side. "Not a bad likeness of the old fella," he said.

I could barely form words. When I was finally able to do so, I said, "Anna Tessier drew this."

Emily came to my side. She looked up at me, her eyes wide. "Are you sure?" She gently pried the sketch from my hands.

"How do you know she did this?" Thomas asked.

"I saw her sketchpad. She initialed all of her drawings like that."

"You never told us that before," Bennie said.

"So Solomon and Anna knew each other," Emily said.

"It means they *know* each other," I corrected.

"You're right," Emily said. She handed the sketch back to me.

"We're onto something here. We have to keep looking." I stared at the sketch, at Solomon's face. My fingers tightened at the corners of the paper. I thought about ripping it to shreds, but Emily put her hand on mine, sensing what I was about to do.

"He can't know we were here, remember?" she said.

I nodded and pinned the sketch back on the corkboard.

We walked quickly through Solomon's bedroom and back down the staircase to the main floor. Our flashlights guided us past the storage room that we used to gain entry. We followed the hallway, checking rooms as we went. Eventually, we came to a solid wood door that was secured with a silver padlock.

"What's behind it?" Bennie asked.

"Something important. Why else would he lock it?" Thomas replied.

I took the small crowbar from Thomas's fanny pack.

"Are you crazy?" Thomas said, grabbing my arm.

"Ah, guys?" Emily said from across the room. "You may want to take a look at this."

We walked across the room to where Emily stood next to a large, rectangular object under a blue tarp. It was the same one we'd seen in the back garden the night we camped out on Watch Hill. It was about three feet wide and at least ten feet long, and was on some kind of base that made it almost as tall as we were.

I pulled out my knife. The others looked down at the blade before meeting my gaze. No words were exchanged; none were needed. This was why we were here.

I began to cut the nylon ropes that held the tarp in place. The blade was dull, impeding the operation.

"That wouldn't cut through warm butter." Thomas took a small pocket stone out of his fanny pack. "Gimme."

"I got it," I shot back.

"Let me sharpen it." Thomas tried to grab the knife but only succeeded in knocking it from my hand. It hit the floorboards and bounced under the tarp.

"Idiot," I said.

"You're the idiot," Thomas responded.

It was then that we heard it, the distinct sound of a vehicle with a hole in the muffler. Years of waiting for boats to pass through the narrows had honed our ability to judge distance on anything with a motor. The truck was close.

Emily moved toward the front window and looked out. "It's him!"

"That's impossible. The ferry isn't due back for another hour," Bennie said, checking his watch.

"Looks like your watch is the idiot," Thomas replied.

"But we saw him drive on board," Emily said.

Our ferry was getting on in age, and it wasn't uncommon for it to turn around and head back to dock if something went wrong.

"Maybe the boat had engine trouble again," I said.

"He's in the driveway!" Emily gasped. "And he's unloading something from his truck!"

"We gotta get out of here!" Bennie said.

I dropped to the floor to search for my knife, but it was out of reach. I felt a hand on my shoulder.

"Leave it, we gotta go!" Emily hissed as Thomas and Bennie made their way toward the storage room.

"My dad gave me that knife," I said, now on my stomach. My hand fumbled blindly under the tarp.

"Please, Pierce," Emily said, softer now, her hand still on my shoulder.

I got to my knees and noticed a small tear in the tarp. I shone my flashlight into the opening and put my eye to the hole. What I saw made me instantly jump backward and drop my flashlight.

"What is it?" Emily asked as she retrieved my flashlight from the floor.

I was rendered mute. She shone the flashlight in the hole and looked in herself.

"Oh my god," she said, her voice trembling. "It's an eye."

The sound of footsteps echoed in our ears. It was my turn to grab Emily by the hand. We ran back toward the small storage room. Thomas and Bennie had already set one of the large metal drums under the window. We held the barrel steady as Emily climbed up and crawled out the window just as we heard the front door open.

"Hurry!" I said as Bennie jumped out the window.

"Go!" I instructed Thomas, who didn't have to be told twice.

Emily and Bennie grabbed his outstretched hands and pulled him through the opening. As soon as Thomas was clear, I jumped up and grabbed the window frame. I could hear footsteps outside the door. The metal drum fell over the second I cleared the window, making a loud clanging noise followed by the sound of glass exploding on the floor. The barrel had rolled into the shelf filled with jars.

We ran as fast as we could up the lane and through the front gate. I looked back as we crested the hill, expecting to see Solomon standing on his porch, watching us or, worse yet, tearing down the road in his clunky, loud pickup. But when I looked back, he wasn't there.

We didn't stop running until we reached our trikes, which we'd hidden in the barrens. Emily and I stared at each other, breathless, wide-eyed. We had both witnessed something that Bennie and Thomas had not.

"What?" Thomas asked as he took in our faces.

"Nothing," I said. "But we aren't finished in there. We have to go back."

NINE

We stood beside our ATVs on the cliff overlooking the large iceberg that Emily had admired the very first day we met. It had been
over an hour since our failed search of Solomon's place, and we
were taking a little time to process what had just happened. In
truth, we were lying low just in case Solomon was on the roads,
looking for the ones who broke into his place. The wind carried a
chill from the frozen giant just offshore. Emily wasn't wearing a
jacket, and it was clear she was beginning to feel the effects of the
cool ocean breeze. She rubbed her arms where the goose bumps
had taken hold. Emily was still getting used to our climate, one in
which you could experience all four seasons in a single day. This
was life on an exposed island in the North Atlantic, subject to the
currents and jet streams that could send us snow in May or make
it rain sideways at almost any time of the year, rendering umbrellas
useless. Only tourists carried the ineffectual contraptions, which
made it easy to spot potential buyers for our cod tongues. But the
same unpredictable weather patterns could also bring about a sudden and unexpected squall, the kind that could pull a man from a
boat and change a family forever.

I took off my jacket and offered it to Emily. She didn't notice my attempt at chivalry but Thomas did and decided to make a similar gesture. He started to remove his own coat by hauling it over his head like a sweater. But in his haste, it got stuck around his large noggin and he proceeded to struggle like a bear with his head caught in a honey jar. Emily didn't see this epic struggle—she was staring out to sea.

I was holding out my jacket to Emily, but it was only when I touched her shoulder that she turned and looked down at my outstretched hand.

"You sure you don't need it?" she asked.

"Yeah, I'm too warm anyway." A total lie.

Emily put it on just as Thomas got his off. It was now inside out, showing the bright orange lining that matched Thomas's face.

"Smooth," Bennie said.

"We can't all have fancy zippers that work every single time," Thomas replied.

Emily rolled up the sleeves of my jacket to make for a more custom fit. Then she touched the frowny-face button that Anna had given me.

"I didn't think you for the frowny-face-button kind of guy," she said.

"It was a gift, from a friend," I responded. I would have liked to say more, but Bennie intervened.

"Everybody comfortable now?" he sneered. "We can't stay here forever. What are we going to do?"

"We have to go back," I said.

"You're cracked if you think I'm going back there," Thomas declared. "You had your chance to see what was under that tarp, but you shagged it up."

"Me? You're the one who knocked the knife out of my hands," I replied.

"You should have just let me sharpen it. It was dull."

"You would know," I said.

"What's that supposed to mean?"

"Exactly." I was fuming inside. It was more than just a knife. And it was Thomas's fault that it was no longer hanging in its sheath by my side.

"Let's just agree it was Bennie's fancy-arse watch that couldn't tell the right time," Thomas said.

"My watch works fine, unlike that stupid ferry," Bennie said defensively. "And speaking of which, isn't your dad the one who's supposed to keep the engine running, Thomas?"

"Yeah, so?"

"So, maybe if he put the bottle down once in a while, he could do a better job and that ferry would have taken Solomon off the island as planned."

A look of shock washed over Thomas's face. His eyes widened and his mouth dropped open though not a single breath passed his lips. There was an old fable we were told as kids. It was a story meant to warn you not to make a crooked face because if the wind blew at your back, your face would get stuck like that permanently. Thomas had proven the validity of the story and seemed frozen in a state of shock. Emily and I looked at each other uncomfortably. Thomas's father was a bit of a drinker. But he managed to get the work done, for the most part, though he, like a few others on the island, was slipping more and more these days. My mother suggested that he had too much free time on his hands. It was a byproduct of a failing fishery. People just didn't have money to spend on a mechanic. And for what little business there was, Thomas's older brothers were forced to pick up the slack at the garage. His father was getting noticeably meaner to Thomas, too. We'd sometimes hear him swearing at his youngest son when we drove up to his place.

"He hardly ever drinks on the job," Thomas said. "And for the record, my dad could put an arse in a cat if he wanted to."

"Great if you're a veterinarian, not so much if you're a mechanic," Bennie quipped.

"Boys, can you stop being childish for one minute?" Emily said, stepping in between us. She looked directly at me. "Do you want to tell them or do I have to?"

I didn't want to admit to anyone what I had seen under that tarp. Not yet anyway. I was still processing it myself. And I feared that it would sound like another tall tale.

"Tell us what?" Bennie inquired.

I took a deep breath. "There was a hole in the tarp," I said. "We saw something."

"We saw a lot more than 'something,' Pierce," Emily said, admonishment in her eyes. "Come on."

"Well?" Thomas asked impatiently.

"It looked like . . . I mean, it could have been . . . It probably was, maybe . . ."

"It was an eyeball," Emily said. "Staring back at us."

As I heard it out loud, it sounded as crazy as I thought it would.

"An eyeball?" Bennie asked. "You been smoking some of Junior Maher's wacky baccy?"

"No, she's right. We both saw it," I said.

"There's someone in there, under that tarp," Emily said.

"Not someone. Anna," Thomas said. "I told you it was a coffin."

"That thing was ten feet long," Bennie said. "It's no coffin."

"Maybe he left room in there for other kids," Thomas suggested.

"It's not a coffin," Bennie repeated.

"Call it what you want, she's in there," Thomas said. "Right, Pierce?"

I looked at Emily, remembering her words to me after church, about not jumping to conclusions without having some kind of proof, that it would do more harm to Anna's family. Emily nodded, as if to say it was okay to speak my mind.

"I don't know," I said. I didn't want to commit to anything just yet. And the idea that she—Anna—could be under there was too much for me to handle.

"Are you saying that of all the other eyeballs you've seen under tarps in the run-down homes of skeety old men, you're not certain this eyeball belonged to the only person currently missing on this friggin' island?" Bennie asked.

"All I know is that we saw something," I said. "We'll know for sure what's under that tarp when we go back."

"Go back? We can't just go back, not now, not ever," Bennie said. "We tore boards off his window and smashed his jars."

He was right.

"It's simple," Emily said. "We just have to wait until he leaves his house again."

"He could come back at any minute, just like last time," Bennie said. "Or have traps set up all over that place now that he knows we were shaggin' around in there."

"See, this is what happens when you watch *Home Alone* fifty times," Thomas said.

"Look, if we're not going to handle this ourselves, then we have to tell the police," Emily said.

"Right. And tell them we might have seen something weird during our last B and E. It'll be a fun story to tell the other kids at juvie," said Thomas.

"He's being a big arsehole," Bennie said. "But he's not wrong."

"All I'm saying is that just because we drive trikes and make a few dollars cutting out tongues and helping out the fishermen, let's not think for a second the police or anyone else is going to listen to us," Thomas said. "They won't because all they see is just some stupid kids who don't know nothing about anything."

Thomas's face turned stern. His eyes drew small and he clenched his teeth, causing the muscles in his round cheeks to tighten. He looked more like the man who inspired the lack of confidence he was showing; he looked like his father. When his dad drank heavily, he'd say cruel things about how stupid Thomas and his brothers were, how idiotic and worthless. He covered the impact of such blows with a thin veil of humor. But at the end of the day, Thomas was probably right: the word of an adult, even one who was from the outside world, would always trump a bunch of local kids on trikes.

"If the police won't listen, then we should tell adults who will," Emily suggested. "Like our families."

"I can't tell my folks. They'll ship me off to another school. You'll never see me again," Bennie said.

"Promise?" Thomas replied.

"It has to be your mom, Pierce," Bennie said, ignoring Thomas's jab.

"My mother?" I recoiled at the thought.

"Yeah. She's calm, sensible. And unlike me and Thomas, your father is not around to administer punishment when it turns out all you saw under that tarp was your own ugly reflection."

He was right about one thing: in our world, mothers acted as judges while fathers doled out punishments. In the absence of the latter, my mother did what she always did—she took on additional roles and managed everything. She was known across the island for being someone who wasn't afraid to speak her mind, which she did on many occasions, especially at the plant whenever she'd perceive an injustice. She would take on coworkers and management alike. She never swore or raised her voice; she just stuck to the facts. And she could throw down with the best of them. I once saw her confront Wes Bartlett, the plant's foreman, over doing away with bonuses. He was so flustered after talking with my mother that he had to go home for lunch, something he hadn't done in forty years working at the plant.

"You don't know my mother," I said. "You have no friggin' clue."

"I'll go with you," Emily said. "I mean, if you want. Just to back up your story."

"Okay," I heard myself say.

"Good, let us know how it goes," Thomas said, starting up his trike. When Bennie got on behind him, he peeled away.

Once they were gone, I looked at Emily. "You don't have to do this," I said.

"We're in it together now," she replied.

We hopped on my trike and once again she wrapped her arms around my waist. But it felt different this time. She was holding on just a little tighter. I started up the trike and we drove along the narrow winding bike paths that took us back to the western portion of the island. The wind had changed once again and was now blowing a warm breeze from the marsh. I started to feel confidence build inside me. With Emily around, it was like all the regular rules were no longer in play. Anything seemed possible.

As we turned onto the old power-line path that led to my house, I spotted a vehicle parked in the middle of our gravel driveway. I stopped the trike abruptly, causing Emily to crash into my back, which sent me into the handlebars.

"Why are we stopping? Please tell me this isn't another fairy thing," Emily said.

I looked through the binoculars to confirm my suspicions before handing them to Emily.

"Is that what I think it is?" she asked.

An old red pickup with a missing antenna was parked in my driveway directly behind my mother's car. She rarely came home for lunch, but this marked another strange bend in the usual way of things.

"He's got Mom!" I gasped. "Hold on," I instructed as I hit the throttle and peeled down the path toward my house.

My old yellow trike shook as we careened down the power-line path at full speed. Each rock we struck sent vibrations up through the handlebars and into my arms. I could feel Emily's hands digging into my ribs. She was holding on for dear life. I'd never gone this fast down this stretch of terrain. What was Solomon doing at my house?

"Slow down!" Emily shouted over the engine. "We'll be no good dead!"

I ignored Emily and navigated the treacherous pathway filled with potholes and jagged rocks. We had a couple of close calls, but I managed to keep the machine upright. At the bottom of the path, I made a sharp left turn that nearly finished us, but by some divine intervention the three-wheeler didn't flip over. I hit the throttle one last time and tore up the dirt driveway, screeching to a halt just inches from Solomon's bumper.

Emily quickly jumped off the trike.

"Don't ever do that again!" she snapped, and punched me square in the arm.

"I'm sorry," I said, but I didn't really mean it. All my focus was on what was going on in my house.

As we walked past Solomon's truck, I saw the driver's-side window was rolled down. Inside, it was messy with newspapers and nautical maps scattered over the dash and floor mats. And wedged between the seats were two menacing-looking fishing gaffs complete with barbed hooks.

Precautions had to be taken. I hurried over to our woodpile and removed the axe from the splitting block.

"What are you doing?" Emily asked.

"Just in case."

"In case of what?"

"In case there's a killer in my house, Emily. A killer alone with my mother."

Emily's face softened. "Just don't go in swinging, okay?"

We ran up the front steps, swung open the screen glass door, and rushed through the porch to the kitchen.

I'll never forget the bewildered look on my mother's face when she saw me enter the kitchen with a girl by my side and an axe clenched in my right hand. She was by the sink, pouring a cup of orange pekoe from our old, cracked porcelain teapot. Solomon was sitting at our chrome kitchen table, a plate of date squares on a place mat in front of him.

"Pierce?" my mother said, looking from me to Emily to the axe in my hand.

"Mom," I said in my best man voice. "Are you okay?" My fingers tightened around the handle.

My mother poured some sugar into a special bowl that was part of a set she got as a wedding gift sixteen years ago. She carried it over to the table and set it down.

"Am *I* okay?" she asked as she walked toward Emily. "Hello. And who are you?" My mother's eyes were oscillating between Emily's face and my jacket, which Emily was still wearing.

"Oh, hi, I'm Emily, Bennie's cousin." Her sunny smile was having no effect on my mother's chilly disposition.

"So, you're Sandra's daughter." Her eyes widened. "Quite the change from New York City, I guess," my mother said as she calmly took the axe from my hand and laid it next to the stove.

Solomon was looking at me with his dark eyes. If he was affected by the sudden intrusion of an axe-wielding kid, he didn't show it. He merely reached for the tin of milk beside the date squares and stirred his tea nonchalantly with one of our spoons. I was transfixed by his large hand on the teaspoon and by the high-pitched clinking noise he made with each rotation.

"Mom, what's he doing here?" I pressed.

"Pierce, mind your manners," my mother replied. "You're in enough trouble as it is."

"What do you mean by 'trouble'?" I asked.

Solomon reached into the breast pocket of his old tweed jacket that was draped over the back of his chair. He pulled out my knife and placed it on the table.

"I found it where you dropped it, in my house." He took a sip of tea from the mismatched cup and saucer that I usually drank from.

"You don't know that's mine. How come you're here making assumptions and stuff?"

"Well," said Solomon as he gently placed the cup back on the saucer. "Nice of you to carve your name on the handle. And I do believe you're the only Pierce on the island, so it wasn't hard to track you down."

My mouth went completely dry. I'd forgotten about the name on the handle. My mother was staring at me with her hands on her hips.

"You broke into this man's house, Pierce." She had that tone in her voice, the one that went straight to my heart and made it bleed invisibly, the one she only used when she was extremely disappointed in me.

"You don't understand, Mom, he's the one who—"

"—who should be upset at *me*," Emily finished. She gave me a look that clearly begged for me to shut my trap before I made matters worse.

"I was with Pierce," she continued. "We . . . well, we visited Mr. Vickers's place together. It was just the two of us." Emily was lying and telling the truth all at the same time. I couldn't understand why she was leaving Thomas and Bennie out of it.

"You know, most visitors knock on the front door and, if they're fortunate enough, get offered tea and delicious date squares." Solomon grinned and raised his cup to my mother in a way that made me want to punch him in the face.

"Of course, Mr. Vickers, you're right that we should have knocked on your door," Emily conceded. "But the place looked abandoned, all boarded up. I heard stories about the fairies that were seen around there, and I wanted to check it out for myself."

Solomon laughed at the mention of fairy lore.

"We're sorry, Mr. Vickers. We both are. Right, Pierce?" Emily said, now looking at me.

"Yeah," I muttered. "Yeah, we're . . . sorry."

Solomon and I locked eyes. He had the same look that Sister Ida would get when she was trying to figure out if a student was telling her the truth about why they were late getting back from lunch. Only the most daring could avoid confessing. Thomas always said that nuns would make the best cops.

"So, you were just curious, and therefore you broke into my place?" Solomon said. "Did you find anything of interest?"

"It was pretty dark," I said. "We didn't stay long."

My mother shook her head. She'd heard enough. "I don't know what got into you, Pierce Jacobs. Or maybe I do," she said, looking at Emily.

"It's quite all right," Solomon said. "There wasn't too much damage—nothing that can't be fixed."

"Mr. Vickers, you have been so kind as to not get the police involved," my mother said. She came over to where I was standing and put her hand firmly on my shoulder. It felt cold and in no way comforting, which was an indicator of what would come next. "But my son will clean up the mess he left behind. And he will pay for any damages he has caused."

"Mom, you—"

"We can do that," Emily jumped in.

My mother grinned at her tightly, then turned her cold gaze on me.

"Good," Solomon said, finishing the last of his tea. "I'm glad to have the help. Then I will see you both tomorrow morning. Seven a.m. Don't be late. I know where you live, well, one of you anyways." He flashed a smile and then grabbed another date square, stuffing it in his mouth. He looked at me while he chewed, then wiped his mouth with our good linen napkin that was also part of that wedding gift from long ago. After he swallowed, he stood, threw on his jacket, walked through the porch and out the front door.

My mother looked at me.

"Mom, you have to let me explain," I pleaded.

"Let me see," she began. "You and your new friend here broke into a stranger's house, destroyed some of his things, and ran back here with an axe? That sound about right?"

It did sound right, and it sounded even crazier when she said it out loud.

"It really isn't Pierce's fault, Mrs. Jacobs," Emily said. "We were just curious."

"If you were 'just curious,' why did you vandalize that man's house?" my mother asked me, ignoring Emily completely.

"That was an accident," I clarified.

"Did you take anything?" my mother asked.

"No!" I replied.

My mother started to clear the table. She always began cleaning up in the middle of an argument with me or my father, her way of preparing for the onslaught. Dad couldn't stand her being mad at him and would make every effort to make things right. This usually involved getting her to laugh at one of his stupid impromptu dance moves. She could never stay mad at him and would eventually let out a giggle or, if warranted, a full-on belly laugh. It was disheartening that I couldn't make her feel better the way my father used to. It was yet another skill he didn't have time to pass on to me.

"You do realize this is not how I planned to spend my lunch hour," my mother said as she grabbed her white smock. "I'm not done with you. Be here when I get home, Pierce."

"Mrs. Jacobs," Emily began, "I know I haven't made a great first impression, but—"

"No, no, you haven't," Mom interjected. "You should probably go home, Emily. And leave my son's coat."

My mother walked toward the door. She stopped just short of the threshold and looked back at me. "Your father would not have approved," she said, delivering the final crushing blow before closing the door behind her.

Once I was sure my mother was gone, I turned to Emily. "Why did you say all that?" I snapped. "That wasn't the plan."

"Solomon being here changed the plan," Emily pointed out. "He got here first with his side of the story, so your mom would never have believed ours."

"You don't know that," I argued.

"No, but what I do know is that we're kids who think we saw an eyeball under a tarp. Solomon would have had a perfectly good explanation, which would have satisfied your mother because, like Thomas said, he's an adult who just had his house broken into by little thugs."

"You're listening to Thomas now? Did you hit your head on the ride down here?"

"You mean when you almost killed us both?" Emily huffed. "Luckily, my head's just fine. But thanks for asking." Her not-so-subtle dig got me worried that she would never get on my trike ever again. That too would be Solomon's fault. It added more fuel to the fire burning inside me.

"So, you don't believe what we saw under there?" I asked, starting to feel a little betrayed.

"Truth is, I don't know what we saw. You don't either. And if Solomon is hiding something, we would have tipped our hand before we could get to the bottom of it," Emily said.

"Oh, I think we've more than tipped our hand. Solomon was just in my kitchen eating my mom's date squares," I said.

"Look, everything turned out well for what we wanted," Emily countered. "Now we don't have to break in again because we've been invited." She took off my coat and handed it to me.

"Which means?" I asked.

"It means I'll see you tomorrow morning at seven at Solomon's place."

TEN

At 6:55 a.m. the next morning, I stood in front of Solomon's place waiting for Emily to show so we could begin our penance. In my hand was a plate wrapped in tinfoil, which contained a fresh batch of date squares, my mother's reaffirming gesture of gratitude to Solomon for not involving the authorities on the matter of her delinquent son. Word travels quickly in a small community, and something like this would have been a stain on our family forever. Ross Coles and the Arseholes would have had a field day coming up with a nickname suitable for the crime. Thankfully, I would not be forever reminded of my sins.

I was tired. It had been a long night. My mother had delivered on her promise to discuss yesterday's goings on in greater detail after her shift at the plant. She was particularly curious to know why I ran into the house wielding an axe.

"I thought he was in here threatening you, or worse," I said. It was a half-truth, which I figured was better than no truth at all. I could tell my mother wasn't quite buying my story, but she let it go.

"You have to be more responsible. You know better than this," she said.

"I know, Mom. I'm sorry, I'll make it right." Emily had cast doubts in my mind about what we'd actually seen at Solomon's place, and I needed to be sure before I burdened my mother with the weight of it.

"He's a strange man, Mom," I said, hoping she'd read into this without my having to say much more.

"He's a stranger; he's not strange. There's a difference, you know," she said. "And be careful around that girl, Emily. It seems she's got a rebellious streak in her, which can't be easy on her mother. Lord knows she's been through enough."

"Her mom has? What do you mean?" I asked.

"I mean it's time for bed," she replied, pointing in the direction of my room. It had been a long day for both of us, and she was at the end of her rope with me.

I lay awake most of the night staring at the pitch-pine ceiling, thinking how unfair it was that Emily was taking the brunt of the blame when I was the one who put her and my friends up to breaking into Solomon's place. I wanted my mother to like Emily. I *needed* her to like her.

The wind on the ride over had done a number on my hair and I found myself regretting not getting up earlier to wash it. Even a hat to cover it would have been sufficient. I usually didn't care about such things, but Emily's arrival somehow had changed all that. I wet my fingers and ran them across my head a few times in an attempt to at least get everything going in the same direction.

"That's not going to make you any prettier."

I turned around to find Thomas standing there, grinning from ear to ear, with Emily and Bennie next to him.

"What are they doing here?" I asked Emily, a little embarrassed.

"Safety in numbers," Emily said.

"I tried telling her you guys don't need us," Thomas muttered.

"Or I could just tell your folks that you were part of it and let them decide on the appropriate punishment," Emily threatened.

"No need to get on like that," Thomas said. "We're here to help."

"What's with that?" Bennie asked, nodding to the tinfoil-covered plate in my hand.

"Mom's date squares," I replied.

"What, now we have to bring that sleeveen gifts? Give us one, I'm starved," Thomas said, his hands reaching for the plate.

I pulled the plate away from his clutches. "When was the last time you ate only one of anything?"

"This is stupid," Bennie said, his eyes focused on a boarded-up second-story window. "We should go. All of us. Right now."

"See, that's smart thinking right there," Thomas said.

"Fine. I'll see you cowards later," Emily said as she made her way up the crumbling wooden steps to the large double doors, just as we had done the day before. Only this time, Solomon was expecting us.

"Come on," I said to the boys, who begrudgingly followed me.

Once we were on the landing, we all stared at the old wooden doors with the brown peeling paint.

"Go ahead, knock on it, Bennie," Thomas instructed. "You're the one with those bony knuckles."

"You're the one with softball mitts for hands," Bennie fired back. "You do it." I knew my friends—their playfulness was a cover-up. They were scared, as was I. None of us wanted to show it in front of Emily.

"You both should grow a pair, or do you share a set between you?" Emily said.

She went to knock on the door, but it flung open before she could follow through. Solomon stood on the threshold, his dark eyes studying us. He was now clean-shaven and wearing the red-checkered flannel shirt that we'd seen hanging on a nail in his makeshift bedroom the day before.

"I was expecting two little criminals, not four," Solomon said.

"They're our friends and they want to help," Emily replied.

Solomon studied Thomas and Bennie with the same focus as we did when looking for a puncture in a trike tire. He then turned his deep gaze to me.

"That for me?" Solomon asked, motioning to the plate in my hand.

"That's from all of us, date squares," Thomas jumped in.

"I'll hazard a guess that you didn't bake these. Thank your mother for me, Pierce." Solomon reached out and took the plate from my hands. "Now, let's try using the front door this time, shall we?" He motioned with his hand for us to enter.

One by one we passed Solomon, who stood just inside the doorway, eyes trained hard on us. Once inside, the door slammed shut behind us and Solomon turned the loud and rusty bolt, locking us in.

"Wait here," he instructed as he walked down the hall, disappearing into a side room.

"Wait here?" Thomas repeated in a hushed tone. "I can't believe this. We're in his house. And so is he!"

"Yeah, that's generally how it works," Bennie ribbed. "What's your point?"

"Point is, saucy-face, I'm out of here."

Thomas turned to the door, but Emily grabbed him by the arm. She had a viselike grip, which I knew from personal experience.

"He's not going to do anything. Pierce's mom knows we're here."

"Emily's right," I said. "It's way brighter in here now. Maybe we can find something we missed last night."

"This place is even creepier with the lights on," Bennie remarked.

It was an accurate observation. Everything we couldn't see the day before was now exposed in an ominous light given off by mid-century wall sconces and old freestanding work lamps. They were powered by a gas generator that emitted a low hum, making it seem like the building itself was actually breathing. We could see that we were in a large rectangular room with worn gray vinyl floor tiles and plaster walls with jagged lightning-bolt cracks. Above our heads was a plank ceiling covered with badly flaking white paint. A dozen or so electrical cords with empty light sockets hung down like tentacles along each side of the room. It was as if they were waiting for someone to walk below them so they could snatch up their prey.

The room's contents were in keeping with the overall chilling feel of the building itself. Directly in front of us was a large oak desk with torn and tattered bedsheets strewn across the top. Just off to the side of it was an ancient-looking medical baby crib with long, tubular metal legs with caster wheels. It was filled with old paint cans, one of which had leaked its crimson-red contents over the side, making it look like some wounded four-legged creature. And halfway down the room, four single, white metal cots with missing mattresses were pushed up against a wall.

"This was the reception area of the cottage hospital," Bennie said, pulling the sheets off the desk, which created a cloud of dust around us.

"How do you know that?" Thomas inquired.

"I asked Dad about the place last night. Don't worry, I didn't tell him we broke in," Bennie assured us. "He showed me a picture in one of his medical books from back in the day. This desk was just inside the door and there were cots on both sides of the room, just under those electrical cords."

"This is creepy," Thomas declared, now standing next to the pediatric crib that had been repurposed to hold old paint cans and brushes. An entranced Bennie walked over to where Thomas was standing.

"During tuberculosis outbreaks, there were kids of all ages in here," Bennie said, running his hand over the rails of the crib.

As visually captivating as these macabre items were, there was only one thing in this hospital of horrors that I was interested in seeing. Unfortunately, the blue tarp and whatever was underneath it was nowhere in sight.

"Where is it?" I asked. "Where did it go?"

My friends followed my gaze to the place where we'd seen the rectangular object less than twenty-four hours ago. It was gone.

"We need to get out of here, right now," Thomas said as he made another move to the door. Once again, Emily stopped him cold.

"No, we didn't cut through the ropes, remember?" Emily reminded us. "He doesn't know we saw what was under that tarp."

We were interrupted by a squeaking noise coming from down the hall.

Solomon emerged from the shadows, dragging something behind him. As he got closer, we could see that he had a broom in one hand and was pulling a galvanized wash bucket and mop with the other.

"Here," Solomon said, passing off the cleaning tools to Thomas and Bennie. "You two give this space a good cleaning."

"Us? They're the ones who broke in," Thomas said, playing up the lie that it was just me and Emily.

"I have another job for them. This way," he said, motioning us back down the hall.

"We didn't even make a mess out here," Bennie huffed.

"Don't say I didn't warn you," Thomas whispered. "It was nice knowing you."

Emily and I walked down the hallway, passing the door with the large padlock. We met up with Solomon just outside the supply room that we had used to gain entry to his place. He pushed open the door, revealing the mess we had left behind in our hurried escape. The large black drum we'd used to climb through the window had tipped over and rolled into the metal shelving of glass jars, causing them to topple and break. There were shards of glass everywhere.

"You two left quite the calling card," Solomon said.

"Yeah, again, we're really sorry," Emily responded. The more she apologized, the angrier I got. Why were we supposed to feel sorry? This old man had something to do with Anna's disappearance. And now he'd hidden the evidence that would prove it. If there was anyone who should be riddled with guilt and apologies, it was Solomon Vickers. Yet here he was acting all high and mighty about a few broken jars.

"I'm guessing there's not much else to get up to in a small place like this," Solomon said. "Which is why I'm taking this in stride, in case you're wondering. You liking it here?"

I didn't like that he was asking Emily a question, but there was nothing I could do about it.

"This island has its charm," Emily said.

"You're from New York, right?" Solomon asked. "Been there a few times myself."

"Really?" Emily's face brightened. That too made me boil inside. Emily was highly intelligent, and she knew he was a threat, so how could she be falling for his charms? But there was something else to this encounter, and maybe she was onto it. I suddenly recognized in myself the same feeling I sometimes got when Thomas and Bennie would bugger off and do something without me. The feeling had a name: jealousy.

"I quite like the MoMA," Solomon continued.

"Me too! We used to go on evenings when there was free admission," Emily said.

"What's a MoMo?" I asked.

"MoMA. Museum of Modern Art," Emily replied.

Solomon smiled at me in a way that made me feel stupid. I looked away.

"Well, best get at it." He picked up two pairs of orange PVC-coated gloves and handed them to us. "Throw the glass in the drum. And mind your fingers. We don't need anyone getting bloodied up."

Solomon turned and walked to the door, shutting it behind him.

I waited for the sound of a lock, but it never came. I looked up at where we had pulled off the weathered planks to gain entry, but the opening was boarded up tight. Even though the door wasn't locked, I felt trapped.

"What a mess," Emily said, looking around the room. "He has every right to be pissed." There was so much glass on the floor that it looked like the frozen gully we'd go skating on in winter. There had to be over a hundred glass bottles on those shelving units and not a single one was left intact. The legs on the metal units them-selves were badly bent from the impact of the drum, rendering them unfit for future use. Still, I felt little remorse.

"That old man could be a killer. What choice did we have but to do what we did?" I could feel my anger finding its target, now that he was out of sight. "I don't think we should be talking with him about what museums we like and how cool New York is." I gave Emily a withering look.

"You're the one who handed him a plate of cookies."

She had a point. I felt my anger break apart like shifting sea ice in the spring.

"Sorry, it's just all so weird," I said, trying to make up for my outburst. The last thing I wanted was for Emily to be upset or in any way disappointed in me. The only other person whom I couldn't stand being mad at me was my mother, and I was currently walking a thin line on that front.

"Let's just clean this up and get back to the others," Emily said as she slipped on the gloves and picked up a plastic dustpan that was next to the barrel.

We worked in awkward silence for the next half hour with the only noise coming from the shards of glass we deposited in the barrel. My mind was now on Emily. I didn't like the idea of her being mad at me. I was like my dad that way—I didn't enjoy con-flict. Dad always looked for a way to restore the peace.

"Funny," I said.

"What?" she asked.

"The first time we met, you were cleaning up broken glass."

"You saying I'm bad luck or something?"

I stopped working and looked Emily in the eye. "Actually, since you met me, you've been involved in a break-and-enter, the destruction of private property, a showdown with some bullies, and an almost fatal ride on a trike, so it seems like I'm *your* bad luck." It was a veiled apology but it was sincere, and Emily's wide grin and laughter told me she accepted it.

We were good again.

We continued cleaning until we finally got every last shard of glass off the floor and into the barrel. But as I removed my gloves, a trickle of blood ran down my left hand and wrist.

"You're bleeding," Emily said, taking my hand in hers.

Emily located the source, the knuckle of my pointer finger. She tore off a piece of paper towel from a roll that was next to some cleaners and proceeded to put pressure on the cut. She noticed a few other small scars on my fingers.

"Are these from cutting out cod tongues?" she asked, running her fingers gently over the old wounds.

I nodded. We used knives for everything from gutting fish and baiting lines to removing birch bark to help start a fire and opening cans of soup when camping. I'd carried a knife around for as long as I could remember. Knives were an absolute necessity. All of us boys had abrasions on our hands. As we got older, we became more skillful with them, but even then, it was impossible to completely avoid the odd nick or cut. It just came with the territory. Plant workers, like my mother, rarely cut themselves by virtue of years of experience. They were surgeons with the blade. So were the fishermen, whose hands were tough as leather from years of exposure to salt water and sunlight. Their skin seemed almost impervious, and they used really sharp blades.

For a second, I remembered my father standing in front of me, teaching me how to sharpen my own knife. "You'll do more damage with a blunt one than a sharp one," he'd said.

He had just given me my knife. It was a summer evening, and I'd just turned eight. I was excited because I was old enough to cut out tongues down on the wharf, and I couldn't wait to test the knife out on a few fish. It looked great in my hand. It had a flat birch handle with a walnut finish and a six-inch, slightly curved steel blade. I admired how my father could put an edge on any piece of metal using his grandfather's whetstone. His face showed great focus as he ran the steel over the stone at a slight angle, with one hand on the handle and the other on the blade.

"Light pressure," he'd say, smiling at me. "Run from the heel of the blade to the tip a half-dozen times, then flip it over and do the other side. If you cut your feet off, you're doing it wrong." That was Dad. He had a way of making me laugh when I least expected it.

He showed me how to sharpen the blade a few more times over the course of that summer and the next one. I never really got the hang of it, but he never got frustrated with me. "It takes practice, son. Like with most things, you have to live to learn."

Emily was still holding my hand when my father disappeared from my thoughts, and I felt a shooting pain in my finger.

"Sorry, just making sure there's no glass in there," she said before reapplying the paper towel.

Just then, the door opened. Thomas and Bennie were standing there, staring at the two of us holding hands. Again.

"When's the wedding?" Thomas asked as Bennie shook his head in disapproval.

"He cut his hand on the glass," Emily replied, pulling her hand away from mine.

"I'm sure he did," Bennie said.

"Shag right off, Bennie," I replied. "I'm bleeding here."

"Poor baby," Thomas said. "There's a crib in the next room."

"You guys can't be finished already?" Emily said.

"Solomon told Thomas he wasn't cleaning the mess, just moving it around," Bennie replied.

"Whatever," Thomas answered with a groan. "He said we could go, and I don't want to spend another second in this place."

"Did you find anything?" I asked.

"Yeah. Dust. Imagine that," Thomas replied as he and Bennie turned and walked out of the room.

I looked at Emily. "We can't just leave," I said.

"We don't have a choice. They've been kicked out, and we're done in here." She tossed the paper towel into the metal drum and playfully shoved me out the door.

Once in the corridor, I saw Thomas and Bennie having what appeared to be a serious conversation, looking back at us to make sure we were out of earshot. Then they made their way to the front door.

I hurried my pace, ready to ask them what all the whispering was about, when Solomon appeared from behind the door with the padlock, which he reattached to the hasp.

"Where do you think you're going?" he asked, blocking our exit.

"We're done," I said.

"Great. Then I want to show you something," he said.

"No thanks," Thomas replied.

"Yeah, we're good here," Bennie added.

"Don't be rude," Emily said. "We'd love to see what you'd like to show us . . . sir."

Solomon led us down the hall once again, past the room that Emily and I had just cleaned, then past the stairs that led up to the loft and Solomon's makeshift bedroom and office. We continued down the hall until we came to a set of steel double doors that were rusted at the bottom. Solomon pushed on the exit bars and the doors flew open, revealing sunlight. We were in the back garden, the very one we had seen on Watch Hill the night we'd camped out. Right in the middle of the yard lay the rectangular object under the blue tarp. Emily and I exchanged an uneasy look. A feeling of dread washed over me.

Solomon sauntered toward the object, which was some forty feet away. None of us followed him. We were frozen in place.

"That's what he wants to show us?" Bennie whispered. "What the hell is it doing back here?"

"Isn't it obvious?" Thomas replied. "He's going to force us to bury Anna's body. Then he's going to kill us and bury us in the same hole in the ground."

"You watch too much TV," Emily said. "We don't even do that in New York . . . much."

"Come on!" Solomon shouted from the middle of the yard.

"No friggin' way," Thomas said. Bennie nodded in agreement.

"Fine, go home if you want," Emily said. "But I'm going to find out what's under that tarp." She started walking toward Solomon.

The three of us boys shared a look.

"You know this is stupid, right?" Thomas said to me.

I nodded and followed Emily. Thomas and Bennie were soon by my side. Once we were gathered by the object, Solomon took out a large pocketknife and flipped it open. Instinctively, we took a step back.

"I get that you're all wondering why I'm on this island and what I'm doing out here on my own," Solomon said.

"It's a bit strange," Emily said.

"But it's none of our business," Thomas added.

"Then why did the four of you break in here yesterday?" Solomon asked.

So he knew it was all four of us.

Thomas and Bennie looked down at their feet.

"I saw four kids running away yesterday," Solomon explained. "And you were staking out the place up on Watch Hill that night."

I looked behind me, gauging how far we were from the house. If we ran, we wouldn't all make it. And even if we did make it, then what?

"I know you're curious to see what's under here," Solomon said.

"Yes, we are," I replied, my voice coming out as a dry croak.

The four of us nestled closer together, like a school of fish sensing a predator.

Solomon cut the ropes around the tarp, his sharp blade making short work of the twine bindings. Once he was done, he grabbed the nylon sheet with his free hand and pulled it off.

None of us were prepared for what we saw underneath—a massive, alien creature whose body filled the full length of a ten-foot rectangular tank. It was gray and hairless. Long tentacles lined with hundreds of suction cups were attached to its bullet-shaped head, which jutted out from an elongated flesh tube. These appendages were all coiled up in the acrylic tank, which was filled with a clear solution. Removed from the body of the beast and sitting in its own oversized jar was a softball-sized eyeball, the very one that had peered out at us from the hole in the tarp.

Emily leaned in for a closer look. She looked up at me and smiled as though everything was suddenly okay. But I was just as confused as before, only in a whole new way.

"Genus *Architeuthis*. The giant squid," Solomon proclaimed. "Back twenty-five years ago, some fishermen pulled it from the waters near a smaller island not far from here."

"We've all heard that story," Thomas said. He could not look away from the terrifying creature in the tank.

"The Beast in the Bay," Bennie interjected. "That's the thing that tried to pull the crew of a trap boat overboard. It was the Kieley family, a father and his four sons." Bennie looked at Emily, his eyes wide. "This thing wrapped its tentacles around one of the men and began to pull him over the side. His oldest brother had to use an axe to free him from its rubbery clutches."

That wasn't true, not according to my father anyway. He met one of the Kieley brothers later in life. According to my dad, the brothers said the giant sea monster was already dead when it drifted into their net, and the youngest brother almost fell in trying to pull it on board. Over the years, though, the tale had grown as big as the squid itself.

"My dad told me some people from the university took it away before anyone could get a good look," I said, gazing down at the creature.

"It wasn't some conspiracy," Solomon said, chuckling. "Or some superstition about sea monsters. The university had to gather it up before it started to decompose. It's a rare species that was valuable to them—to all of us. They built this makeshift tank to preserve it, and it's been in storage here ever since."

"It's friggin' huge," Thomas said, his eyes almost as wide as the creature's.

"It's actually shrunk a little over the years, but in its day it measured over twenty feet with those tentacles fully extended," Solomon recounted. "But this species can get much bigger."

"Bigger than *that* thing?" Bennie asked in disbelief.

"Back in 1878, a fisherman near Glovers Harbour caught one that was fifty-five feet long and weighed over two tons."

Our jaws dropped.

"That's twice as long as Dad's boat," I said. "How many more of those things are out there?"

"We don't know," Solomon admitted. "They're deep-sea dwellers, so no one has ever seen one in its own habitat."

It occurred to me that if some unfortunate soul ever did stumble upon one, it would be the very last thing they would ever see.

"Okay, but why is it in this place?" Emily asked, tearing herself away from the eyeball in the jar.

"The university was using the old hospital as a marine research station for a few summers back in the sixties," Solomon said. "They've finally allotted some funding to deal with what's been stored out here. I'm prepping the squid for transport back to the city, where it can be properly studied."

"You a big squid expert or something?" Thomas asked.

"I guess you could say that. I'm a marine biologist."

"News to us," I said. This was a small place where everybody knew everything about everyone.

"I kept it quiet, just told people I had a summer place here to fish. There are some sensitive materials in here. I didn't want any kids breaking into the place." Solomon smirked at that last comment.

This was not at all what I expected. I was relieved that Anna was not under the tarp, but it did little to quell my suspicions that Solomon was not who he appeared to be. Sure, he was educated and had a fancy job, but it didn't mean he was innocent. I still felt he had something to do with Anna's disappearance. The facts remained—he showed up when she went away. And he had her artwork in his place.

"Why did you bring this thing outside?" Emily asked.

"See that clear liquid?" Solomon nodded to the tank. "It's a diluted solution of formaldehyde. It came in those barrels you knocked over. It's toxic, so I move it back and forth using the caster wheels at the base and a makeshift pulley whenever I'm doing research on it. The ventilation is much better out here. So is the light. The tarp keeps the elements off it. Not quite what you thought I had under here, right?" Solomon looked directly at me the way Sister Ida did whenever she gave me an opportunity to fix some numeric miscalculation I made on the chalkboard during math class.

My emotions were shifting faster than the tides around our island. Anna was not under that tarp, but where did that leave us—and her? She was still missing. Disappeared.

"We wouldn't have guessed in a million years that you had a sea monster under there," Emily said, smiling at Solomon in a way that made me cringe.

"I probably might have guessed if I'd had like three guesses," Thomas boasted. "But I'm smart like that."

"You wouldn't have got it even if we gave you the words 'giant' and 'squid,'" Bennie shot back.

My friends had many more questions about the creature in the tank, and Solomon was more than willing to indulge them with answers. Thomas and Bennie were lapping up every word like a pair of thirsty dogs. I couldn't really blame them. This was the greatest show-and-tell we had ever witnessed. But as he spoke, Solomon looked mostly at me, as if I was the only one there. It was like he was trying to figure me out and win me over, which made me even more paranoid about him. Emily was mostly watching my reactions too. She was trying to get a read on me.

"Are you okay?" she whispered when Solomon turned his back to fold up the tarp. I nodded a yes, but I really wasn't okay. I was looking for answers, but all I got were more questions.

Solomon went on to tell us incredible facts about the giant squid. How they had the largest eyes in the animal kingdom. How they had eight arms and two longer feeder tentacles equipped with sharp suckers to snatch prey down deep. Then he spoke of the folklore surrounding the species.

"These creatures were the thing of legends," Solomon explained. His voice was gruff and his words were calculated. "They were recounted by sailors who swore to have seen them on passages across the ocean."

"I betcha they hauled ships down to the bottom," Thomas said to Bennie, both giddy with the idea. And for a second, the thought that such a monster could pull my father from his boat flashed through my mind.

"Don't be stupid," I huffed. "They don't just grab things on the surface and drag them away."

"I agree," Solomon replied. "But it makes for way better tales around a fire."

I had to hand it to him. It took Solomon less than one recess period to entrance my friends. He was an incredible storyteller, more engaging than any teacher we'd ever had. The only times they broke eye contact with him was when they'd playfully attack each other using their fingers to simulate tentacles. Emily asked most of the questions, showing her maturity, though she clearly got a kick out of the boys' childish behavior. I fought the urge to engage as deeply as they did. For some reason, it felt like I was being disloyal to Anna.

The wind picked up a little, carrying a chill from the ocean, which prompted Solomon to look at his silver pocket watch. My father had a similar one that his father had given him. Its polished, hinged cover would sometimes reflect light back to me onshore as he checked the time while steaming through the narrows. That watch was supposed to have become mine one day, but unfortunately, it vanished at sea with my father.

"You have to go now," he said, pointing to the side gate that led directly to the road. Clearly, he didn't want us to pass through his house again.

"Really?" Thomas asked. He wanted more. No adult had ever held his attention for so long.

"We're in no rush," Bennie added. "What else you got?"

"That's all for today, but if you're interested, there's more to show you. You could come back another time."

"Tomorrow morning," I said, a statement, not a question.

His steely eyes found mine. "Sure," he responded. "Why not."

"But we're going back to work on the wharf tomorrow," Bennie said.

"Tomorrow," I repeated, ignoring Bennie's objection.

I turned and walked toward the garden gate. I glanced back to see if my friends would follow suit. They took one last mental photograph of the sea monster before scurrying off to join me.

As we walked along the side of the old structure, they spoke as if we had just seen the year's big blockbuster movie.

"Can you believe that thing has a beak for a mouth to chop up prey?" Bennie said.

"Did you see the size of the suckers on those tentacles?" Thomas asked. "What a hickey that would leave."

"Like you would know," Emily scoffed, which resulted in an exchange of childish giggles.

Thomas noticed that I had gone quiet.

"Smile. I'll pay for the stitches," he said.

"What?" I asked.

"You've been a sook all day."

"And what's with going back in the morning?" Bennie asked. "There's money to be made on the wharf."

"I don't care about that right now," I replied.

"All of a sudden you don't care about fixing up your father's boat?" Bennie said.

"We have to follow this through first," I answered. "Something's off about him."

"I don't know, he seems like a pretty cool guy," Bennie replied.

"And Anna wasn't under that tarp, remember?" Thomas said.

"But the picture she drew was in that place, or did you forget about that? And the bones I saw in his boat? No giant squid explains those."

"And that locked door," Emily added.

"So, you're on his side again?" Thomas chided. "Surprise, surprise."

"All I can say is that if that was my art hanging on his bulletin board, I'd sure hope that you two wouldn't just roll over and have your bellies rubbed like a couple of puppies," she fired back.

"We're no puppies," Thomas said.

"Woof, woof," Emily replied.

"You guys don't have to come, but I'll be back here tomorrow," I said as we walked up to our trikes in Solomon's driveway.

I hopped on mine and Emily, without pause, jumped on the back. The boys shared a look.

"Have fun," Thomas said sarcastically. "More money for us at the wharf without you."

I started up the trike and drove down the narrow path. As we rounded the turn, I could see Thomas and Bennie still standing there, looking as confused as I felt about what I was doing and who I was becoming.

ELEVEN

I had returned home by midafternoon and was surprised to see my mother working in the narrow garden at the side of our house. She was on her knees, removing weeds and rock from the earth before adding strips of seaweed. The kelp that we gathered from the rocky beaches was full of rich nutrients, which made for an excellent fertilizer. Given the terrain, root vegetables were staples in our diet. My parents would plant potatoes, carrots, beets, turnips, and cabbage in the spring and summer, before reaping the rewards in the fall. It was enough to augment what we could get at the shops. I hadn't seen my mother digging in the garden for three years, not since our world had changed.

"You're home early," I said.

"Not much fish again today, so they told us to go home," she replied as she hosed the salt off a piece of kelp before working it into the dirt. "I thought I'd get the garden ready for next year."

"Why?" I asked, thinking we were getting by just fine with store-bought produce and the odd can of mixed peas and carrots.

"Because it's been long enough, that's why," she said, taking off her string knit gloves and tossing them on the ground near the bucket. That was the very first time I had heard my mother reference my father's death in terms of passage of time. As I looked at her scratched and weathered hands, I began to realize just how difficult the past few years had been on her. Planting a garden ran deep. Creating new life was her way of trying to move on.

"The rocks are coming up nicely," I joked, pointing at a jagged stone sticking up from the dirt.

"Cute. Now try another muscle besides your tongue." She nodded to a pick on the ground a couple of feet in front of me. I grabbed it and began to turn over the soil so she could add the seaweed. We worked the earth together, as a team.

"And how did it go with Mr. Vickers?" she asked, her eyes never leaving the ground.

"We cleaned up our mess," I replied as I removed a large rock from my mother's path. "Did you know he was some kind of ocean expert?"

"Marine biologist. And yes, I knew. I wouldn't have sent you over there unless I knew a little about the man." My mother looked up at me, her eyes squinting in the afternoon sun.

"And did he tell you he had a giant squid in a tank?" I asked, hoping to get her thinking about how strange that was.

"Of course," she replied.

"Why didn't you tell me before I went over there?"

"Because you're not a child anymore. And sometimes it's better to find things out on your own." She was sounding more and more like my father, which was not surprising given the fact she had to play that part now too.

"He invited us back tomorrow to see more stuff," I said.

She paused to look up at me. "Are you going?"

It was a good question. Earlier, I was certain I'd go, but now, I was harboring second thoughts.

"Yeah, like you said, no fish means no tongues, so not much else to be at," I reasoned. I couldn't tell her that I had ulterior motives for going back because if I did, she'd shut me down. "Are you okay with that? With me going back?"

"I think it's important to take every opportunity to expand your mind, especially when you live in a small place," my mother said. She picked up the trowel and began digging around the root system from an alder bush we'd cut down some time ago. "Will Emily be going too?"

"Yeah. You know, Mom, she really is a good person," I said.

"She hides it well," my mother countered as she removed the old roots and tossed them off to the side, sprinkling me with a little soil in the process. Her words were like a boot to the stomach.

"Are you going to tell her mom about the break-in?" I knew I was testing her patience on the subject.

"You're asking if I'm going to tell her mom that her little girl broke into a stranger's home her first week on our island?"

I waited, meeting Mom's eye.

"Not this time," she replied with a sigh. "And needless to say, there better not be a next time."

I was relieved to hear her say that. I would never get my mother to see how incredible Emily was if she was grounded for the rest of her stay.

"What's she like? Her mom, I mean."

"Sandra? I went to school with her," Mom answered. She took a long piece of kelp from a red bucket and ran it under the hose. "She was smart, always had top marks in school. Then she moved to Toronto after university, then to the States after she got married."

"Her mom and dad aren't together anymore," I said, which was pretty much the only thing Emily had told me about her family.

"I know. That happens sometimes," Mom replied.

Divorce was a rarity on the island. I only knew of two kids in our community whose parents had split up. Anna Tessier and Joey Sheppard. I'm not sure how the other kids treated Anna, but Joey was in my class. Ross Coles and the Arseholes poked fun at him because he was perceived as being different, and being different to a bully is like chum in the water for a shark. It will attract their attention. But the only change I saw was that Joey was around a lot less since he had to spend time off the island to be with his father. He didn't seem sad to me. I suspected that sometimes having one parent was different from having one parent at a time.

"We really should be fully planting the backyard," my mother said, laying the last of the seaweed. This was a not-so-subtle hint to let go of my father's boat. My immediate reaction was to tell her that I would never agree to that, but given my recent transgressions, I had very little bargaining power and was hoping my silence would suffice for now.

"Okay, Pierce. For now," she said, reading my thoughts the way only a mother can. "I need to talk to you about something else." She stood up and wiped the sweat from her brow with one of my father's handkerchiefs. "It's about Anna."

Hearing that name made my heart pound. And there was something about the way she said it that implied she knew something that I didn't.

"Did they find her?" I asked.

"Not yet." She watched my face carefully, gauging my reaction. I never told her about my encounters with Anna. She had no idea I was friendly with her. It was my one big secret in a small place.

"Pierce, I know you're worried about her," she continued. "Anna's been missing for six days now and we're all praying for her safe return. But we have to be open to the idea that she might not come home."

These were not the words I wanted to hear, especially from her. This was the second time in my twelve years of life that my mother had to have that talk with me.

I couldn't keep the rage out of my voice. "Have they stopped looking?" I asked, remembering the hurt, anger, and betrayal I felt when they called off the search for my father.

"No one has stopped looking," she said. "They've covered every square inch of this island. But there's been no sign of Anna here or on the mainland. I'm worried for her and her family, but I'm also concerned for you."

"I'm not the one missing," I said.

"But because you and I have gone through something like this, it's bound to bring back memories, which can be confusing and even painful," she said. "And maybe that's why you're worried about this girl you barely knew." Her words were as salty as the strips of kelp she was putting into the dirt. I didn't want to hear any more. For me to equate the loss of my father with Anna's disappearance was like two storms converging. It was too much heartbreak to handle at once.

"Promise me, if you ever feel overwhelmed, you just have to tell me. Okay? We can't change what happened to your father, but if anything were ever to—"

"You're gonna need more seaweed," I said, pointing to the red bucket.

She nodded, then gently rubbed away the dirt she had inadvertently spattered on my cheek.

"There, all set," she said. She picked up the red bucket and took a long look at the garden before walking back to the house.

TWELVE

I was an only child, and I felt it acutely, more so after Dad died. Almost all the kids I knew came from big families. My father knew of one family in particular that had thirteen children between the ages of two and twenty.

"They had to stack them like a cord of wood every night just to have enough room to sleep," my father would joke.

But in our parts, all hands were needed. Each child helped out in one way or another, whether it was the older ones looking after the younger ones, or working on a wharf or in a boat. As a rare only child in a place where big families were the norm, I used to think that it would be nice to have a sibling. But then I'd see how Thomas's brothers treated him, and I felt fortunate that our home was an arsehole-free zone.

In our little saltbox house, my bedroom was my own. I didn't have to share it with siblings. It was a place of comfort, and though it was modest, it had everything I needed. Across from my twin bed was a cherrywood dresser with antique brass handles and a framed mirror with a crack near the bottom, caused by Bennie, who threw a shoe at Thomas when he cheated at Monopoly. Dad demanded that we play outside shortly thereafter, and Mom made sure we followed the new rule.

In the corner of the room was a small handmade pine bookcase that held my books and board games. The walls were covered in faded golden floral wallpaper that contained numerous pinholes from where my movie and sports posters once hung, but I removed them shortly after my father died. They just didn't seem important anymore. To the side of my bed stood a highboy on which my twelve-inch black-and-white TV sat. It had two large knobs and was encased in white plastic. It was great for video games but would only get two channels, one of which was the local station based out of St. John's. I had watched in secrecy the reports on the search for my father. The station sent a reporter to the island to cover the event, which was the top story on the evening news. Every day of the search, I watched the first broadcast, then the rebroadcast at midnight, naively hoping that somehow the story would change. But it never did. After three days, that reporter left to cover a workers' strike on the west coast of the province. It didn't matter. He never told the full story anyway. He never uncovered the truth that I was the one, the fisherman's son, who was responsible for the fisherman being lost to the sea. The details were etched into my memory as clearly as one of Anna's drawings.

I went to bed early with the plan of getting up before dawn to go out in the boat with my father. "I have to test the bilge pump. I could use a hand," he said to me one day after school. He noticed I had been particularly quiet, the result of Ross booting me right in the arse at recess, sending me flying into a bunch of older girls who reacted like I was some kind of virus.

"I'll go with you!" I sat straight up from my usual slumped position. "Are we going fishing too?"

"Maybe one or two for the table. But you'll have to get up really early," he said with a smile. Just like that, he rescued me from my funk.

Being only nine, I was still too young to go fishing for the full day; that wouldn't happen until I was at least twelve or thirteen. But it didn't matter. I was still excited. To go out before daylight was extremely grown-up. I had gone out with him before to jig a fish, but only on very short trips closer to shore and only in the afternoons. And I did go out with him a few times in the evening to catch some squid in the cove. But this time was different. This was work. I'd be getting up before dawn, just like a real fisherman. Just like him.

But we'd have to be back home in a few hours. My parents were going to a wedding on the mainland that day, and it would take a ferry ride, followed by a long drive, to get there. They'd be staying overnight, which meant I'd be staying with Bennie and his family.

The evening before our trip to sea, I said good night to Mom and Dad as usual. My mother was hemming a new pair of my father's dress pants for the wedding the next day. Though he was about average height, she playfully suggested that it would be easier on her if he just wore a higher-heeled shoe.

"I don't have your gorgeous legs to pull it off," he replied as he sipped on his fifth cup of tea that day.

"You still up for an early rise?" Dad asked me.

"Of course," I said.

My parents shared a knowing smile. At the time, I thought it was doubt about me getting up at such an early hour, but later I would come to understand that it was love and contentment for everyone and everything in that room. For safety and comfort. For family.

"You just make sure you're home in time to get your arse into these dress pants," Mom warned Dad as she bit off the thread.

"You think I'd miss a chance to have a scuff out on the floor with you, high heels and all?" my father replied, winking.

"Yuck," I grunted as my parents carried on. I couldn't imagine why anyone would dance with a girl, even if it was my mother.

"Go on to bed out of it," my father chortled. "Can't have a tired crew tomorrow."

Crew. I liked the sound of that. It got me even more excited. I walked over to the table, pulled my knife out of its black plastic sheath, and ran my thumb laterally across the blade. It was sharp and ready for action. Content, I slid the knife back into the sheath. Then, to my parents' surprise, I grabbed my rubber boots so they'd be nearby the next day and went off to bed.

I remember hearing a gentle tap on the door early in the morning. It was still dark out. My window was open and a sweet-smelling breeze billowed the white polyester curtain like a sail. I found the movement rather hypnotic and it would help me find sleep on most nights. But this wasn't one of them.

"It's time, son," my dad said.

I hadn't slept a wink in anticipation of our big day. I threw on some old clothes and my rubber boots, which I'd strategically positioned near the end of my bed. Once dressed, I joined my father in the kitchen, where he was listening to the weather forecast on our old clock radio while sipping black tea.

He looked at me, his eyes bright. "You're all set," he said, smiling as he dropped two spoonfuls of cocoa powder into a cup before adding hot water from our chrome kettle. Despite my mother's protests, my father had replaced the electrical cord on it twice already using cords from other appliances. They were of a generation where anything that could be fixed was fixed. And things that couldn't were simply repurposed. Replaced wooden steps would become firewood. Outgrown clothes would find their way into a quilt. Even our garbage box was an old chest freezer painted marine gray to prevent further rust.

"Something to warm you up," Dad said, handing me the cup of cocoa.

I was too tired to even acknowledge it, but I happily took it between my hands. I was struggling to keep my eyes open. The kitchen was exceptionally warm that morning and the darkness outside confused my young mind. How could it be morning if it was still night? What was day if the day was still dark? Instead of taking a seat at the table, I decided to perch myself in the plush orange-cushioned glider chair in front of the woodstove. From this vantage point, I could rock and still see my father as he sipped his tea at the table.

"Should be a fine day on the water," he said.

"I'll take my knife, just in case we catch a few fish," I announced in a very adult way. I pulled it out of its sheath and flicked my thumb over the blade to test its sharpness yet again.

"Don't think your mother would appreciate that," he said, pulling on his rubber boots.

"Maybe just one or two for the table," I replied, using his own words against him.

"If we're late, she might make you go to the wedding too. Might be fun, you could even find a pretty girl to dance with."

"Gross," I replied as I sat back in the chair, and followed with a big yawn.

Dad chuckled as he filled up a two-liter soda bottle with tap water. "Maybe we will have time today to catch just one fish, but don't tell your mother."

We were two men getting ready for a trip to sea. The kitchen was peaceful, calm. We were speaking in hushed tones so as not to wake my mother. But the feeling also brought a heaviness to my eyelids. The warmth of the fire was too much to fight.

I don't remember much after that, but clearly, I fell asleep. I felt a hand on my head and I heard a voice. "My boy." Those were the last words I heard my father say.

The next thing I recall is waking up in the chair next to a cold cup of cocoa. The clock radio told me it was well after nine. Dad was long gone. He'd done what any good father would do—he went out to do a man's job and left his sleeping son in the comfort of his grandmother's patch quilt by a warm woodstove.

My mother came into the kitchen wearing her robe. The sunlight through the window cast a glow around her. She looked pretty with her hair down, like a movie star. She told me that my father would be home any minute or at least he better be and that we men had it so much easier when it came to getting dressed up.

"All you have to do is slap on a jacket and you're good to go." She read the disappointment on my face and told me not to worry. "You'll have plenty of opportunities to go out in the boat with him again."

But she was wrong. Two hours had passed and my mother's emotions drifted away from anger to genuine concern. This was not like him. Given the ferry schedule, my father knew exactly when he had to be home to make it to the wedding. And by now, almost all the other boats were in from the fishing grounds. She called her brother, my uncle Donny, and he and some others from the community went out to search for him.

My mother left me with the neighbors so she could wait on the wharf. But I managed to slip away. I quickly made my way up the harbor and watched from a distance. My mother was standing on the end of the breakwater, staring out through the narrows, anxiously waiting for his return. It was the closest she could get to the ocean and still be on dry land. She was dressed in her finest, with her hair blowing in the wind.

An excitement came over her when she spotted Uncle Donny's boat off in the distance steaming toward the harbor. He had my father's boat in tow. Perhaps it was as she had hoped, just some mechanical failure that left my dad stranded most of the day. But as my uncle entered the harbor, it became clear that my father was not on either vessel. My mother's eyes frantically searched the boats before her gaze fell on my uncle, who quickly finished tying them to the wharf.

"Where is he, Donny?" she demanded, her body rigid and her hands forming tight fists. She looked like she was preparing for a fight. The large overhead lights that ran up the side of the wharf came on as darkness began to sneak into the bay.

"Half the harbor will be out there searching soon, and we've radioed the coast guard. They're on their way," he responded as he hopped up on the wharf and approached his sister.

"No," my mother replied sternly, shaking her head, as if calling him out on a lie.

"I'm getting some lights and going back out," he replied, his hands holding her arms firm as he looked directly into her eyes. "We'll find him, Diane." But I know now what he probably knew then.

I remember hearing the sounds of old diesel engines echo across the water. I looked around the harbor and saw a dozen or so boats heading out to sea and even more being prepared from the stages and twine lofts. I wondered why, since it was too late to go cod fishing. Maybe the squid were in. We'd catch those at dusk.

I walked up to my mother in time to watch the tears stain her face.

"Where's Dad?" I asked. But she didn't answer me. Instead, she dropped to her knees and hugged me harder than she'd ever done before or since. I still remember the sweet smell of the perfume that she only wore on special occasions.

An exhaustive search turned up nothing. And the only clue left behind were a few fish found on board his boat. My mother prepared me as best she could for the worst. I remember her eyes as she knelt down in front of me. They were so filled with tears that they looked like the glass marbles that my parents played with as small children. Then the words poured from her lips.

"Your father won't be coming home tonight."

It was concluded that after he tested the pump, he decided to go fishing for a couple of hours, something he would not have done if I'd been with him. Authorities suspected he was a victim of a rogue wave, or some combination of that and a slip and fall. It didn't matter exactly what happened because either way, the ocean had swept away my world.

For months after, I would have horrific nightmares of walking out my front door only to find myself standing in the middle of the ocean. It was still like a pond. I'd look down and see thousands of fish and other marine life of all shapes and sizes swimming just a few fathoms below. They were all tethered to fishing lines connected to cork floats that were bobbing up and down on the surface at my feet. I'd turn back toward my house, but it was no longer there, replaced by a massive wave that swallowed me whole. I was engulfed in complete darkness. The only sound came from the popping of my ears the further I sank. Though I couldn't see them, I could feel the sea creatures brushing against my arms and legs. I would wake with a pounding chest and a shirt soaked in sweat.

As I got older, I began to unpack the moments leading up to the tragedy. I relived our last night together over and over again in my mind until the guilt completely took hold. Though my father's death was ruled an accident at sea, I never saw it that way. I believed he was a victim of a son who couldn't stay awake.

THIRTEEN

The next morning, I stopped by Bennie's before making the trek to the far end of the island. I knew that the boys were against going back to Solomon's, but I thought Emily was firmly on board with the idea. Bennie's parents were at work, but they now had house guests, so I thought it best not to barge in. For the first time ever, I rang the doorbell and listened as the faint musical interlude played inside. After a minute or so, the door swung open. But it wasn't Bennie or Emily standing there. It was Emily's mother, Sandra. She looked tired. Her short hair was sticking straight up in places, and she was still wearing a blue flannel housecoat.

"Yes?" she asked in a raspy voice.

"Is Emily home . . . I mean Bennie," I replied, not wanting to be disrespectful.

She smiled. It was the same smile as Emily's. "You're Pierce, Diane's son," she said.

I nodded.

"My god, you're the spit of your dad," she said, studying my face. Though I looked more and more like my father the older I got, no adult had ever said that to me, perhaps thinking it would just stir up those feelings of loss. But it didn't. What I felt was a sudden rush of pride.

"Thanks," I replied with a legitimate smile.

"Emily and Bennie left a while ago to meet a friend on the other side of the island."

Her words hit me hard. The smile quickly disappeared from my face. They went without me. My mind racing, I muttered a thank-you before jumping back on my trike and peeling away.

A rage brewed inside me as I raced across the barrens to confront my so-called friends. It had rained earlier, which further dampened my mood. Normally, I loved the feel of the island after a downpour. That earthy smell mingling with the ocean air. The way the water would cling to the brightly colored clapboard of the houses, making it seem like they were freshly painted. Everything just seemed greener and more alive than before. But this time was different. The trek through the wet and bumpy terrain was a messy one given the speed at which I was going. Heavy brush and water-filled potholes soaked the legs of my jeans.

I pulled up to Solomon's house a little after ten, consumed by feelings of anger and betrayal. I jumped off my trike and barreled up the steps, then pounded on the door with the side of my fist like it was a hammer.

The door swung open, but it wasn't Solomon who greeted me. It was Thomas. And he was eating one of my mother's date squares.

"What's all the racket about?" Thomas asked, stuffing the last bite into his mouth. I struggled to comprehend what I was seeing.

"You're here too!" I huffed.

"We were invited, remember?" he replied. "Did you bring any more baked goods?"

"What? No," I snapped.

Thomas swung the door open. "No worries. Bennie brought a loaf of homemade bread."

I followed him inside to the large rectangular room where Bennie was drinking tea from a ceramic mug with the Memorial University of Newfoundland logo. He was standing next to a faux walnut folding table upon which was placed a stainless steel air pump Thermos, some mismatched mugs, condiments, and a plate of toast.

"You guys told me you weren't coming back," I said.

"Yeah, we weren't," Bennie replied as he spread some jam on his toast. "But there was no talking Emily out of it, and we couldn't very well let my cousin come here on her own."

"And where is Emily?" I demanded. For some reason, I felt her betrayal the deepest.

"Well, look who decided to show up." I turned and saw Emily walking down the hall. She was carrying a box of slides and a projector, which looked to be even older than the one at our school.

"I stopped by Bennie's place, but your mom said you were gone," I said, trying my hardest not to let my anger seep into my voice.

"I called your house, but there was no answer, so I thought you were already here," Emily said. She must have phoned when I went out back to hang clothes on the line. But still, she could have called back. She could have waited for me.

"I wouldn't have come over without you," I blurted. I looked from her to the boys, who were still stuffing their faces with the last pieces of toast.

"Okay," Emily replied, squinting as though she was trying to figure out who I was.

"You've been missing out, man," Bennie said between bites of toast.

"Solomon has been telling us the best stories," Thomas added, licking the jam from the butter knife before offering it to Bennie, who shook his head in disgust.

"Oh, Solomon's telling stories?" I said. "And where did you get that?" I asked Emily, nodding to the slide projector in her hand.

"Upstairs," she replied, placing it on the table near the mugs.

"You let her go alone?" I scolded Bennie.

"Let me?" Emily said sharply.

"I offered to go with her, but she said she didn't need any help," Bennie replied as he poured some hot water over a tea bag before handing the cup to Thomas.

"I would have gone, but I didn't want to," Thomas added, blowing in the cup to cool off the liquid.

"Not that it's any of your business, but I wasn't alone," Emily noted. "Solomon was with me."

I couldn't believe what I was hearing. We were here to find a young girl, not be entertained by the one person who just might be behind her disappearance.

"Being with Solomon is worse than being alone," I countered. The idea that Emily was with this stranger unsettled me. I already had a missing friend; I couldn't handle losing another.

We were interrupted by a loud clanging that almost caused me to jump out of my skin. We turned and saw Solomon coming down the hallway with a metallic-gray rolled-up projector screen in his hand. It struck the floor, creating the same sound as before, prompting him to use both hands to properly balance it the rest of the way. He looked . . . different. He was dressed up, wearing dark pants with a beige collared shirt and a black wool vest. He looked like one of our teachers.

"Good, you're here," he said, his eyes scanning me and coming to rest on my mud-covered jeans. I brushed the dirt away and immediately hated myself for doing so.

"You invited me," I said, shoving my dirty hands into my pockets.

"I figured you'd be the first here, not the last," he said. "But don't worry, Pierce, you didn't miss much." Solomon walked across the room, opened the legs on the portable screen, and plopped it down like he was staking his territory with a flag.

"Miss what?" I asked.

"Solomon's going to show us some more sea monsters," Bennie said, beaming.

Solomon? So they were on a first-name basis now? Was that all it took, a bit of tea and toast, and the promise of a slide show? I could understand Thomas and Bennie falling for these blatant attempts to gain our favor, but I thought Emily was immune to such tactics. I thought she knew things, about people, about the world.

"Like I was telling your friends, I have some astonishing photos of marine life from the waters around here and other parts of the world," Solomon boasted. "Let's get started, shall we?"

Thomas and Bennie grabbed a couple of folding chairs and planted them, followed by their arses, just a few feet away from the projector. Emily pulled up a chair next to the projector and motioned for me to do the same, but I chose to stay on my feet, a silent protest against my so-called friends for making me feel like the odd kid out.

I watched closely as Solomon began his selection process,

holding the slides to the light to see the image before carefully placing each one into a slot in the carousel. His movement was so deliberate, so meticulous; it was as if the slides themselves were living, breathing creatures. A horrific thought crossed my mind: had he dressed up for Anna and given her the very same presentation?

Solomon flicked a switch and the projector groaned to life.

"Would you like to see the devil?" Solomon asked as he stepped into the dusty beam of light, projecting an ominous shadow on the screen behind him. A quick look to my friends confirmed that they were as confused by his comment as I was. Emily looked from Solomon to me, her eyes wide and her mouth slightly open.

I remembered when I was younger, looking on in horror at the image in my grandmother's illustrated bible of a hooved creature with the head of a goat and large horns devouring sinners in the fires of hell. Many sleepless nights followed.

"You really need to see this," Solomon said. He took a couple of steps toward us, causing Thomas and Bennie, who were closest to him, to recoil in their chairs. But he stopped when he reached the table.

Solomon pushed a small button on the slide projector and an image appeared on the screen. It was an underwater photo of a large black diamond-shaped creature with a flat body, wings for fins, and a spiny tail. Thomas and Bennie let out a chorus of oohs and aahs. Emily sat up in her chair and leaned in closer to the screen.

"This is a Mobula ray from a dive I did in the Sea of Cortez down by Mexico," Solomon explained. "This one was fourteen feet long."

"It's freaking awesome!" Thomas proclaimed.

"It's got underwater wings," Bennie added, flapping his arms and striking Thomas right in the face, causing Emily to let out a belly laugh.

"Those are pectoral fins. They use them to propel themselves along. It also gives them the ability to jump several feet out of the water," Solomon said.

I crossed my arms and cleared my throat. "That isn't the devil," I said, even though the thought of that creature breaching the surface sent shivers up my spine.

"Not in the biblical sense," Solomon replied. "It's been nick-named the devil fish due to the hornlike cephalic fins on its head." Solomon pointed at them with his index finger, breaking the beam of light.

"The devil fish. An actual cool nickname," Thomas said, no doubt thinking about his own, less flattering alias.

"Despite the size of this Mobula ray and the menacing name-sake, these fish are harmless filter feeders. Remember, you can't judge something by outward appearances alone." He turned away from the screen and looked right at me.

I took a deep breath. "Do you have a kitchen here?" I asked.

Solomon looked confused. "There's a small one in the back that almost qualifies," he said.

"Is it behind the door with that big padlock?"

Solomon met my eye.

"I don't keep my kitchen under lock and key," he said. "Is that something you folks do around here?"

"Only when Thomas comes over," Bennie joked.

Thomas and Bennie snickered, but Emily's face showed concern.

"What's behind that door?" I asked, pointing down the hallway.

Thomas's and Bennie's smiles quickly faded.

Solomon became eerily quiet. His eyes were as cold and black as the sea creature on the screen.

Emily stood up. "I guess we're all curious," she said, standing next to me. "We don't mean to be rude or anything," she added.

Solomon shut off the projector. The absence of the labored fan made the room forebodingly quiet. The sound was replaced by the hum of the lights when he flicked a switch on the wall, illuminating the room.

"What, show's over?" Thomas asked, prompting a subtle elbow to the kidney from Bennie.

Solomon didn't respond. Instead, he took a few steps toward me and studied my face much like Emily's mother had done earlier. After a long pause, he reached into his vest pocket and pulled out a small brass key.

"Here," he said, passing me the key. "Go see for yourself."

I took it, willing my hand not to shake.

A wave of tension washed over us. Thomas awkwardly put his mug on the table, hitting the other ones so hard that we all flinched. Bennie began adjusting his watch strap, as he was prone to do whenever he felt anxious.

"Go on," he insisted. "Open the door."

"I'll go with you," Emily said.

"Sure, Emily. You can go with Pierce, as long as you can keep a secret." Solomon turned to Thomas and Bennie. "What about the rest of you? Can you keep a secret?"

"Is it the good kind or the bad kind?" Thomas asked.

"Sometimes you have to find out these things on your own," he answered.

His words shook me. They were so similar to the ones my mother said to me in our garden the day before.

"Yeah, I don't know about this," Bennie interjected. He stepped in front of Emily like an overprotective bodyguard. But she was having none of it and pushed him to the side.

"Where's your sense of adventure?" Solomon chirped. "Have at it."

I led the way down the corridor. The floor creaked with every footstep, almost as if the house itself was warning us to stay away. Solomon remained behind, and as soon as we were out of earshot, we began to speak in the hushed tones we used at church.

"Well, Pierce, that was as subtle as a smack in the back of the neck with a sculpin," Bennie whispered, which resulted in a slap to the head from Thomas.

"Sorry if I interrupted your tea time," I replied. "But you seem to have forgotten why we're here."

"I don't know," Thomas said. "This feels like a whole lot of stupid."

"Do you really think he'd give Pierce a key if he didn't want us to see what's in there?" Emily said.

"Right. So that 'keep-it-a-secret' is about some old mops hidden in a broom closet," Thomas scoffed.

Our debate ended abruptly as we arrived at the door with the large padlock.

"The key probably won't even work," Thomas said. "He's just shagging with you."

I put the key in the lock with one hand while steadying the large hunk of metal with the other. I slowly turned it until I heard a clicking sound, and the shackle was released from the lock.

"Okay, so it works," Thomas said.

I looked behind me, back down the long hall where I saw Solomon walking slowly behind us, about ten feet away. He gave no clue as to what lay ahead. I turned my attention back to the door.

I removed the lock from the latch and handed it to Thomas, who unceremoniously tossed it on the floor. It hit the ground with a loud thud, startling us all.

"Sorry," Thomas said, gauging our reactions.

I put my hand on the octagonal glass knob and turned it. I took one last look around at the others, then to Solomon, who was now standing directly behind us. He nodded.

"Go ahead," he said.

I pushed open the door, which revealed a staircase descending into complete darkness.

"Stairs?" Thomas whispered. "Are we walking into a dungeon?"

"So much for your mop theory," Bennie said.

"There's a light switch just to your left," Solomon said.

I reached up and clicked the light on. We all peered down a wide staircase made of rough lumber, leading to a small section of concrete floor some ten feet down.

"What's down there?" Emily asked.

"You'll have to find out for yourselves," Solomon said. "Just remember our agreement—this is a private matter."

"Can't you just tell us first?" Bennie asked. Thomas nodded in agreement.

"Odd. You were brave enough to break in here. And I've given you ample time to express your doubts—that is, if you have any," Solomon said. "I give you a key to snoop around, and suddenly you lose all courage." He looked at me, sizing me up, his face impossible to read.

"I'm good to stay up here. I've seen lots of basements," Thomas said.

"It's all of you together or none of you," Solomon countered. He approached the open door and put his hand on the knob. "But it's up to you. If you don't want to see what's down there . . ." He began to shut the door.

"No," I replied, stopping the door with my hand. "We need to see what's down there." I forced the door ajar, freeing it from Solomon's grip.

"Hold on to the rail," Solomon cautioned. "Wouldn't want anyone to get hurt."

"Do you have a flashlight or something? It looks really dark down there," Emily said, shaking the rail to test its reliability.

"There are light switches below," Solomon replied.

"You're not coming?" Bennie asked.

"Why would I? I know what's down there," he said, a grin on his face.

Emily and I looked at each other. We would lead the way, followed by Thomas and Bennie.

The staircase was wide enough that we could walk down two abreast. It was solid with very little give, which made me think it could support a lot of weight if need be. It was a strange thought to come to mind. Given the poor lighting and steep incline, we made use of the two-by-four handrail as we made the descent. I looked back when we were about halfway down and saw Solomon standing at the top of the stairs, holding the door open with his foot. The padlock that Thomas had dropped on the floor was in his hand. He could easily trap us all down there.

When we reached the bottom, we found ourselves standing on the light-gray concrete floor. We could only see three feet ahead of us; after that it was lingering darkness.

"Careful now," Solomon called out from above. "Don't go fumbling around in the dark."

"I don't see any switches," Thomas said. I could hear the panic in his voice.

"What's that?" Bennie asked, pointing to an outline in the dark that was just a few feet away. It was over five feet tall with a narrow square frame and had what looked like a large head perched on top. "Is there someone down here?"

"Hello?" I called out. "Who is that?"

Thomas rooted around in his pocket and retrieved his key chain, which had a small novelty horseshoe light suspended from the ring. He pointed it into the black void and clicked the tiny plastic button. A thin beam of light lit up a row of sharp white teeth, causing us to let out a high-pitched shriek. Just then Emily flicked on the switch, flooding the space with fluorescent light. What we thought was a human figure was actually a large, elongated animal skull on top of a wooden filing cabinet. It had rows of peg-like teeth in each jaw.

"What is that thing?" Thomas asked.

The sound of hard-soled shoes connecting with wood echoed behind us. Solomon was descending the stairs with that same unreadable grin on his face.

"Don't be afraid," he said when he reached the last step. "It's just a pilot whale skull."

"Did you kill it?" Bennie asked.

"No," Solomon responded. "So much can be learned from what washes ashore."

Once we regained our composure, we looked around. We were in a large, open basement with high ceilings and exposed beams. The space was filled with cabinets and metal racks lined with oversized jars containing frightening-looking fish and various other sea specimens suspended in clear liquids. There were also taxidermied marine birds arranged according to species in open shelving units constructed out of rough lumber. Some were lying flat while others looked as if they could take flight at any moment. Microscopes and steel medical instruments were spread out on a metal table that had a magnifying lamp attached to it. The entire scene reminded me of the mad-scientist lab our school created one year for Halloween. Only this was all too real.

"Holy frig!" Thomas said.

"What is this place?" Emily asked.

"The university stored these specimens and some equipment down here after they closed their makeshift lab upstairs some twenty odd years ago," Solomon replied. "And as administrations turned over and priorities shifted, all of this was forgotten. Don't mind the dust."

My friends barely heard Solomon's history lesson. Instead, they began to explore the room, so full of curiosities, picking up jars and marveling at their contents. I kept my eyes on Solomon as I feigned interest in a small jar that contained seaweed, the kind my mother was fertilizing the garden with.

Solomon stood with his arms folded, smiling the way my father would when he watched me tear into the presents under the Christmas tree.

Then Thomas saw something that made his eyes turn into saucers. "No way!" he gasped, holding up a large jar with a hideous, insectlike sea specimen, pale yellow in color with eight long legs suspended in a milky fluid.

"Let me see!" Bennie insisted as he attempted to snatch it from Thomas. Emily walked toward them as if she was in some kind of trance. I kept my distance but couldn't keep my eyes off the strange creature floating in the jar.

"*Colossendeis colossea*," Solomon declared. "The giant sea spider. They feed on other sea creatures like worms and sponges by using a straw-like organ on its mouth called a proboscis to puncture prey and suck out their fluids." Suddenly I felt sick to my stomach.

"Imagine that thing crawling out from under your heater," Bennie said.

"Man, I'm just glad he's in there and I'm out here," Thomas added, before tapping the glass with his pointer finger as if he was trying to wake the grotesque creature from its slumber.

"Just try not to break it," Emily cautioned as she took the jar from Thomas's hands and carefully returned it to the shelf.

I continued to scan the room. Along with the many shelving units of specimens were a dozen or so twelve-gallon buckets with fastened lids sitting next to some empty fish tanks. Each one had its contents written across the front in black marker. From what I could make out, these buckets contained everything from harp seal organs and fin whale blubber to daggertooth fish and a goblin shark. I couldn't imagine a greater horror than opening any one of them. Then something less hidden caught my attention in a far corner. A bunch of long, ivory objects were laid out on a black tarp on a table some thirty feet away. As I got closer, the realization hit me. They were bones, the very ones I'd seen in Solomon's boat. They were neatly laid out to form a small skeleton, about two and a half feet in length. The arms and legs were spread out from the torso but the hands and feet were missing, as well as part of the sternum. And there was no skull, just some vertebrae leading to emptiness. My mind went into overdrive trying to fill in the missing pieces. Then, it all became clear.

On the wall above the table was a poster of a large penguin-like bird. It was black with a white belly and had a long hooked beak, tiny wings, and large webbed feet. The words "Great Auk" were written across the top. I reached out to touch the bones.

"Careful!" a voice warned, and I jumped.

"Sorry. It's just that they're arranged that way for a reason," Solomon said, his expression stern. "So it's best not to touch them." His large hand landed on my shoulder. I shrugged it off, but I didn't move from his side.

"I saw these in your boat," I said. "Why are you collecting bird bones?"

"These are not from just any bird. The great auk was a flightless sea bird." Solomon ran his hand over the image, smoothing out the edges as he spoke. "But they're extinct now, from over-hunting." My father had spoken of extinction that day out on the water when we saw the humpback whales.

"There are only twenty-four complete skeletons in the world. I want to construct another one from the bones of different auks," Solomon continued.

"Why?" I asked. They were gone and there was nothing anyone could do to bring them back.

"Education. We need to see the consequences of our actions. If we understand what we did to the great auk, we might not do it to another species like the northern cod."

"What do you know about our fishery, you're not even from here," I fired back. My body stiffened as if readying for a fight.

"I know the reports say you've landed fewer fish every year for the past ten," Solomon replied, with what I perceived to be a smug grin. "It's happening elsewhere. And with the shortfall in cod, those in power are talking about harvesting what they're calling 'underutilized species,' like some of those your friends are so fascinated with over there. And if those fisheries are not managed properly, I don't think I need to tell you what's going to happen."

I looked over at my friends across the room. Bennie was holding two spiny sea urchin shells up to his eyes and gazing through the holes. Emily was examining a huge lobster claw. It was blanched nearly white with only a hint of orange remaining on the calcified shell. She held the strange appendage up to her face. The boys laughed hard as she herself became a hybrid creature—part girl, part lobster.

"Kids," Solomon said, as if reading my mind. "Can't blame them, I suppose." Solomon was speaking to me differently now, like we were a couple of dads at a playground watching our kids chase one another around the swing set.

"Not what you thought you'd find down here, was it?" Solomon asked as he rubbed his neck with his hand, before stretching it from side to side, showing a little of his age.

"Not even close," I replied.

"Can I have this?" Thomas said, taking the giant lobster claw from Emily.

"No," Solomon replied. "That came from a lobster that was over one hundred years old."

"Well, it's not like the lobster needs it anymore," Bennie chimed in. Solomon shook his head and laughed.

"Told ya," Emily said as she took the claw from Thomas's hand and returned it to the shelf.

"If you're all interested, I could use some help organizing this collection before I send it back to the university," Solomon said, his eyes resting on me.

"I'd love to help," Emily said as she and the boys joined us. "That would be amazing."

Thomas and Bennie conferred for a minute in hushed tones.

"We're in," Thomas said. "But this sounds like work."

"Because it is," Solomon replied. "For which I would pay you." That's all it took, the promise of a few dollars, and just like that they forgot about Anna, leaving me as the lone holdout.

"But like I said before, it's all of you or none of you," Solomon said as he began straightening the jars on the shelf. "So what say you, young Pierce?"

Thomas and Bennie nodded at me. Emily, who was standing in between them, put her hands on the soft spot of their shoulders and squeezed. It was her not-so-subtle way of telling them it was my decision to make. But it really wasn't much of a choice. If I said no, not only would I never hear the end of it from the boys, but it would pretty much put an end to any hope of finding a connection between this stranger and Anna.

"Okay," I said, which caused Bennie and Thomas to do some impromptu dance moves behind Solomon's back.

"Good. But remember, don't tell anyone besides your parents," Solomon warned. "I don't want anyone else breaking in here."

This request sounded both reasonable and suspicious at once. I was finding my relationship with Solomon to be similar to walking on one of our rocky beaches: the shifting stones kept you from getting too comfortable. My opinion of this stranger to our island changed with every step. Was he for real or was I, like Anna, just falling for his charms?

FOURTEEN

That evening, I pulled up to our driveway on my trike to find my mother taking clothes down from the line. The intensifying wind whipped and snapped the sheets as dark clouds moved in. I had agreed to Solomon's offer to come work for him, but I knew I had to clear it with my mother. After all, as she herself had pointed out on many occasions, this was not a democracy. She had complete veto power over everything that had to do with me.

"Sounds like a good idea," she said as she removed the flailing cotton bedsheet from the clothesline that ran parallel to my father's boat. The plastic-coated wire rope was attached to tall wooden poles driven into the ground at each end of the yard, both with a six-inch aluminum pulley attached at the top. We had a dryer in the house, but this was always the preferred method. Not only was it economical but nothing beat the smell of clean clothes fresh from the outdoors.

"Solomon's well educated. Maybe this job will spark something, get you thinking about your future," she continued as she handed me the end of the sheet, which we proceeded to fold together.

"What do you mean 'future'?" I asked as I dropped the folded sheet into a blue plastic laundry basket. "I finish school, then I go fishing." This was the first time I had broached the subject with my mother. I was hoping to bring her around to the idea the closer I got to graduation.

"Finish high school, yes, but then there's university or trade school," she replied as she folded a towel and handed it to me to deposit in the basket. This was also the first time I had heard my mother mention such options.

"No, I don't need any of that," I fired back.

"You're twelve. You don't know what you need, you're not supposed to," she said, her voice soft as she tossed some wooden clothespins in the basket. "There's nothing wrong with fishing for a living or working in a plant. It's good, honest work. But things are changing, Pierce. You have so many more opportunities than your dad and I did."

My mother knew what she was talking about. More people were leaving the island to go to school or find other work. But I didn't want to be like them. I wanted to be like my father. And his before him. It was my right, my obligation.

"And you're so bright, all your teachers have said so," she continued. I had gotten mostly As and Bs through school. Bennie was always at the top of the class while Thomas struggled, being so much better with his hands than with his head.

"You don't get it, Mom. But Dad would have," I said as I pulled a towel off the line, causing the clothespins to snap in two.

My mother's lips drew tight. "Your father wanted something more for you too," she replied, staring at the overturned boat. "He knew you were smart. He knew you'd make something of yourself more than . . . well, more than that boat over there."

"You're just afraid, is all, that I'll disappear too," I fumed as I felt the first raindrop on my skin. How could she not want me to carry on where my dad had left off? I owed him that much. In fact, I owed him so much more.

"Yes, I'm afraid." She reached for my arm, but I pulled away. "I'm afraid that we won't be able to put food on the table or heat the house or buy gas for that . . . for that stupid car out front," she said as she threw the rest of the clothes into the basket. "But then I think maybe there's another way, for both of us."

"What other way?" I asked as the dark clouds opened up and the rain came pouring down.

"Like Uncle Donny," she replied.

Her words hit me like I had just jumped into a freezing-cold pond. My uncle and his family up and moved off the island well over a year ago. He found work in the city. I never understood at the time why he left. I'd learn later in life that he had something called degenerative disc disease that required special therapy, and, more important, he'd moved to put an end to an arduous way of making a living.

"You can't possibly be suggesting that we move away," I said, as if she had suggested we go to the moon.

"It's just something to think about."

"I don't want to think about it. Ever. This is our home," I said before grabbing the basket of clothes and heading back to the house.

I went to bed a little after supper, which we ate in near silence as the rain pounded the side of our house. The next morning, I got up early to go work for a man I didn't entirely trust. I walked out of the house assuming my mother had already left but was surprised to see her working in the garden. The ground was muddy from the rain.

"No fish today," she said, and shot me a smile. I nodded before jumping on my trike and heading off to Solomon's place.

As I crested the hill behind my house, I could see the entire community. My eyes fell on the fish plant, not so much for what was happening but for what wasn't. The normally bustling operation with its forklifts, trucks, plant workers, and kids standing around with knives and buckets was eerily silent. Unfortunately, this was becoming a regular occurrence, but I hadn't really understood the impact until that very moment.

At the far end of the wharf stood Ross Coles and the Arseholes. They were using hockey sticks to shoot rocks at seagulls bobbing on the water. Boredom always brought out the very worst in them. The image stayed with me as I made my way across the island. About halfway there, I encountered a small group of people from our community. They were using long sticks to part the bushes and thick grass as they made their way across a field, searching for Anna. Katherine Boyer, the only female fisherperson on the island, was leading the way. She saw me and pointed a warning with her stick to the police car parked off to the side of the road. She knew my trike would be confiscated and was kind enough to warn me.

I switched directions and took the long way around to Solomon's place.

FIFTEEN

Solomon's basement was dark and damp and smelled like mildew. Emily and I were sitting next to each other at an eight-foot folding table, while Thomas and Bennie were on the other side.

The boys' parents had approved of their new employment, as did Emily's mother. They knew fish was scarce. They also knew it would keep our idle hands out of trouble.

I watched as Thomas and Bennie playfully elbowed each other for more space. The three of us had been inseparable pretty much since kindergarten, often clinging to one another against the bullies of our world. But things were changing between us. Or maybe I was the one who was changing.

I had barely spoken since I arrived half an hour earlier. I was thinking about the fight I'd had with my mother. The idea that we might someday have to leave this place left me cold inside.

"So, you met my mom," Emily said, interrupting my thoughts. I felt a rush of blood to my head, making the hairs on the back of my neck stand up. With all the goings-on, I'd forgotten about my awkward encounter with her mother the previous day. I'd left as quickly as I came, leaving with little more than a mumbled thank-you.

"She thought you were a little . . ." Emily searched for the right word, and I feared she'd settle on the four-letter profanity that started with an *s* and finished with a *t*.

". . . intense," she concluded.

Intense? I was instantly upset at myself for not making a better first impression.

"She seemed nice," I replied. "Too bad I didn't seem so."

"It's okay, you'll see her again," Emily said.

I smiled, liking the prospects of a next time.

"Hey," Thomas whispered from the other end of the table. "My mother dropped off a boiler of soup at Anna's place last night."

"Any word?" I asked.

"Nope," Thomas replied, looking over his shoulder at Solomon, who was just out of earshot. He was pulling out some notepads from a cabinet at the far end of the room. "But guess who my mother saw driving past her place in a red pickup?" Thomas whispered.

"Solomon?" Emily asked.

Thomas nodded.

"What was he doing there?" I asked.

"Isn't it obvious?" Bennie interjected. "The old man wants to keep an eye on things, see if anyone's on his trail."

Our conversation ended abruptly when a couple of notepads came crashing down in the middle of the table. Solomon was standing in front of us, holding an oversized jar in his hand. It contained what he called a deepwater octopus, suspended in formaldehyde. This creature, like the giant squid, was void of color. Solomon put the jar down, then leaned on the table. He still wore a long-sleeve collared shirt, but the top two buttons were open, revealing a white undershirt. He pointed to a handwritten label attached to the front of the jar. His fingers were long and bony, and there was a gold band on his ring finger. It was the first time I'd noticed it. Was he married? And if so, where was his wife?

"Each label contains information on the species, including a brief description of the specimen, the date it was acquired, as well as where it was found and the name of the person who collected it," Solomon said.

"Why are we doing all this?" I asked. It seemed like "busy-work," as my mother called it, like when Dad used to make me sort old lumber in the shed while he fixed a leak on our roof.

"We need to prepare everything for transport back to the university in St. John's, where all of this will become part of a larger collection," Solomon replied. "Now, carefully take the specimens down from the shelves, record the information on the bottle in a notepad, and place them in the crates."

"Pretty straightforward," Emily said, grabbing one of the two notepads and a fancy looking pen from the middle of the table and placing it in front of us. She popped the cap and smiled at the sight of the gold nib. "A fountain pen," she said. "This will be fun."

Bennie and Thomas grabbed the other pad of paper and some pencils.

"We'll race ya!" Bennie said.

"No, this is not a race and anything broken comes out of your pay," Solomon said.

He walked to the other side of the basement, where he focused his attention on the wider flat cabinets that were filled with plants and algae pressed onto paper sheets and glass microscope slides. He treated the specimens with great reverence, examining each of them through the magnifying lamp. He looked like a mad scientist preparing for an ungodly experiment.

Emily and I worked from our side of the table while Thomas and Bennie worked from theirs. The boys performed well as a team. Thomas retrieved the specimens from the shelf, while Bennie recorded the information. Emily and I took turns writing down the details on the labels, though I barely took my eyes off Solomon, who continued to work on those cabinets on the other side of the room.

"You're terrible," Emily said, shaking her head at me.

"What?" I asked, confused.

"Your penmanship. It's terrible," she said, pointing at the paper in front of me. "I can hardly read what you wrote."

"I suppose you can do better?" I fired back, a little annoyed.

"Watch and learn," she replied. She picked up the fountain pen and began to write out the information from the label of a specimen bottle that contained a large starfish.

Her penmanship was so fluid, so rhythmic. Her hand danced across the page, leaving behind the most beautiful cursive writing I had ever seen.

"Where did you learn to write like that?" I asked.

"My grandmother on my dad's side," she replied, her eyes still focused on the page. "She's the one who took me to art galleries and museums. And she taught me calligraphy."

"What's that?" I asked. The only other word that I knew that was even remotely similar was "geography," which I didn't much care for.

"What I'm doing now, silly," she replied. "It's just another name for fancy handwriting. Here, you try it." Emily flipped the page and handed me the pen. I took it in my hand and pressed it to the paper. Blue ink drained onto the page.

"It's all about upward and downward strokes," she said, putting her hand over mine and guiding it over the paper. "Keep your pen at an angle. And then go light on the upstroke, then heavier on the downstroke." She pressed down on my hand with a little more force. "See?"

We took our hands away to reveal my name. *Pierce*. It was the nicest I had ever seen it written, before or since. When I looked up, Thomas was staring at us.

We spent the rest of the day cataloging the creatures in the glass bottles, everything from soft-shell clams and longfin hake to viper-fish and snipe eels. There were thorny skates, green sea urchins, rough sea anemone, small crabs, shrimp, and mud stars. Of course, we had seen some of these species before, even though we may not have known their proper names. They were considered bycatch, or unwanted fish, caught in nets and inadvertently brought back to the wharf, where they would be discarded. We sometimes came upon them in various stages of decomposition, with missing eyes, rotting flesh, and oozing fluid.

I took down a bottle from the top shelf that contained a bunch of giant spiral shells and placed it on the table. I was about to record the information into the ledger, but the name on the label jumped out at me. Emily sensed something wasn't right.

"What is it?" she asked.

"Look," I said, pointing at the name of the person who'd collected the specimen. Solomon Vickers.

"It's a waved whelk," Solomon informed us. He was kneeling in front of a filing cabinet containing seaweed samples. "It's a type of marine snail."

"I know, it says that here," I replied. "But it also says that you collected it."

Solomon walked over and took the bottle from my hand. "Oh, yes, I remember that dive now," he said as he studied the label.

"So, you worked out of here for a summer?" Bennie asked.

"A couple of them, some twenty-five years ago," he replied.

"Then you were here when they brought in the giant squid?" Emily surmised.

"Yes," he replied.

"Why didn't you tell us?" I asked. If he had a connection to this place, why was he only bringing it up now?

"It's not important," Solomon said. He picked up a box of cataloged specimens. "What is important is that we get this collection out of here. There are more empty crates in the room around the corner," he said, motioning to Thomas and Bennie as he headed up the staircase.

"Come on, I'll supervise." Thomas poked at Bennie, who responded by booting him in the arse. The two boys disappeared around the corner.

"That was weird," I said, staring at the name on the bottle. "Why didn't he tell us before that he worked out here years ago?"

"You mean he should have told us everything about himself the day after we broke into this place?" Emily quipped.

I slammed the bottle down. "Why are you always taking his side? He's a stranger!"

"I'm a stranger too. You know that, right?"

"You're different," I replied.

"How? You don't really know me." I didn't know her. But before I could try to articulate my feelings, I was interrupted by the sputtering of the overhead lights.

"Probably just the generator. Low on gas," I said a split second before the lights went out, leaving us in complete darkness.

"Hello! What's going on!" Emily called out. But there was no response.

"Thomas! Bennie!" I shouted. Still nothing. Then it hit me. This was Solomon's doing. This was his plan all along—to separate us, then trap us in the basement.

"Guys!" I shouted into the silence. "He's doing this on purpose," I whispered to Emily. I picked up the fountain pen and gripped it firmly in my hand like a knife.

"No. It can't be. I think you were right the first time, just the generator," Emily said.

"I'll go check it out." I got up, but Emily grabbed my arm and pulled me back down on the chair.

"Do you really wanna go poking around in the dark in a basement filled with glass jars of creepy-crawlies?"

"I have no choice," I said. "He has my friends."

Just then, the lights came back on. Standing over us was a five-foot-tall creature with a matte-black, hairless head and one elongated eye. Its two huge flippers were reaching out to grab us. Our screams echoed throughout the entire basement. They were followed shortly after by laughter from the monster itself—Thomas, wearing a black rubber diving hood and mask, with swim fins on both hands.

"You should have seen your faces!" Thomas giggled as Bennie came out from around the corner.

"We found this gear in the back," Thomas said.

"It was in a trunk with these," Bennie added as he threw some old Polaroid pictures on the table, photos of men and women standing on a wharf near a boat.

"Not cool!" I yelled. "You scared us half to death, idiots!"

"That was the point," Thomas replied.

"Who are these people?" Emily asked, picking up the Polaroids off the table and scanning through them.

"Well, look at that!" Bennie said, taking one of the photos from Emily's hand. It was a picture of a man and woman dressed in wet suits, their arms around each other. "That's Solomon!"

I ran across the room and retrieved the magnifying lamp. Bennie plugged it in while Emily held the photo under it. We all leaned in for a closer look. It was indeed Solomon but a much younger version of himself. He looked to be in his late thirties or early forties, and the woman with the long, red hair standing next to him was about the same age. A date was written on the bottom in red marker: September 28, 1966. Solomon was wearing the same wedding band he had on now. The mystery woman was also sporting a ring on the fourth finger of her left hand.

"What's going on?" Solomon asked as he came barreling down the stairs. He looked at Thomas, who was wearing the mask and flippers, then at Emily, who was holding the photo of him and the woman.

"Give me that." He snatched the picture from her. "You're supposed to be working with the specimens and, for the record, I'm not one of them!" His face was suddenly flushed. He hadn't exhibited anger when we broke into his house, but we were seeing it now.

"This mask doesn't belong to you," he scolded, tearing it off Thomas's head.

"It was just a stupid joke," I shot back, while Thomas rubbed his forehead.

"These are not toys!" he yelled, holding the picture above our heads. "Get back to what I'm paying you to do. And no more scavenger hunts, understood?" Solomon scooped up the diving gear and the rest of the pictures before heading back upstairs.

"He's right, you shouldn't have been fooling around down here," Emily said, sitting back down at the table.

"Listen, if someone leaves diving gear lying around, then they're not allowed to get sooky if someone else uses that gear to scare the crap out of others," Thomas countered. "That's the rule."

"Oh yes, everyone knows that rule," I said sarcastically.

"Let's just finish up and get out of here," Bennie said, sitting back down and picking up his pencil.

We spent the next couple of hours cataloging the last of the collection, sharing with each other the particularly weird and creepy specimens. Solomon's outburst had one good outcome: it brought us closer together. It was like when Ross Coles and the Arseholes would attack one of us, the others would rally around him, either drawing fire or helping with an escape route. As for Solomon, he didn't say much for the rest of the day. He split his time between bringing the crated specimens upstairs and boxing up the contents of the file cabinets while remaining a distance away from us.

I took down the last remaining jar from the shelf. It contained an eight-inch-long, football-shaped sea cucumber. Emily was recording the information on the label when Solomon came back downstairs.

"That's the last of the jars," Emily declared, collecting both notepads.

"Good. Put those on top of the boxes over there," Solomon instructed, nodding to a half dozen banker boxes stacked against the far wall.

"I'll do it," I said. I took the notepads from Emily and walked to the far end of the room while the others crated up the last of the specimens.

I placed them in an open box that contained a number of large blue binders, one of which had the words "Giant Squid" handwritten on the spine. I picked it up and began to flip through the pages.

It had all sorts of information on the sea creature, everything from its habitat to the predators that hunt it, which was illustrated by an image of a sperm whale. There was a map of the world showing where these dead giants had been found. But unlike most things in the basement, the materials looked to have been compiled recently.

I scanned the binder until I came upon a drawing of the squid we saw in the tank. The artist's technique looked familiar. It had the same wavy lines I'd seen in other drawings. The initials in the bottom right corner confirmed my suspicions: A.T. Anna Tessier. This was the second time I had seen her work in this place, the first being Solomon's portrait. But this one proved something definitively— she had been inside his home.

I pulled the drawing out from the plastic sleeve and marched directly over to Solomon. "Anna was here!" I shouted, holding her drawing up. "And don't tell me it's not her work because I know it is."

Emily took the sketch from my hand and studied it.

"A.T. Same initials as the drawing we saw in your bedroom," she said.

"So, you lot made it all the way upstairs the day you broke in," Solomon replied calmly.

I kept my eyes on him, fearful that he was like one of those large rats down at the wharf at night. They were huge, the size of cats, and had long, hairless tails, slimy, scruffy-brown fur, and razor-sharp claws and teeth. I began to wonder if we'd soon see Solomon's claws now that we had him backed against a wall.

"Easy, we're not the ones on trial here," Thomas said.

"Trial?" Solomon repeated with a chuckle.

"Maybe we should just call the cops, let them ask the questions," Bennie added.

"Or you could just ask me about this drawing like mature young adults," Solomon replied.

I had heard enough.

"Did you do something to her?" I asked, my finger extended toward him. The accusation lay there like a rotting fish.

"No," Solomon said. He was completely composed. He didn't even blink.

"I don't believe you," I replied. How could I, with the evidence right there in front of us, complete with the missing girl's initials right smack in the corner?

"Hold on, everyone," Emily said. "Solomon, why do you have Anna's drawings in your house?"

"Because she gave them to me." He gently took the sketch from Emily's hand. "I would see her sometimes out near the cliffs, all alone, drawing. Anna's very talented."

"I know that," I said, thinking he had no right to even speak her name.

"I asked her if she could help me with my work by sketching some of the marine specimens, including the giant squid."

"So, you don't know where she is?" Bennie asked.

"No. And I'm worried about her too. That's why I was in church on Sunday, to support her family and get an update. I spoke to her mom last night. I wanted to give back some of her sketches."

I looked at Bennie, his theory debunked. He looked away.

"And is there an update?" Emily asked.

"Nothing yet," Solomon said.

"You're lying," I replied. "We saw the cops here a few days ago."

"That had nothing to do with Anna."

"Then why were they here?" I demanded.

"That's none of your concern. And it has nothing to do with a missing girl." He looked at Anna's sketch, then handed it back to me.

I took the sketch and stared at it. My arm was shaking a little, so I held it with both hands. The thought that Anna was in this place alone with this old man was scarier than any of the specimens we had cataloged.

"Maybe we should go," Emily said, discreetly putting her hand on the middle of my back and nudging me toward the stairs.

"And we should settle up now too," Thomas added, sticking his hand out. Bennie stood next to him and followed suit.

Solomon ignored them. Instead, he took out a cream-colored handkerchief and wiped his face before carefully folding it and putting it back into his pocket.

"I understand you're worried about your friend," he said. "And I'm sure me losing my temper earlier didn't help ease your suspicions of me. I'm not one to covet material possessions, but those pictures you found earlier . . . they mean something to me. But that's no excuse for my anger, though. I'm sorry."

"Who is she?" I asked. "The woman in the photo."

"My wife." He turned his wedding ring with his thumb. "That wet suit, it was hers. We worked here together, all those years ago."

"And where is she?" I asked.

"She died," he said.

Thomas and Bennie shot each other a look before dropping their eyes to the floor.

"And no, despite your playground rumors, I didn't kill her. Or Anna. Or anyone, for that matter. Sometimes things happen in this life that are outside of our control." Solomon let out a sigh and plopped down onto a chair. His face was drained. I knew that look. My mother wore the same one on warm summer evenings and cold winter nights when she longed for her husband. And like Solomon, she still wore a reminder on her finger too.

"I'd like you to finish the work you started," he said, looking up at me from his chair.

"We did what you asked. Isn't it time you pay up?" Bennie asked, looking around at the now empty shelves.

"We find cash best," Thomas added.

"The work is done in here," Solomon said. He took out a pouch of tobacco and sprinkled some of its contents onto paper before licking the end and rolling it up. "But not out there." He stood and pointed at the vast ocean that roared just outside the lone basement window.

"Work on the ocean?" Emily asked.

"Yes," he said as he struck a match and lit his cigarette. "I'm heading out just after dawn. I would very much like it if you all came with me."

He wanted us to join him at sea. But I hadn't been out in a boat since my father's death.

SIXTEEN

The very last time I was in a boat on the open water was early August, a month or so after my ninth birthday. The squid were in the cove earlier than expected that year, so after supper my father took me out with him to jig a few. He would use them as bait to catch cod the next morning. "We'll go catch a few fresh ones," he'd said, winking at my mother, who just shook her head.

There was a story to it, one that had become something of a running joke, though my mother did not find it so amusing. Sometimes my father would buy a block of frozen squid from the plant, which he'd let thaw overnight in the boat. The previous summer, he bought a twenty-pound block and put it in the trunk of our car with the intention of taking it to the boat that evening. But he got distracted when my uncle Donny asked for some help fixing a leak in his roof. They spent the better part of the evening working on it. The next day, an unexpected squall prevented any vessels from leaving the harbor. My father forgot about the block of frozen squid, which baked in the oven-like trunk of the car for two whole days. My mother and I discovered my father's memory lapse on grocery day as we made our way to the ferry.

"What's that smell?" she asked, her nose crinkling.

"It's coming from the back," I replied, pinching my nose between my thumb and forefinger.

We jumped out of the car. When my mother popped open the trunk, we got the full impact of the rotting fish. Gagging, Mom slammed the trunk shut, uttered a few choice expletives, and drove back home to murder my father. It was one of the few times she was legitimately mad at him.

That evening, he had to tear out the carpet from the trunk before hosing it down with some heavy-duty cleaners. Eventually, my mother found the humor in the whole debacle, though she never made stuffed squid for dinner ever again.

Shortly before dusk, my father and I headed out through the breakwater with the intent of filling a few buckets with bait. It was beautiful on the water. The setting sun became a pale tint of orange as it began to sink under the horizon and we were blanketed by a warm breeze. My father and I were one of twenty or so boats anchored outside the narrows.

"Mind yourself now," Dad warned playfully, turning the crank on an oversized reel mounted to the side of the boat, his hand over mine.

The squid came up over the side in rows, their tentacles wrapped around the bright red jiggers. Soon, a flurry of black ink sailed through the air as the squid hit the bottom of the boat. One got my father right in the eye.

"You bugger," he muttered, playfully jumping up and down with his hands over his face.

I laughed so hard I thought I was going to wet my oilskins. When we had enough to fill three ten-gallon buckets, my father removed our hands from the reel. I looked down and saw plenty more squid swimming just below us.

"Why are we stopping? There's still more down there!" I said.

"We only take what we need. We look after them, they'll look after us, understand?" He put his big hand on my shoulder.

A while later, we steamed toward the harbor, content with our few buckets of squid. We passed by a number of boats, including one belonging to Ross's father, Joseph Coles. Standing next to him was Ross himself with his nineteen-year-old brother, Dennis. They were each holding hand reels with a number of squid jiggers attached. Ross's line was all tangled up in his hands like a spider's web.

"Gimme that!" his father snarled, trying to undo the mess. "You're useless, you know that? Useless!" He concluded his tirade with a few other choice words that would fetch someone a good strapping followed by a month of Hail Marys if uttered in our school.

Ross ignored us and looked down at his rubber boots.

My father locked eyes with Joseph Coles as we passed. Joseph Coles was quick to look away.

As we finished navigating through the maze of boats, my father let me steer us toward the breakwater, his hand on mine on the tiller stick. He was quiet, which meant there was something on his mind.

"The Coleses. They're not very nice, are they?" I said.

My father looked down at me. "Joseph had a hard life. But it's no reason to pass that along to his sons."

He pushed my ball cap down over my eyes. My father didn't speak much about his own father, who died when I was three. My mother would only say that he was a strict man with a quick temper. She also told me my father was much closer to his grandfather, my namesake.

"Son, do you think you can get us home?" he asked, nodding toward the opening in the breakwater.

"I got it," I replied.

He took his hand off mine and I guided us into the safety of the harbor.

SEVENTEEN

Early the next morning, I found myself gazing down at Solomon's boat. I was wearing a pair of rubber boots and holding my yellow oilskin pants. Just about everyone I knew owned the rubber-coated rain gear, which was essential for work on the water. Getting cold and wet at sea was not an option. Thomas was already aboard, wearing his bright orange oilskins. He was helping Solomon store a Coleman stove and cooler in the fore cuddy, a small, covered storage space near the bow. The boat was smaller than my father's and had a fiberglass shell with a small outboard motor. When it wasn't riding the waves, it was tied up at the far end of the harbor near the other boats, which had by then long departed for the fishing grounds.

I had discussed Solomon's proposal of further employment with my mother the night before. After a long pause, she finally spoke. "You're old enough. This is your decision to make."

Understandably, she was a little nervous about my venturing out on the water. I heard her pacing the floors long after I went to bed that night. But I think she knew that our home was one that depended on the ocean for pretty much everything.

"Good morning, Pierce," Solomon said. He continued to prep the boat without looking up.

"You need a special invitation or something to get on board?" Thomas asked, looking up at me with his hand shading the sun from his eyes.

"Just waiting for the others," I replied, taking every second I could to keep my feet on dry land.

"Your wait is over," Emily announced, sidling up next to me. I could sense her excitement, which added to my anxiety. I didn't want to disappoint her or for her to think less of me for not being as seaworthy as the others. Bennie was right behind her, carrying a couple of pairs of oilskin pants.

"Morning," I replied.

"Put these on," Bennie instructed as he handed Emily a pair of dark green oilskins. "They'll keep you dry out there."

All three of us slipped on the rain gear over our jeans and pulled the suspenders up over our shoulders.

"Well? Am I officially one of you now?" she asked. "Or do I still have to make out with a fish or something?" She was referring to a traditional ceremony performed by those not from here, which involved a recitation, a drink of rum, and kissing a cod, followed by the presentation of a certificate acknowledging one's newly minted status as an honorary islander.

"You look fine," I replied, but I was distracted by the thought of going out to sea.

"You're a real chatterbox today," she noted. But before she could say more, Bennie got things rolling.

"Emily, you watch how I do it and then follow me down," Bennie instructed. He was acting less like a cousin and more like an overprotective big brother. It was understandable. Bennie was the youngest in his family. His brother, who had already moved away to university, and sister were much older than he was. He was relishing the idea that he was now the older sibling with wisdom to pass along.

"Sad. He thinks I've never climbed a ladder before," Emily said loud enough for Bennie to hear.

"It can be tricky," I replied in Bennie's defense as we watched him very slowly get down on his hands and knees in front of the ladder. He then proceeded to methodically search for the first rung with his foot, moving at a snail's pace. Normally, Bennie would hop down with such stealth that his feet would barely graze the ladder, but he wanted to show Emily the safest way possible. He looked absolutely ridiculous with his exaggerated slow-motion movements.

"Is he serious right now?" Emily asked.

"You've never seen a robot get into a boat before?" I replied.

Emily laughed hard and my anxiety drifted a little farther away.

"All right, you two," Solomon called out. "We're wasting daylight."

Emily descended the ladder as if she'd done it countless times before, and I was next. I climbed down slowly, making sure both of my feet were firmly on the same rung before moving to the next, while my hands gripped the rails.

"Very funny, juice arse," Bennie said, thinking I was imitating him. I wasn't. When I finally made it to the vessel, Solomon was watching me intently. We locked eyes for a second. I turned away, and when I glanced back at him, he was handing out life vests to my friends.

"We don't wear these," Thomas said, pushing it away. This was strange but true. Fishermen didn't wear life jackets. In fact, a good percentage couldn't even swim. That's just the way it was on our island.

"You wear them on my boat," Solomon replied, shoving the vest into Thomas's chest.

"So, I assume we're going to collect some more specimens?" Bennie asked.

"You could say that," Solomon said. "Now put those on."

"Are we going to catch a giant squid?" Thomas asked.

But that was all Solomon had to say. We were learning quickly that he was as unpredictable as the weather.

Solomon gave an animated demonstration on how to properly secure the red flotation devices. Emily snickered at one point, comparing him to a flight attendant before takeoff. I laughed even though I had never been on a plane and had no idea what she was talking about.

Once we were all suited up, Solomon had us sit in twos on each side of the fishing room where freshly caught fish would be kept. Bennie and Thomas sat together with their feet dangling in the after standing room, which was the space closer to the stern that you'd stand in when jigging fish, while Emily and I were in the forward standing room, which was closer to the bow. Next, he fired up the outboard motor and unhitched the boat from the wharf. We began to steam out past the safety of the breakwater and through the shelter of the narrows. Seagulls soared overhead as we cut through the waves. Emily closed her eyes and took long, deep breaths.

"It smells so incredible out here," she said.

"It does," I replied, focusing on the horizon.

"Are you okay?"

"I'm fine," I lied.

"You don't seem fine."

"Just a little seasick."

But I wasn't. Unlike my father, I'd never had a problem with motion sickness. In that way, I took after my namesake, my great-grandfather. My dad, on the other hand, got sick for two straight weeks when he first started fishing with my grandfather. "Just awful," he'd recounted over supper one day. "Didn't matter if I had food in my belly or not. Though I tried to eat before I went out because the dry heaves are the worst." My father worked through it even though he threw up on fish on two separate occasions as he was pulling them out of the water. He referred to this as "adding insult to injury." Though his seasickness was pretty bad in those early days, my affliction seemed so much worse. My heart was beating fast ever since we left the harbor, and there was a ringing in my ears. I was frightened to death to be out on the water.

"Sorry you're not feeling well," Emily said.

"Do me a favor? Don't tell those two back there. They'll never let me live it down."

"I won't."

We steamed for another thirty minutes, past a number of anchored fishermen who were trying unsuccessfully to fill their boats. I could see the concern on their faces.

"Will they catch anything?" Emily asked.

"Been a bad year so far, but it'll pick up," I said as Solomon brought the boat to a stop a good distance away from the others on the water.

"Drop the anchor," Solomon instructed.

Technically, I was closest, but I was reluctant to move.

"Should I do that?" Emily asked.

"No, I'll do it," I replied, springing to my feet.

"Too slow, I got it," Thomas declared as he stepped around me to the bow. He grabbed the four-pronged, wrought-iron grapnel and tossed it over the side. It took twenty fathom of green nylon rope with it to the bottom. I felt my stomach turn as I watched the anchor and rope sink into the deep. I turned to Solomon. When he saw me, he averted his eyes.

"So, what are we catching?" Bennie asked.

"A giant squid?" Thomas suggested. "Or maybe a giant something else?"

"Think smaller," Solomon replied as he lifted up the gangboards that covered the fishing room. Down below was a three-foot-long plastic cylinder tube with wire, round flat weights, and rubber plug valves on both ends.

"Where's the hook?" Emily asked.

"No hook," Solomon replied. "This is called a Niskin bottle. We use it to collect samples of water from various depths so we can study salinity, which just means the amount of salt it contains. We also look at the concentration of nutrients like phosphates and nitrates."

"Hold on," Thomas said. "We didn't come all the way out here just to collect salt water, did we?"

"We're collecting microscopic plants and animals called plankton."

"We thought this was going to be important work," Bennie said.

"Plankton are extremely important," Solomon said. "Phytoplankton generate half the oxygen on earth. And zooplankton, such as small crustaceans called krill, feed bigger animals, including the humpback whales. And though they're tiny and not as awe-inspiring as some of the specimens you've seen, we couldn't exist without them."

We spent about a half hour collecting seawater from varying depths, then pouring samples in small bottles before attaching handwritten labels to each one. Emily, Thomas, and Bennie took turns dropping the device overboard, then releasing a flat weight called a messenger on the wire that would open the bottle and collect the water at the desired depth. I recorded their findings. The work actually distracted me for a while, and I found myself almost enjoying the experience. I had to hand it to Solomon. His passion for his work was infectious.

He sat on the gangboards next to me, smiling at some kittiwakes soaring overhead. "It's a pretty special place," he said.

"It's okay," I replied. I was sitting alone next to the man who less than twenty-four hours ago I'd accused of having something to do with Anna's disappearance. What did he want from me? An apology?

"I didn't always love the sea," he continued, rubbing his weathered hands together. "After my wife died, I didn't want to be anywhere near the ocean."

"Did she drown?"

"No," he replied. "There was a car accident. The other driver was asleep at the wheel." He looked off to the horizon, squinting as if he was trying to make something come into focus. "One minute they're there, and the next they're nowhere. It makes you wonder, how does that happen?"

It was the first time I'd heard anyone articulate exactly how I felt about my dad's death. I looked over at my friends. Thomas and Bennie were goofing around, trying to impress Emily with how fast they could pull the bottle up from the depths. Bennie had given Emily his watch so she could record the times.

"My wife and I loved working together," he continued. "Above and below these waters. But when she died, I didn't want to be out here anymore."

"It reminded you of her," I said.

"Yes," he replied. "But, as time passed, I realized that I belong out here."

I knew what he was trying to tell me, and I didn't like it. I wasn't ready to make peace with my loss.

"We got enough salt water on board yet?" Thomas called from the stern.

"Or do you want us to collect some air too, maybe a few rocks from the bottom?" Bennie added sarcastically.

Solomon took out his silver pocket watch to check the time.

"That's lunch," he declared, and then stood up.

"Now we're talking," Thomas said, dropping the Niskin bottle at his feet.

"What are we having?" Emily asked. Her hair was stiff from the salt of the ocean, her face a blush pink. The sea looked good on her. Day by day, she was transforming into one of us.

"Lunch is a fish feed, of course," Solomon said.

"Yes, b'y!" Bennie exulted, fists in the air.

Emily looked at me blankly.

"It's a fish stew with potatoes, onion, and fatback pork." It was delicious at the best of times, but it tasted even better out on the open water.

Solomon retrieved the vegetables and pork from a cooler in the cuddy, while Thomas and Bennie set up the Coleman stove and a large aluminum pot.

"Where's the fish?" Emily asked.

"About a hundred feet straight down. This will help," Solomon replied, producing a hand line and jigger made of monofilament line wrapped around a homemade square reel with a Norwegian treble hook and a stainless steel sinker attached to the end. It had a red tube sleeve over the shank so no bait was required. My father had a habit of making his reels out of my hockey sticks, which were the perfect width, so I was careful not to leave my sticks lying around.

"Pierce, can you help?" Solomon asked.

"Sure," I said as I took the reel from his hands. My anxiety had all but passed. I was feeling much better.

"You're relying on him to help catch one?" Thomas protested. "He couldn't catch a cold if he stood stark naked on Watch Hill in February. I'll show you how it's done." Thomas held out his hand, waiting impatiently for me to pass him the reel.

"Pierce can do this," Solomon said. "It's in his blood." He nodded at me as he sharpened his knife on a stone.

"Watch and learn, Thomas." I grabbed hold of the reel with one hand and grasped the attached nine-ounce jigger with the other, then made my way from the gangboards to the after standing room, where my friends were.

"You don't have a few potted meat sandwiches on board just as a backup, do ya?" Thomas asked Solomon, who kept running his blade over the stone.

"We got this," I whispered to Emily. She smiled sweetly, then grabbed the reel from my hands.

"*I* got this. Now, what do I do next?"

"You drop your jigger over the side," I said.

Emily released the hook and sinker overboard. It made a plunging sound as it hit the water.

"Let it go all the way to the bottom. Then you pull it up a few feet and move the line slowly back and forth like this." I tugged the fishing line in a fluid motion across the gunwale of the boat, exactly how my father had shown me. "Nice and steady," he'd said, putting his hand over mine as we pulled the line back and forth. "They'll grab hold when they're ready to."

"Now you try," I said as I handed the line to her and she began to jig for her very first fish.

Bennie and Thomas were seated on the gangboards, smirks on both of their faces.

"That's good form," Bennie said.

Solomon gestured for some help, and Bennie started cutting up some potatoes and onion on a board, and dropping them into an old aluminum stockpot.

"Hold on now, the girl hasn't caught anything yet," Thomas said. He stood with his arms crossed as though he was the foreman and this was his wharf.

As the line drifted with the boat, Emily recast from time to time.

"Nice and steady," I said, putting my hand over hers.

"How many people does it take to jig a shaggin' fish?" Bennie called out. He was smiling, but Thomas's cold stare made me let go of Emily's hand.

"I got something!" Emily shouted.

"Then pull it in," Solomon replied.

"Hand over hand. Let the line drop at your feet," I said.

Emily began to haul the line aboard like she'd done it all her life.

"It's pretty heavy!" she said, her face showing the strain.

"It's okay, I'll take it from here," Thomas announced, reaching across me to take the line from her hands.

"Shag off, I got it," Emily replied.

Bennie beamed. "Cousin, this place is rubbing off on you."

Emily continued to haul up the line, despite the burning sensation she undoubtedly felt on her fingers as the monofilament passed over them. She looked down into the clear water and saw the glint of the nickel-plated jigger emerging from the deep. Attached to its treble hook was a large codfish.

"I see it, it's huge!" Emily said.

"Keep going," I replied, and she did just that, only faster now, motivated by the sight of her catch.

A ten-pound cod appeared at the surface, the hook firmly in its mouth. Emily pulled the fish aboard, where it landed with a thud near her feet, its body convulsing as it struggled to breathe. She grabbed the jigger with both hands and held the attached fish at arm's length for a better view. Its scaly skin glistened under an unfamiliar sun. She stared in disbelief, spinning it around as it clung to the hook.

"Nicely done," Solomon said, sticking his knife in the gangboard.

"Good size too," Bennie remarked.

"Yeah, yeah, enough talk, let's get at it." Thomas took the fish off the hook and gave it a quick tap to the head with a gaff before handing it over to Solomon.

"Not bad for my first try," Emily said.

"Not bad at all," I replied.

We gathered around Solomon as he proceeded to fillet Emily's catch, first by making an angular cut around the head. Then he ran his blade on a slight angle along the dorsal fin to the tail, using the backbone as a guide. I watched Emily's eyes follow the razor-sharp blade. With a few strokes of the knife, he cut the entire fillet away from the backbone. Solomon did the same on the other side, producing two large fillets. He then removed the skin and dropped both fillets into the pot with the potatoes, onion, and salt pork. He threw the rest of the fish overboard, where the pieces were immediately devoured by aggressive seagulls. My father used to do the same thing whenever our family cooked a feed on the water.

"Birds gotta eat too," he'd say. "And it keeps them happy so they don't poop on your head." Dad punctuated this joke by grabbing me by the noggin and messing up my hair. This would always get a rise out of my mother, who'd hit him with a rubber glove until he released me. On those Sundays, we'd eat and tell stories, anchored in the cove under the late-day sun.

Now Solomon stirred the simmering pot. Its contents were transformed into a stew, which he poured into a large aluminum tray on the gangboards, as was our way. We each took a fork and dug in. My appetite had come back. I even had a fork-to-fork battle with Bennie over the last piece of fish. Emily settled the dispute by swooping in and grabbing the piece for herself.

"The presentation is questionable, but it's pretty yummy," Emily remarked, stuffing the last morsel of her catch into her mouth.

"Dad always said everything tastes better on the water," I replied. I caught Thomas staring at us again. He quickly looked down at the tray, then picked it up and poured the remaining liquid overboard.

"Hey," Bennie said, holding a piece of homemade bread in his hand. "I was gonna dip my bread in the pot liquor."

"There's alcohol?" Emily asked. "Are we getting drunk in this boat?"

"No," I said. "Pot liquor is the leftover broth."

"Oh." She began laughing, which had a contagious effect on me.

"Nothing funny about it," Bennie griped as he flicked his bread out on the water, where two gulls fought over it.

"Here," Thomas said, handing Bennie the jigger. "If ya want

more, just jig another one or stick your head in. There's tons down below."

"Not anymore," Solomon said as he took the jigger from Bennie's hands. "You're all on the wharf every day. You can see what's happening better than any scientist."

"And what's happening exactly?" Thomas asked, before letting out a crude after-dinner belch.

"We now have the technology to take every last fish from the sea. We can even process it on board in large factory trawlers. It's only a matter of time before we run out of fish."

"Come on. Look at the size of the ocean," Thomas proclaimed, stretching his arms wide. "And there's like another four or five like this."

"Fish lay thousands of eggs all the time," Bennie added.

"Yes, but fewer make it to adulthood," Solomon replied. "We're now dragging nets across spawning grounds. Make no mistake, there will be consequences."

I listened in silence. I remembered my father saying similar words.

After lunch, we washed off the pot and forks before putting everything back in the cuddy while Solomon stood in the bow and rolled a cigarette. Bennie and Thomas threw a bucket of seawater over the gangboards while Emily and I packed away the Coleman stove. The tides had changed and the water was starting to get a little rough.

"Pierce, could you give me a hand?" Solomon called out.

As I carefully made my way to the bow, an ocean swell caused the boat to roll just enough to make me lose my balance before I caught myself and readjusted my stance. My heart began pounding. I couldn't breathe. I was frozen in place, unable to move, just like that day that Anna found me stuck on the ladder between water and wharf.

"Here," Solomon said, passing me the thick green nylon rope that was connected to the anchor at the bottom of the ocean. I took it in my hands and immediately felt safer. I looked at him. He nodded, then turned away. Hand over hand, I slowly guided myself to the bow.

"Thanks for helping me with the grapnel," he said. "My shoulders aren't what they used to be." He made it sound like I was doing him a huge favor, but we both knew that wasn't the case. He grabbed the other end of the rope, and together we began to pull the anchor up from the depths.

"I haven't been in a boat in a while," I said as I felt the rough fibers pass through my palms.

"I'm guessing the last time you were out here was on that boat behind your house," he replied. His comment caught me off guard. "Such a shame that it's just sitting there, rotting away."

"It's not for sale if that's what you're getting at," I said.

"I know. Your mother told me your plan about fixing it up."

"So you think I'm crazy too." I was bracing for a lecture.

"No, I think it's a good idea," he said. "A boat is meant to be in the water."

"Exactly," I replied.

"I'm pretty handy with a hammer, so if you ever want some help with getting it back into shape, just let me know."

"Sure," I said, but I couldn't meet his eye. Instead, I looked over at my friends, who, arms stretched wide, were regaling each other with stories about the biggest fish they'd ever caught.

We finished pulling up the anchor and Solomon led the way back to the others, giving me the freedom to move at my own pace. I sat down next to Emily, who had a strange look on her face. I grabbed the jigger and began to reel up the line, which was still a tangled web at the bottom of the boat. Solomon was satisfying Thomas's curiosity for all things mechanical by showing him the inner workings of the outboard motor, while Bennie looked on with a tin of drink.

"You should come over tonight," Emily said to me. "For tea."

"For tea?" I asked, confused.

"You know. Tea," she said. "A cup of tea with some sweets on the side."

"Yeah," I said. "Of course." After a weird pause, I said something that I'd never said in my entire life. "Sounds lovely."

As the wind picked up, carrying with it a fragrant smell from the barrens, I felt giddy and nervous. That's when I saw something in the distance just over Emily's shoulder. An eighteen-foot speed boat was heading our way. As it got closer, the young faces aboard looked familiar.

"Is that Ross Coles and the Arseholes?" Bennie asked as he and Thomas got back into position on the other side of the gangboards. Solomon was busy in the stern carefully pouring gas from a red jerry can into the small fuel tank.

"Yup," Thomas confirmed. "That's them."

They're riding low in the water," I said.

"Maybe they have fish?" Emily suggested.

"They're not fishermen," Thomas said. Thankfully, I thought. And even if they had a load, they would not be allowed to sell it at the plant.

"Where are they off to?" Emily asked.

"Good question," Bennie replied. "The harbor is back the other way."

As they steamed past us, I noticed something odd in how the

boys were positioned. Ross was at the tiller, which was fine enough. But Jody and Rounder were kneeling down in the middle of the boat on either side of a fishing net. They were keeping a close eye on something underneath it. They looked over at us with complete and utter contempt, like the time we stumbled on them drinking beer up behind the school.

"What's with the net?" Thomas asked.

"I don't know," I replied.

Solomon finished filling the fuel tank and instructed us to sit down. He fired up the engine, spun the boat around, and headed back to the harbor.

As we got closer to the breakwater, Solomon called me to the stern. "Here, you take us in," he said, putting my hand on the tiller. I was reluctant at first, but I felt a familiarity with the outboard engine. It was similar to the motor that was in my uncle Donny's boat, which he and my dad had let me steer on a couple of occasions. The vibrations running up my arm reminded me of riding my trike. Suddenly, I was in control. A strange thought passed through my mind: maybe, just maybe, I would make a good fisherman someday.

"Nice and steady," Solomon said. And for the first time since my father's death, I guided a boat through the narrows and past the gray fish plant to the far end of the harbor.

As Thomas and Bennie tied the boat to the wharf, a man in his late thirties appeared at the dock. His dark hair was neatly parted to one side. He wore a beige trench coat over a white shirt. In his hand was a large manila envelope. I couldn't make out what was written on it, but I did notice an official-looking red and gold shield emblem in the top corner.

"Who's that fella?" Thomas asked as we took off our life jackets.

"Take the water samples out of the fishing room," Solomon

ordered as he climbed the wooden ladder to the wharf. He approached the strange man, speaking to him in hushed tones. The man presented him with the envelope he was holding. Solomon opened it, took out a single page. When he was done reading it, he looked at the man, who simply nodded and walked away. Solomon turned his attention back to us.

"I won't need you tomorrow," he said before walking away from us into his stage.

EIGHTEEN

I stood in front of the bathroom mirror just above our powder-blue sink, desperately trying to gain some kind of control over the cowlick protruding from the back of my head. I was sporting a beige button-down, short-sleeve shirt with a pair of brown cords, neither of which I had worn since the end of school. I felt nervous about having tea with Emily and her mom, not sure if this was what one would consider a date. And if it was a date, much like with my trike, I had no idea of the mechanics behind what made it run.

My mother poked her head into the bathroom and watched as I struggled with the comb. She knew I was heading to Bennie's and undoubtedly suspected the effort I was making was all for Emily's sake. Instinctively, she took the comb from my hands, ran it under the water, and began taming the beast on my head.

"Just like your father's," she said, smiling at me in the mirror.

I remember watching Dad run a steel-bristled brush through his thick mane, though any attempt at taming it was futile, just as it was with mine. Mom used to fix his hair too, struggling with a pink plastic comb, which finally broke at the handle one day, sticking straight up from Dad's head.

"Think anyone will notice?" he'd asked.

Mom and I had burst out laughing.

Now she hummed while she worked on my hair. Something was on her mind.

"What I said about moving away," she began. "You know I was just tired, right?"

"I know," I said. Still, it was a relief to hear it.

My mother finished up, handed back the comb, and told me to say hello to Emily's mom.

I got to Bennie's place a little after seven. It was still light out, which was good because I decided it was best to walk. A ride on the trike would undo all the effort on my hair. It would also ruin my pants. I even considered wearing some of my father's cologne, which my mother still kept in her nightstand, but then I remembered Thomas's gross misuse of his brother's at church and decided against it.

"You look nice," Emily said with a smile as she greeted me at the door.

"Thanks," I replied. "You look best kind too."

"Thanks. I think," she said with a giggle.

"It means you look really good," I mumbled, a little embarrassed that I had to spell it out.

Though I'd seen Emily pretty much every day since she'd been on our island, I was suddenly nervous. I was sweating and I felt a pounding in my chest to the point that it affected my speech. I sounded almost out of breath. Emily looked different too. Instead of her jeans and plaid shirt, she was wearing blue slacks and a short-sleeved white top. Gone was her ponytail, replaced by long, flowing hair that ran down her back. She also smelled different, like the wild roses that grew near the graveyard. This made me regret not wearing Dad's cologne.

Emily led me through the large kitchen with its oak cabinets and cream-colored laminate countertop, through the dining room past the long cherrywood table under the basket-style brass-and-crystal chandelier, and into the living room. It was there that her mother, Sandra, sat sipping on a cup of tea. I had been at Bennie's place many times before, but we never hung out in the living room. It didn't have a TV, and the floral-patterned sofa and matching love seat looked brand-new. Bennie said it was used only for company, which, I suddenly realized, meant me that night.

"Nice to see you, again, Pierce," Emily's mother said, getting up and giving me a hug, something I was not accustomed to from anyone besides my mother. I had received a number of the awkward embraces from other people at my father's funeral, but nothing really since.

Emily's mother wore a light-green summer dress, a direct contrast to the flannel robe she had on that day I first met her. Her short hair was neatly styled, and you could see the strong mother-daughter resemblance. But unlike Emily, her face was made up with rouge and lipstick.

"Yeah. Hi," I replied as she poured me a cup of tea from a brown glazed ceramic pot. I was thankful it was just regular tea like at home and nothing that required much thinking on my part.

"Where's Bennie?" I asked, my eyes searching the house.

"Went to town on the mainland," Emily replied as her mom handed me the cup.

I took it in both hands so as not to spill it and sat in the love seat across from Emily's mom. Emily poured herself a cup and sat next to me.

"You two have been on some adventures since we got here," her mother began, offering me a homemade snowball from a square plate. I took one and instead of taking a bite, I popped the entire thing in my mouth.

"Yeah, all four of us," I said in between chews, in case she had a problem with her daughter hanging out with just me.

"Don't worry," she replied. "I'm happy Emily has met new friends."

"They're the ones who should be happy," Emily fired back as she stuffed a snowball into her mouth, making me feel less self-conscious about having just done the same.

"It's nice that you're showing Emily around the island I grew up on," Emily's mother continued. "You know, I went to school with your mom."

"She told me that," I said as I sipped the tea. I usually took it with milk and sugar, but having it black felt more grown-up.

"And you knew my dad too?" I asked, remembering fondly how she said I looked like him.

"Your father was a couple of grades older than us. Handsome boy, like his son."

"Mom!" Emily interjected.

But I didn't mind. I was always happy to hear people say anything about Dad.

"All the girls liked him, you know, but he only had eyes for your mom."

"Mother! He doesn't want to hear about his parents having googly eyes for each other," Emily said. "It's just gross."

"It's okay," I replied. "They weren't shy about it around the house."

"From grade ten onward, when you'd see one, you'd see the other," her mother continued.

For the first time, the realization hit me that my parents had been inseparable since they were just a few years older than I was now. They had been together a lifetime before the sea took Dad away. It gave me an even greater appreciation for what my mother had gone through. For what she was still going through.

As we drank tea and ate more homemade cookies, the topic quickly turned to the talk of the island—Anna.

"The poor thing," Emily's mother said. "Gone well over a week now."

"Nine days," I replied.

"I heard they're calling off the search here and following a few leads on the mainland," her mother continued.

"Anna's not on the mainland. She didn't run away," I said, my voice strangely husky.

Emily cleared her throat before taking another sip of tea.

This was her mother I was talking to, and yet I couldn't manage to change my tone. I tried to think about how she'd given Emily free range of the island. All that could be taken away in a heartbeat, especially if I made a bad second impression.

"I just can't see someone like her doing that," I said, softly this time.

"Why are you so certain?" her mother asked.

"I don't know, I just am," I replied.

Emily shot her mother a look to tell her to drop the subject.

We went on to talk about how her mom planned on coming back to the island after she finished university, but then she met Emily's dad. "One thing you start to learn when you're an adult is that things never work out as you planned." She poured some more tea, but it splashed onto the coffee table. Frustrated with herself, she wiped it up with a napkin.

"Her dad traveled a lot," she said, smiling at Emily. "He was . . .

well-meaning, but he could barely look after himself let alone anyone else."

I kept my eyes on Emily. She was watching her mother as if she
was hearing this for the very first time. It all seemed so unfair. My
father was gone through no fault of his own, and Emily's dad was
still alive but willfully absent.

Emily caught me staring at her.

"I'm happy you came home for the summer," I said. "Both of
you."

"We are too," Emily replied.

Her mom spoke a little more about the island and how little
it had changed in the years she'd been gone. But soon after, her
energy suddenly dropped off. She excused herself and went to bed,
leaving me, Emily, and a half plate of snowballs.

We were both quiet for a bit. I started to wonder if this was
the date part.

"She gets tired easily," Emily said. "She had cancer two years
ago. In her kidney. But they gave her radiation treatment, so she's
better now."

Cancer. I was shocked. Thomas's grandfather died from it just
last year, but he was in his late seventies. I didn't think anyone
younger could get it.

"Glad she's feeling better," I replied as Emily reached over
me for the teapot, her elbow making contact with my knee as she
poured the last drop. We looked at each other and smiled nervously. Then she leaned in and kissed me on the cheek.

"Thanks," I mumbled. I could feel my face getting hot.

"Sorry, I didn't mean that to be awkward," Emily replied.

"No, no, it was . . . fun," I stammered.

"What was fun?" We turned and saw Bennie standing behind us.

"I thought you went to town with your folks," I said, jumping up from the love seat and almost knocking Emily over in the process.

"Nope, I went trouting with Joey Mullins up on the barrens." He grabbed a snowball and threw it into his mouth before plopping down on the love seat between us.

"Catch any?" I asked.

"Nope. What was fun?" he asked again, giving me the once-over.

"Having tea with Mom," Emily replied as she stacked the cups and carried them and the teapot off to the kitchen, leaving only the plate of snowballs behind.

Bennie looked me up and down, eyeing my crisp slacks and my combed hair. "You know she's my cousin, right?"

"Yeah, so?" I asked.

"I've seen the way you've been looking at her, holding hands and all. Just watch yourself."

Bennie had never threatened me before. Usually, we were getting threatened together. But now he was acting like an overprotective father.

"What are you whispering about?" Emily asked when she returned from the kitchen.

"Nothing," Bennie and I said in unison.

Emily stared at us. But before she could follow up, we heard someone barrel through the kitchen.

"Bennie! Bennie! My eyeballs are burning!" Thomas shouted. He was soaking wet from head to toe. His normally curly red hair was now flat to his head and dripping with a mysterious brownish liquid. Then the unmistakable putrid fishy smell hit us. I knew immediately what it was.

"You're rotten!" Bennie yelled as we jumped up.

"What is that smell?" Emily asked, grabbing a lace napkin from the tea setting to hold over her nose and mouth.

"Cod liver oil," Bennie responded. "Don't touch anything!" Bennie ran to the kitchen.

"Why are you covered in it?" I asked.

"Ross and the Arseholes dunked me in a barrel of it down by Loyola Pinsent's stage," he replied. Back then, fishermen would fill barrels with fish livers and water, then let it all ferment for months before removing the layer of oil that would rise to the top. The foul-tasting elixir was used to both treat and prevent everything from colds and flus to rickets and gout. As bad as it smelled, it tasted even worse.

Bennie ran back into the room with a roll of paper towels and a bowl of warm soapy water. Thomas ripped some sheets from the roll and started to wipe his eyes.

"I told them I couldn't see and that's when they threw me in the harbor."

"Stop shagging around," I said.

"Do I look like I'm kidding?" Thomas asked, squinting to see us through a veil of sticky sludge.

Bennie and I shared a horrified look. Our friend had been thrown into that rancid water. That was no joke. He could have easily disappeared beneath, never to be seen again.

"I managed to pull myself up onto a dory and only for that, I would have drowned," Thomas said. His tears left tracks through the sticky cod liver oil that covered his face.

"Here, let me do that," Emily said, taking the paper towels and dipping them into the soapy water before gently dabbing it around his eyes.

"All over a few dollars they think we owe them for those cod tongues?" Bennie asked.

"It was a warning," Thomas said. "Ross told me we all had to keep our mouths shut about seeing them in the boat today."

"So they were up to no good," Emily said.

I suddenly remembered Ross's heinous lopsided grin as he watched that conner swimming around outside the breakwater with a cork tethered to its back all those years ago.

"Wait, what are you dressed up for, Pierce?" Thomas asked, now able to see again. "And you're all in the living room. Are those snowballs? You guys were having a party while I was fighting for my life?"

"It's not like that," I replied.

"Looked like that to me," Bennie added.

"You're the worst friends ever." Thomas waved Emily away and stormed out of the house.

"Thomas, wait!" Emily shouted. But he'd already slammed the door shut.

We were quiet then, all three of us.

"They could have killed him," I said. I was thinking about those awful nightmares I used to have months after Dad died, dreams about sinking into the darkness beneath the waves.

"You don't think I know that?" Bennie replied. "You should go now. I gotta open some air fresheners before my folks get home."

Bennie walked toward the stairs that led to the garage. Emily and I were alone again.

Our date was ruined. My heart sank a little. "I'll see you tomorrow," I said before leaving through the kitchen.

It was a lonely walk home. Both Bennie and Thomas were mad at me. A divide as big as the one separating our island from the mainland was coming between me and my friends. I touched the spot on my cheek where Emily had kissed me, but any pleasure from that moment was gone now. One thought pushed all others aside: what was Ross hiding that was so important he'd almost drown Thomas to keep it a secret?

NINETEEN

It was an eerily quiet morning on the wharf. My friends and I sat a few feet apart on our overturned buckets, watching in silence as the boats came through the narrows. Many sailed past the plant with no catch to process while others had only a couple of hundred pounds or less on board, a far cry from the two thousand pounds of cod they had grown accustomed to landing just a few years back. It was becoming all too apparent that this was another bust of a fishing season.

Ross Coles and the Arseholes made quick work cutting the tongues out of what little fish did hit the wharf. Meanwhile, we kept our distance. This was survival of the fittest now, and we were in no position to challenge them even if we wanted to. Thomas sat a little farther away from the rest of us. He was still upset at us for having a social gathering, or as we referred to it "a time," without him. But I knew there was more going on. We were just an easy target for the anger and humiliation he felt over what Ross, Rounder, and Jody did to him the night before.

Bennie sat in between Emily and me like a chaperone at a school dance. I knew what he was doing and was a little insulted. Emily didn't seem herself either. She was gazing off into the distance as if in some kind of trance. Why was she so far away?

We watched as yet another thirty-foot trap skiff passed by without any fish to speak of, while a smaller boat in its wake landed with a humble catch. At its rudder was Joseph Coles, Ross's father. He was alone. Ross's older brother, Dennis, who usually fished alongside him, had left for the mainland earlier in the summer. Rumor had it that it wasn't an amicable parting of ways. In fact, Bennie told us that his dad had to use six stitches to close a cut above his eye a week before he left.

Ross made his way sheepishly to his father's boat. Joseph barked something at his son as he jumped up on the wharf. Though we were a fair distance from them, we could hear the word his father uttered at the end of their exchange: "Useless."

Ross made his way down the ladder, scowling at me before disappearing out of sight.

"You know they went out," Bennie said when Ross was gone.

"Who went out?" I asked.

"Anna and Ross," he said.

I jumped to my feet, pointing my finger in his face. "That's bullshit," I said. I couldn't imagine Anna ever being interested in someone like Ross Coles.

"Joey Mullins told me when we were up trouting, so there you go."

"Joey Mullins tells lies," I replied. "There's no way she'd ever go out with the likes of him."

"The likes of him?" Thomas repeated. He got off his bucket and stood between me and Bennie. His eyes were drawn tight, his breathing heavy.

"Are you being serious right now?" I asked. "He slammed your head into a barrel of cod liver oil before throwing you into the harbor over there."

"He's a total skeet, but that doesn't mean all people like him are skeets," Thomas responded. "Not all of us are built for fancy tea parties."

Though they were different in many ways, Thomas and Ross were similar in a few. Both were rough and tumble, not great in school, and more inclined to use their hands than their heads. Even their families were comparable, each with a bunch of brothers and no sisters. And more importantly to Thomas, they had slightly less than most.

"Boys," Emily said, looking off into the distance. "I think they're stealing fish."

Thomas, Bennie, and I followed Emily's gaze. Jody and Rounder were standing in front of the wooden cutting table, obstructing Joseph Coles's view, while Ross stuffed some fish into a five-gallon bucket. This was unheard-of. None of us kids had ever taken fish without asking. If they got caught, the consequences would result in a lifetime ban from the wharf. And if Ross's dad caught them, the consequences would be much worse.

"Are they that hard off for a few dollars?" Thomas said.

"Maybe. There's eight mouths to feed in Rounder's family alone," Bennie replied.

"Where is he going now?" Emily asked as Ross disappeared around the corner. Jody and Rounder followed shortly after.

"I'm going to find out," I said, and began walking toward the back of the plant.

"Don't," Thomas pleaded. "Leave it alone."

Despite his warning, I continued to the large white loading doors of the plant. As I turned the corner, someone grabbed me by the shoulders and threw me up against the wall. My head bounced off the cold concrete. It took a few seconds for the dizziness to subside, but when it did, Jody and Rounder were standing in front of me. And from behind a wall of large fish boxes appeared a smiling Ross Coles.

"You were watching us," Ross said as he scooped up some ice from one of the gray boxes that was prepped to transport fish off the island.

"I'm just going home, Ross," I said as I tried to walk away only to have Jody and Rounder grab me by the arms.

"Shag off!" I barked, still trying to break free.

With one fluid motion, Ross pulled my knife from the sheath attached to my belt.

"No. You were definitely watching us," he said as he flicked his thumb across the blade. "That's a good way to lose an eye." Beads of sweat rolled down my face as he brought the knife up to my face, stopping an inch from my right eye.

"Let him go," I heard a voice say.

Ross lowered the knife, and I turned my head to see Emily standing between Thomas and Bennie.

"Look at this crowd of losers," Rounder said as he and Jody let go of my arms.

"How was your swim last night, Riblet?" Jody asked.

But Thomas remained silent as he looked down at the ground.

"You could have killed him," Bennie said, stepping forward.

"Easy now, little man," Ross said. "If I wanted to drown him, he'd be drowned. That was a warning to all of yee to keep your mouths shut."

"About what?" Bennie asked. "What are you hiding?"

"Or who are you hiding?" Emily said.

Ross's eyes turned cold. He walked up to Emily, my knife gripped firmly in his hand. "My old man was right about girls like you," he said, now inches from her face. "Too smart for your own good."

"You had something in that boat!" I shouted. "You had it pinned down with a net."

He started to laugh. "And you think we had that missing girl?"

"Anna," I said. "Her name is Anna."

"I know exactly who she is," Ross fired back.

"We don't know nothing about any of that," Rounder said. "We were just out for a spin to Clayton's Island."

"Shut up!" Ross yelled at Rounder, who suddenly looked as frightened as we were.

"Where is she?" I asked, fear giving way to anger. "If you know something, anything, you should say!"

Ross spun around and quickly pinned me to the wall with one arm while holding the knife to my throat with the other. My friends moved to help but were blocked by Jody and Rounder.

"I could cut your throat like a fish," Ross growled. I could feel a trickle of blood run down my neck.

"Stop it!" Emily yelled.

"Hey!" a voice called out.

A man appeared in our midst—Wes Bartlett, the plant's foreman. "Stop your skylarking back here!"

Ross removed the blade from my throat.

"Keep out of my business," Ross whispered in my ear. He dropped the knife to the ground and walked back toward the wharf. Jody and Rounder followed, grabbing the bucket of stolen fish as they left.

Wes lit up a fresh cigarette off the smaller one in his mouth. "You all right?" he asked.

"Yeah, I'm fine," I said. Wes nodded and headed back inside the plant.

Emily and the boys rushed over to me.

"You're cut," Emily said.

"It's just a scratch," I replied, rubbing my neck as I tried to catch my breath.

Emily ran to the cooler and scooped up a handful of ice. "Just breathe," she said, applying the ice to my neck.

"I hate them so much," Thomas said, breaking his silence, which lasted the entire ordeal. "What do we do now?"

"We can't go to the cops," Bennie said. "All we've really seen them do is steal a few fish."

"We have to find her," Emily said.

"We have no clue where she is," Thomas said.

"Ross didn't like it when the bigger one mentioned that other place. What was it called?" Emily asked.

"Clayton's Island," I replied. "No one lives on it anymore, but some of the older kids go out there to drink and camp out." In the 1960s, the government resettled all the residents of the island to larger communities, rendering the place a ghost town.

"We need to go there," Emily said.

"And how are we supposed to get there?" Thomas asked.

There was only one way. "Solomon," I said.

"So, you suddenly trust him now?" Thomas asked.

It was a fair question. But things had changed. I'd seen another side of him when we were out to sea.

"I do," I replied.

"Pierce, you should talk to him," Emily said.

"Why Pierce?" Thomas asked, clearly put out that she hadn't picked him.

"Because Solomon talks to him like an adult," Emily replied.

"Okay," I said as I grabbed my knife off the ground. "Get your gear ready. I'll meet you all at Bennie's. If I can convince Solomon, we'll leave right away."

TWENTY

I jumped on my trike and drove as fast as I could to Solomon Vickers's place. The wind was blowing a gale at my back. It almost felt as if some strange force was hurrying me along. As I got closer to the far end of the island, I began to think about what I would say to convince him to help us. He was logical. He'd spent the better part of his life analyzing hard evidence, something of which my friends and I were in short supply. I would need to choose my words carefully. As my father used to say, "Mind your tongue. It can be as sharp as any blade and can cut even deeper." This was the sage advice he bestowed on me one night after I refused to eat my mother's cooking, telling her she needed to try harder. We'd had fish every night that week, and like a fool, I never thought to wonder why.

It was difficult to concentrate on what I would say. I could still feel the blade against my throat, Ross's words echoing in my head—that thing he said about girls like Emily being too smart for their own good. What did he mean by that?

As I pulled into Solomon's driveway, I could tell immediately something was off. The tailgate on his red pickup was down and a couple of large cardboard boxes were resting on top of it. As

I walked past the truck, I saw some books and clothing in the boxes. I continued up the steps to the large wooden doors only to find them slightly ajar. I could hear a familiar noise coming from inside—the fan and the clicking of the slides in a carousel. The old doors creaked as I pushed them all the way open.

"Solomon?" I called out. No reply. I waited a few seconds before walking inside.

I navigated my way through the maze of crates, my eyes drawn to the only light in the room—from the old slide projector propped up on a folding table. Sitting in front of it with a remote in one hand and a ceramic mug in the other was Solomon. His thick, silver hair was greasy and his red flannel shirt was unbuttoned. At his bare feet was half a bottle of whiskey.

He remained completely motionless as I walked up to him. What was on the screen had his undivided attention—a slide of him and his wife. The image looked fairly recent. Solomon's hair was more salt-and-pepper than the brilliant white I was accustomed to. He and his wife were kneeling on the shoreline next to what appeared to be a number of curved bones several feet in length. Red granite cliffs were visible in the background.

"Solomon?" I said.

"Rib bones from a bowhead whale," he replied, his eyes still on the screen. "We took them from the waters off Red Bay, Labrador. It was home to a Basque whaling station."

It was an odd greeting, but at least it was something.

"People hunt whales?" I asked.

"Not anymore, for the most part," Solomon replied before pouring himself more whiskey from the bottle.

"Laura, my wife, and I collected those bones seven years ago for the provincial museum's education program. She was a curator there. That was the last trip we made together before her accident. She's been gone five years to the day." Solomon gulped the whiskey in his cup.

"I'm sorry," I said. "I saw some stuff in your truck. Are you leaving?"

"I have a confession," he replied.

A confession? I felt my heart sink.

"Over there, by the squid." Solomon motioned with his mug. "It's all there in black and white."

My mind began to spin. I walked slowly across the dimly lit room to where the giant squid came into sight. Its enormous, detached eye watched my every move from its jar. On top of the tank was a manila envelope addressed to Solomon. I recognized the red and gold shield emblem in the top corner, the same insignia on the envelope the man in the trench coat had presented to Solomon down on the wharf.

I gently picked it up and opened it. Inside was a letter with the words **"notice of eviction"** written in bold across the top. Solomon had to vacate the property immediately. This was his third and final warning. He would face jail time for trespassing if he prolonged his stay any longer.

I walked back to Solomon with the letter in hand.

"You're not supposed to be here?" I asked.

"Well, I was allowed. Just not for this long," he replied. "The place is condemned and has to be torn down." He took the paper from my hand and smirked as he read it again before handing it back to me. "Back in January I convinced the university to give me two weeks to catalog what was here. Somehow those two weeks turned into six months."

"I don't understand," I said. "Why are you still here?"

Solomon clicked the button on the remote and another slide popped up. It was of his wife, younger now by some twenty-plus years. She was setting out some elongated bones on a folding table. On the wall above her head was a poster of the great auk. I'd seen this exact display before in the basement.

"This was Laura's project, one that she never got to finish," Solomon said, struggling out of the chair and making his way to the screen. "When I saw these bones in the basement, I knew I had to finish what she started."

"You've been looking for auk bones to finish the skeleton," I said.

"It was important to her." He propped himself up against the table for support. "And I wanted to finish it here, where it all started. But now I'm out of time. And as run-down and creepy as you kids might think this place is, I'm having a hard time letting it go."

I knew what he meant. I couldn't imagine leaving this island and all my memories of my father behind.

"You know, for the longest time I blamed myself for her death," he began as he took out a pouch of tobacco and started to roll a cigarette. "I should have been with her that night in the car. Maybe we would have stopped for coffee or taken a different route. Something . . . anything to throw off the timing, just by a few seconds." As he spoke, he stared at the unlit cigarette in his hand. "But recently, I figured out this kind of thinking only fuels the pain. And she would not want that. Nor would she want me smoking again." Solomon dropped the cigarette into his mug.

"How do you move past it?" I asked.

"By getting back on the water. By teaching you kids a thing or two. By working on projects she started so long ago." Solomon pushed himself off the table and walked over to me.

"I know you miss your dad. But the best way to honor those we've lost is to live the very best life we can."

Solomon put his hand on my shoulder and for a brief second I was with my father again. I would think back on these words long after the man who uttered them was gone.

"So what are you going to do now?" I asked, placing the letter on the table next to the slide projector.

"The university is sending trucks first thing Monday morning to pick up our specimens over there."

Our specimens. I liked the sound of that.

"When they go, I go too." Solomon began walking toward the back of the building, but he stopped suddenly and turned back to me.

"Why are you here?" he asked, squinting to see me.

His mind was heavy and his body impaired from the whiskey. This wasn't going to work, not in the way I had planned.

"I was wondering if you'd help me fix up my dad's boat," I said.

A smile appeared on his face. "Yeah, I'd like that very much," he said.

"Maybe we could take it out to Clayton's Island someday?"

"Clayton's Island," Solomon repeated. "I collected some auk bones out that way."

"Is it hard to get to?" I asked.

"Not with a compass and a good map," he replied, nodding toward a rolled-up chart near a pile of boxes. "We'll take a trip out there when we have your boat up and running."

"That would be great," I said.

He shot me a smile before turning and disappearing into the darkness.

I didn't follow him. What was the point? Instead, I grabbed the nautical chart and headed out the door.

I quickly made my way to Bennie's place, where I found my friends waiting for me inside the garage. We didn't have Solomon, but we did have his boat and his chart.

"We're going without him," I said.

TWENTY-ONE

We arrived at Solomon's stage on the far end of the harbor by midafternoon. It was eerily quiet. The boats had come in with little or no catch, which meant the plant was shut down for the day. It also meant that nobody would see a bunch of kids sailing through the narrows without an adult on board.

We threw our oil clothes into Solomon's boat like we had done a couple of days previous and made our way to his red ochre fishing stage located near the water's edge. The single-story shed-like structure used to be owned by Francis Byrne, but he leased it, along with the fishing gear and the boat, to Solomon just before he moved away at the beginning of the year. He had finally had enough of too many subpar fishing seasons.

Just to the side of the stage, resting on an aluminum trailer, was the old fifteen-foot Zodiac that Solomon had brought with him to the island. I could see clearly now why he'd stopped using it, electing instead to lease the fiberglass boat off Francis Byrne. The old inflatable boat had seen better days. Its black, rubberlike coating sported a number of large patches, like the kind we used to repair holes in our bicycle tires.

"At least we're not taking that out," Thomas said, nodding

at the old inflatable as I popped up the wooden door latch and entered the fishing stage. Inside, coils of green rope and black netting dangled from an exposed beam that ran the length of the ceiling. Bleached oars, rusted gaffs, fish prongs, and large orange buoys and floats filled the space. I unzipped my knapsack and took out Solomon's nautical chart. We rolled it out on a crudely built fish-splitting table, each one of us pinning down a corner with our hands.

"Clayton's Island is here," I said, pointing to the small island just north of our own. "Our safest bet is to follow the shoreline heading east until we reach the end of our island." I traced the route with my finger. "Then we steam due north for an hour and we should be there."

"Should be?" Thomas repeated. "And if we miss it?"

"We'll run out of fuel and be adrift at sea," Bennie replied, pointing to the hundreds of miles of open water on the map.

"We won't miss it," I said, sounding confident but knowing there was absolutely no room for error.

"And what if Anna is on that island?" Emily asked. "They're not just going to let us walk away with her."

"I know," I said. If Ross caught us, there was a good chance we'd all go missing too. "We'll have to figure that part out when we get there. There's no other way."

We gathered up a set of oars and the life jackets that were hanging on the wall, and I grabbed one of the two jerry cans of fuel we'd need for our return trip.

When we made our way to the edge of the wharf, I watched my friends descend the ladder into Solomon's boat. I waited for a wave of uneasiness to wash over me, but it didn't come. My heart was beating normally and there was no ringing in my ears.

I knelt down and passed the jerry can to Bennie before carefully climbing down the wooden ladder. For a second I wished Solomon was there to see me climb into his boat without fear.

Once on board, Bennie retrieved the large, brass compass encased in a wooden box in the cuddy and handed it to Emily, who placed it next to our nautical chart. They began studying it a little more closely, making marks on it with a pencil. Meanwhile, Thomas and I made our way to the outboard motor at the stern. It was an older model, forty horsepower, and though it had seen better days, it would get us to where we needed to go.

Then the realization set in. Unlike my father's crank-start, single-cylinder engine, this type of motor needed a key.

"What's the holdup?" Thomas asked.

"Solomon must have the key," I said, deflated.

"Key," Thomas chuckled as he unzipped the gray nylon fanny pack around his waist and pulled out a wrench, a flathead screwdriver, and some electrical tape. He started by disconnecting the battery. He then popped off the casing to the motor and bypassed the ignition switch by rerouting some wires before reconnecting the battery. He struck some wires together a few times. It made a clicking until finally the motor roared to life. Just like that, Thomas had hot-wired the boat.

Emily and Bennie untied the twenty-footer while Thomas pushed us away from the wharf with the four foot fishing prong. Once we were free from the dock, I put the outboard in gear and carefully maneuvered us through the harbor. We slipped by the deserted fish plant as we made our way to the breakwater. My hand tightened around the tiller. My friends looked at me. I knew they were thinking the same thing—was this safe? I opened up the throttle and steamed out into the unknown.

Once outside the safety of the harbor, we headed north until we rounded the farthest point out, then we set a course east, following the coastline for some sixteen miles. There was a light breeze at our back, but gray clouds were forming in the sky. I was hoping the weather would hold.

Emily and Bennie were near the bow, keeping a close eye on the map and compass, while Thomas was keeping watch over me at the helm.

"Give me a turn, you're going too slow," he declared, trying to nudge me away from the tiller.

"Shag off," I said, pushing him away. "The last thing we need is you fooling around out here."

Thomas was highly skilled behind any machine, but he was in equal part reckless, something we couldn't afford right now.

The wind changed and was now in our faces. Emily's long hair billowed behind her like a shirt drying on a clothesline. The skies opened and the rain came flooding down. We scrambled to secure our rain gear.

"This isn't a shower, it's a storm!" Thomas shouted over the roar of the engine.

"It'll pass," I replied, struggling to see through the blinding rain.

Emily and Bennie were huddled near the bow, heads down as the rain pelted off the hoods of their oilskin jackets.

Then we heard it. A loud thud on the starboard side, like an axe striking a block of wood. The collision came with enough force to jolt us all to the other side of the boat.

"What was that?" Thomas shouted as he crouched over the motor.

"Growlers!" Bennie pointed to a field of ice directly in our path. These chunks of glacial ice had broken off the larger icebergs and were big enough to sink the boat.

"Turn her off!" Thomas ordered, his hand reaching for the mess of wires on the motor.

"We can't," I replied, grabbing his arm. "We'll be pulled into the rocks." We were still following the coastline and the current would drag an idle boat to certain disaster.

"Then we need to turn back," Thomas ordered, looking through my binoculars. "They're spread out over a mile or so."

But I knew if we turned back, we would never get this chance again.

"Keep an eye on each side," I said.

Thomas moved quickly to the bow with my instructions, and soon Emily and Bennie were leaning off each side of the boat as we entered the glacial minefield.

"There!" Emily shouted through the blinding rain and pounding waves, while pointing furiously at a huge chunk of ice just off the starboard bow. I pulled hard on the tiller, narrowly avoiding contact.

"Over here!" Bennie called out, hands flailing on the port side. I once again adjusted our course, pulling the tiller in the opposite direction. This continued for thirty minutes as we inched our way down the coastline. My eyes were burning from the salty spray.

"Growler!" Emily called out, pointing dead ahead to a huge chunk of ice sticking some five feet out of the water.

"We're gonna hit it!" Thomas yelled.

Emily sprang into action, grabbing the four-foot-long fish prong that lay flat against the gunwale. It was the very same one that Thomas had used to push the boat away from the dock. She stuck it into the growler like she was harpooning a mythical beast risen from the depths.

"Some help!" she shouted at Bennie, who immediately grabbed hold of the long, wooden handle. Together, they pushed us away from the ice until eventually the noise stopped. We had broken free.

We stared at each other for a moment. There were no cheers or congratulatory high-fives. We all knew just how close we had come to forfeiting our own lives.

"Good to go?" I asked.

They slowly nodded, one after the other.

We sailed onward, carefully navigating our way through the last of the growlers until the rain finally relented and we came upon the source of the deadly obstacle course. It was the iceberg Emily had admired that very first day on the island. But it was different now. It was smaller, half its original size. It was only a matter of time before it would be claimed by the sea.

With the ocean of white in our wake, we were out of coastline. Now we'd have to enter the open water to reach Clayton's Island, with no land to guide our way.

"Due north," Bennie said, holding up the compass. According to the chart, it was pretty much a straight line to our destination. Thomas joined Bennie at the bow while Emily made her way to the stern.

"Nice work with that prong," I said, taking off my oilskin jacket. The weather was changing once again, with a warm sun breaking through the blanket of clouds. "You really saved us back there."

"You weren't so bad yourself," she replied with a grin. "Must be in your blood."

I didn't know what to say to that, so I concentrated on the horizon.

"You're a good friend," Emily said.

It was not what I was hoping to hear.

"I mean, to go looking for Anna like this," she continued.

"She was there when I needed someone," I said.

As we spoke, I steered the boat toward two large groupings of rock that jutted some thirty feet out of the ocean. Two granite pillars were separated by a few hundred feet of ocean. One of the rocks looked like the head of a horse while the other was much narrower, more like a tail. I could feel my eyes fill up. I knew this place.

"What are those?" Emily asked, looking at the formations through my binoculars.

"It's a fishing ground known as the Saddle," I said. "This is where my father was fishing when it happened. My uncle found his boat not far from here."

Emily looked at me. "Is this the first time you've been here?" she asked softly.

"Yes," I said. I looked down at the cold, dark water.

I went quiet then. I concentrated on keeping the boat equidistant from the two groupings of rock.

As the rolling waves carried us farther out to sea, the fog became even denser.

"Is this normal?" Emily asked with concern in her voice.

"We'll be okay," I replied.

"We should see Clayton's Island by now," Bennie called out as he and Thomas scanned the map. I cut the engine and joined them up toward the bow.

"Can't see nothing with this fog," Thomas remarked. "We could have sailed right past it." Thomas picked up the compass and began to examine it closely.

"Maybe this thing is broken," he said, shaking it like a snow globe.

"No, the compass is right, you're the one that's broken," Bennie insisted. "Try shaking your head."

There was a noise, a familiar one that I'd heard all my life coming from outside my bedroom window—the sound of waves pounding the shore.

"Listen!" Emily said.

And just like that, the fog lifted, revealing Clayton's Island some eight hundred feet in front of us. The island was flat and barren, and dotted with weathered houses and small wharfs in various stages of decay.

"How do we get to shore?" Emily asked.

"The old harbor is around the next point," Bennie said.

The jagged coastline of Clayton's Island was now less than three hundred feet away from our boat. The waves were pushing us closer by the second.

"We better get going," I said, moving toward the stern. Thomas followed me and began manipulating the wires to start up the engine again.

"Hurry up!" Bennie shouted.

"Wires must be wet," Thomas said as he frantically tried to dry them off with his shirt.

"Guys!" Emily said, holding up the red jerry can.

Thomas checked the tank.

"It's dry," he announced.

Emily dragged the can over the deck to the stern, where I hastily grabbed it from her and began filling the tank. We were now less than fifty feet away from the rocks.

"Hurry the frig up!" Bennie yelled.

My hands were shaking so badly that gasoline splashed across my rubber boots. But somehow, I managed to get some into the rusted tank as Thomas squeezed the primer bulb.

"Try it now!" I shouted at Thomas, who once again worked the choke and started in with the exposed wires. Less than a boat's length from disaster, the motor roared to life. I grabbed the tiller, opened up the throttle, and pulled us away from the jagged rocks.

We made our way along the coast until we came to the entrance of the harbor. It was small, with a rubble-mound breakwater of large interlocking stones, many of which had fallen into the sea, leaving gaping holes in the harbor's defense system. The island never had a fish plant. Instead, the inhabitants would split and dry their fish on flakes, which were raised platforms made out of limbed trees. Only one small fishing stage was still standing near the water's edge. And tied to it was Ross Coles's boat.

I cut the engine as we made our approach. Thomas and Bennie grabbed the oars and positioned them in the locks on the sides of the boat.

"Now what?" Emily asked.

"We go to shore," I said.

TWENTY-TWO

The very last time I saw Anna Tessier was in late September of 1989. It had been three months since our last encounter, and we were all back at school on our island.

Throughout the summer and fall, I periodically made a trip over to the other side of the island to see if Anna had returned to that same place to draw what I thought of as "our iceberg." On one particular day, fortune was on my side.

Anna was sitting on that same rock overlooking the bay. She was staring at the once towering pyramid of ice that was now a quarter of its original size. It had taken a completely different shape. The elements had gouged out the middle section, leaving two prominent pinnacles on each end. Anna was different too. There was no pad or pencil in her hands. She was staring at our iceberg with such intensity that I wondered if she was the one making it melt.

I didn't even know she knew I was there, not until she said, "What does it look like to you?" without so much as taking her eyes off the thing in front of her.

"It looks to me like a melting iceberg," I said.

We picked up from where we left off months before. You can do that with certain people. My mother used to say that those kinds of people are the ones you ought to hold on to.

Anna turned to me and patted the space beside her. I almost tripped over a root in my haste to join her on the boulder.

"Kinda looks like a saddle," I said. The irony wasn't lost on me, that being the name of the fishing ground where my father had disappeared.

"It looks to me like two people frozen in time." She held her index fingers up, close to each other but not touching. "They're just staring at each other, separated by a chasm neither can cross."

I could have listened to Anna talk all day long even if I had no idea what a chasm was. "Did your friend like her sketch?" I asked.

"I think so," she replied. "She liked my art. She just . . . didn't like me. Not in the way I like her anyways."

I was too young, too stupid, to understand. All I could think was how anyone could not like Anna. It seemed impossible.

"She sounds like a bit of an arse," I said, my legs dangling off the boulder. "I mean, who wouldn't want to be friends with someone who drew an amazing picture of them?"

"That some kind of hint?" Anna asked, smiling.

"No, just saying."

Anna nodded at my trike. "Got anything to eat on that thing?"

I did. I retrieved my knapsack from my trike and took out a bologna sandwich. I carefully unwrapped it and gave half to Anna. As she ate, I admired that wide cuff silver bracelet around her wrist.

"It's my mom's," she said between bites. "The bracelet."

"Pretty," I replied.

"It's a bribe to get me to like my stepdad."

"And do you?" I asked.

"He's best kind," she replied. "But I didn't tell her that. I wanted to keep the bracelet."

We shared a laugh with our mouths full and I thought that this must be what it felt like to have a big sister.

"You know, you had everyone worried," I said. Shortly after our previous encounter, Anna had disappeared for three days before walking through her front door like nothing had happened.

"I didn't feel like coming home," she said, her eyes following a seagull that had just landed on the tallest pinnacle of the iceberg.

"You shouldn't disappear like that," I said, ripping the crust from my sandwich and tossing it near the edge of the cliff. The seagull took flight and headed toward its prize.

"Don't worry, I won't be going anywhere again. Not for a while."

"Promise?"

"Before I do, I'm coming back for my good-luck charm." She reached out and rubbed the frowny-face button on my nylon windbreaker. "I promise I won't disappear again. Not without that."

Then something extraordinary happened. A loud crack echoed like thunder across the bay. The iceberg began to turn, slowly at first, but picking up speed as gravity took hold. Within seconds, it had completely flipped over, exposing its shiny blue underbelly to the sky. It is extremely rare to be witness to such a sight. My father told me he had seen it happen only once while hunting turrs with my grandfather. "We were no further than a hundred feet away," he said, reenacting the encounter with a box of matches. "The glacier, she turned over. The waves lifted our boat right out of the water."

"Can you believe that?" Anna gasped. Her face was beaming. I'd never seen her so excited.

"And look at that color!" Anna continued. "Electric blue! It looks like it's made of glass."

"It's really cool!" I said.

Anna laughed. We finished our sandwiches in silence, our eyes glued to the iceberg, until the sun's movement across the sky told me it was getting close to suppertime. "Wanna ride back?" I offered.

"Oh, I'm not going anywhere. I finally get to sketch the bottom of an iceberg. But thanks for lunch," she said. "No crust next time."

"Remember your promise," I said.

She nodded as she took out her sketchbook and flipped over a new page.

I got on my trike and drove away, not knowing it was the last time I would ever see Anna Tessier alive.

TWENTY-THREE

We tied Solomon's boat up to the only section of wharf left standing on Clayton's Island, before proceeding carefully in twos down the rickety plank walkway that was suspended over the water. We navigated across missing or broken boards, which revealed the rushing waves crashing against the jagged rocks below.

"I wouldn't want to do this in the dark," Thomas said, his arms outstretched as if he was walking a tightrope.

"We won't have to." I looked at Emily, who gave me the same tight-grin-with-raised-eyebrows kind of smile that my mother would whenever I underestimated the amount of time I needed to finish my math homework.

Once safely on dry land, we walked along a narrow, overgrown gravel road.

There was no sign of Ross, Rounder, or Jody. In fact, the entire place seemed void of life. It was eerily quiet. Old tattered fishing nets and broken lobster pots rested in the tall grass. These were essential tools of the trade that meant the difference between life and death. They, like everything else on the island, had been abandoned.

"Where do you think they are?" Emily asked.

I had no answer. No one else did, either.

"You know why there's no people here, right?" Thomas said, tapping Emily on the shoulder.

"I know. They were all resettled to bigger communities," Emily replied.

"That's what they want you to think," Thomas said. "But the truth is the island was maggoty with the fairies. The people might be gone, but the fairies are still here. I can feel them."

Thomas fell quiet as we came upon a large grouping of alder bushes that obstructed our path. They stretched the width of the road and came up to our heads, making it impossible to see ahead. With some effort, we managed to break through and found ourselves overlooking what can only be described as a ghost village.

The community had been smaller and more compact than ours. The twenty or so saltbox-style houses still standing were in very rough shape. Roofs were caved in and most had either missing or broken windows and doors. Others were just rock foundations with no houses on top. We were told in school that some of those people who were resettled winched their wooden houses to the water and then floated them across the bay on homemade barges to bigger communities.

"This is creepy," Bennie said.

"Doesn't feel like there's any life here at all, fairy or human," Emily replied.

I looked through my binoculars at the ghost village below, following the winding road that zigzagged its way through the town until I came to a small church.

"They have to be down there somewhere," I said.

We made our way down the embankment into the town. We all kept watch for any movement like we did when we went hunting for partridge up on the barrens. Thomas eyed the overgrown grass, undoubtedly looking for fairies. Though we didn't see so much as a seagull, I had a strange feeling we were being watched.

We soon arrived at the church. The small timber structure was similar to the one on our island with the narrow clapboards and steep gable roof and wooden shingles, most of which were missing. The top of the central tower had a domed spire affixed with a wooden crucifix, which cast an ominous shadow under the bright sun.

We walked up the narrow steps to the double wood doors. A chain was wrapped around both handles and fastened with a silver padlock.

"That looks new," I said. The lock and chain were the only pieces of metal on the island that were not covered in rust.

"Are they keeping someone in or someone out?" Emily asked.

"We need to find out," I said, tugging on the chain, which was secured tight.

"Doesn't explain where Ross and the Arseholes are," Bennie replied. "Clearly, they aren't in there."

"There's a sandy beach on the other side of the island," Thomas said. "My brothers used to go there to set bonfires and drink beers."

"Just because the boys aren't in the church doesn't mean Anna isn't there," I said.

"Okay. So how do we get in?" Emily asked.

"The windows are too high up," Bennie replied, looking out past the railing at the side of the church.

"There's another way," I said. I poked my index finger through a section of rotting wood underneath the handle on the left-hand side. Bennie pulled out his silver pocketknife and began working away at the decaying plank. Before long, he had gouged out a groove all around the base.

"Pull," I prompted. All four of us grabbed hold and pulled with everything we had. We heard a crack just before we tumbled down the steps, still clenching the wrought iron handle. We got to our feet and stared at the gaping hole where the handle used to be. I pushed the doors open.

"Hello?" I called out into the dark church. "Anna?" No response.

I made my way through the narrow passage and into the vestibule. Thin beams of light poured down through small pinholes in the steep gable roof. It wouldn't be long before it too would collapse due to neglect. I took out my flashlight and shone it on the rows of varnished oak pews and kneelers. The walls were bare. Religious statues were missing from their stands as were the Stations of the Cross that would normally run the length of each side of the church. They were likely taken by the parishioners when they left. I looked back toward my friends and waved them in with my flashlight.

We walked up the center aisle toward a small wooden altar. The old spruce floorboards squeaked with every step.

Something caught Emily's attention. "What's that?" she asked.

I shone my light to the altar, where a homemade sled with a wide wooden box and curved runners was revealed by the beam. It was the kind we attached to ATVs and snowmobiles to haul wood.

"What's a sleigh doing in a church?" Bennie asked.

"Doesn't matter. Nobody's here. We should go," Thomas said, looking around nervously.

"You guys smell that?" Bennie asked. He was standing near the altar. Emily and I walked over to him.

"It stinks," Emily said as Thomas joined us. It was the unmistakable odor that permeated the harbor every summer and fall. "Like rotten fish."

"Because that's what it is," Bennie said.

And that's when we heard it—a scratching noise coming from the other side of the altar. It sounded like someone was crawling along the floor.

"Someone's up there," Thomas whispered.

I slowly pointed my flashlight at the base of the altar. A tiny, round head appeared from behind it, completely hairless with bulging eyes. And just like that, the head disappeared behind the altar again.

"A fairy!" Thomas shrieked. "I told you they were here!"

I walked up the first of two steps leading to the elevated platform. Emily and Bennie followed. We crept around the side in a tight huddle, my flashlight guiding the way while Thomas, armed with a piece of broken railing, brought up the rear.

When we rounded the corner of the altar, the beam of light illuminated a large creature with a teardrop-shaped body. It had ridges across its leathery back and large, clawless flippers in the front and shorter ones in the back. Next to it was a pile of codfish.

"A sea turtle!" Bennie exclaimed.

"Look at the size of it!" Thomas gasped as he reached out to touch its head, but the turtle snapped at him with its razor-like jaws.

"Little shagger!" Thomas said, jumping back.

"This must have been what Ross and the Arseholes had in the boat that day," Emily said, carefully pointing to pieces of netting that were wrapped around its flippers and neck. It was extremely rare, but from time to time these creatures got caught in the fishing nets.

"What the hell is Ross doing with a sea turtle?" Bennie asked.

"Don't know and don't care," Thomas declared, looking at the fingers that he almost lost. "We gotta go."

"I'm with Thomas on this one," Bennie said. "Those boys could be back any minute. Pierce? Pierce?" Bennie repeated, putting his hand on my shoulder.

"We can't leave. Not yet."

"Pierce is right. We haven't found Anna. And we can't just leave this turtle here," Emily said as she knelt down next to the giant creature.

"The doors are open now; it'll find its way back to sea," Bennie said, motioning to the front of the church.

"It's barely moving. I think it's sick," Emily remarked.

"Look at the size of it," Bennie added. "How are we supposed to get it back in the ocean?"

My eyes wandered over to the old wood sled. It all made sense now. "We'll bring it back the same way they got it in here," I said. I walked over to the sled and grabbed the drag harness, hauling it toward the altar. Emily was quick to lend a hand, grabbing hold of the old leather strap.

"Hurry," Bennie replied, grabbing the back of the sled and lifting it up the steps until it lay parallel to the creature.

The turtle must have weighed well over two hundred pounds, and as Thomas had discovered, it could easily remove an appendage with one snap of its powerful jaws. Fortunately for us, the creature was in a weakened state from being out of its habitat for so long.

"Easy does it," I said as I grabbed its rubbery underbelly on one side while Emily and Bennie did the same on the other. Thomas reluctantly got into position next to me and together we managed to get the beast onto the sled.

We made our way to the bottom of the steps and down the

center aisle, past the vestibule, and through the double doors at the back of the church. Once outside, we struggled our way up the incline—with Emily and I pulling in the front and the boys pushing from the back until we were through the grove of alders and emerging on the other side of the bushes in full view of the harbor.

"It would have been easier to bring the ocean to the turtle," Thomas said as he flopped to the ground. Bennie took the binoculars from around my neck and scanned the cove for signs of Ross Coles and the Arseholes.

Emily looked down at the turtle. "It's in a bad way," she said. The bulging eyes were the only things moving on the beast. It was a matter of time before they closed for good.

"Keep going!" I insisted, grabbing the harness and pulling it forward. The others got back into position and we started our descent. It wasn't long before the runners on the sled hit the old wooden planks leading to the stage. We'd made it. Our boat was just a few feet away.

"Hope this thing appreciated the effort," Thomas said as he stood over it, his sweat leaving wet spots on the creature's back.

"Not home free yet, we still gotta get it in the boat," Bennie said, looking down at the water.

"Let's just push him off here and be done with it," Thomas replied.

"It'll be crushed on the rocks," Emily said, putting her foot on the sled.

It was a fair point. We had to quickly find a way to get it on the boat and out to sea. I looked around and spotted a ten-foot wooden pole fastened to the dock next to the stage. Attached to it was a four-foot metal arm to which was fixed a rusted pulley with anchor rope.

"We can use this," I said, lowering the rope with the crank.

"You sure that can hold him?" Bennie asked.

"It's got to," I replied, knowing full well that this was far from a sure thing. The fact that it was still standing was a testament to those who constructed it. But I also knew there was a good chance that Ross used it to offload his prize, so it had to be still functional.

I went down to the boat to retrieve a green cargo net from the fishing room and threw it up to Bennie, who laid it out next to the sled. Once in place, the four of us lifted the sea turtle onto it. Thomas and Bennie then ran the rope connected to the pulley through the wide loops on the net. Emily and I began to carefully turn the handle on the screeching winch. Once the sea turtle was a couple of feet off the wharf, Thomas and Bennie swung it out over the boat. As it dangled above, the pole started to creak. The boys jumped down to help guide it to a safe landing.

Emily and I were lowering the creature down toward the gang-boards when we heard a loud snap.

"It's gonna break!" Thomas yelled.

"Look out!" Bennie shouted, pushing Thomas to the other end of the boat just before the pole and pulley came crashing down. Emily and I rushed to the edge of the wharf. The broken pole was lying across the middle of the boat.

"You almost killed us!" Thomas shouted as he and Bennie poked their heads up from below.

"Is the turtle okay?" Emily asked, her eyes searching frantically for any sign of movement.

"It's fine," Bennie replied as he and Thomas pushed the broken pole over the side of the boat.

The plan worked. We were going to return this creature to its home.

But no sooner had the thought crossed my mind than something struck the wharf with enough force to take a chunk out of the plank I was standing on.

I turned around and saw Ross, Rounder, Jody, and two other older kids glaring at us from the top of the hill. Their arms were drawn back with rocks clenched in their fists. Ross clutched a small hatchet in his left hand.

"It's Ross!" I shouted as a barrage of stones hailed down on us from above. One skipped off a plank and struck Bennie on his wrist. He screamed out in pain as he clenched his bloody arm. I looked back again and saw the five kids charging down the hill toward us.

"Let's get out of here!" Thomas shouted as he untied the lines. Emily and I quickly climbed on board. Thomas and I went to the stern while Emily tore off a piece of her shirt and wrapped it around Bennie's wrist to stop the bleeding from the impact of the rock. Thomas went to work on the engine, and after a few clicks, the motor came to life.

"Wait," Thomas said, jumping out of the boat.

"What are you doing?" I shouted. "They'll kill you!"

But Thomas ignored my warning. He pulled his knife from the black sheath on his belt. He calmly cut the line to their boat and threw it to me before climbing back in.

"Now we can go," he said.

I nodded and pulled us away from the stage with their boat in tow just as Ross and the Arseholes made it to the end of the wharf.

"Hey, that's our boat, you little fuckers!" Ross shouted. We were now fifty feet away from shore. I let the motor idle.

"Come get it!" Thomas said defiantly.

"I'm not playing here, Riblet!" Ross yelled.

"Neither are we!" Bennie yelled back, still squeezing his arm.

"Keep the stupid turtle, just leave us our boat!" Rounder pleaded, which drew a dirty look from Ross.

"I think we'll keep both!" Emily called out, putting her hand on the creature's back.

"You're all dead!" Ross yelled. "There's nowhere to hide back home!"

"We're not afraid of you, you . . . arseholes!" We all looked at Emily. Her hands were clenched, her eyes focused on Ross.

"We'll let someone know you're out here!" I shouted.

As I put the engine in gear, it went completely dead. Thomas quickly checked the wires and I opened the gas tank. It was bone dry. I picked up the red jerry can.

"It's empty," I said, looking at the others.

I had forgotten to put the cap back on and the remaining gas had spilled out onto the floorboards. To make matters worse, the current was pulling us back to shore.

"Grab the oars!" I shouted at Thomas.

Thomas's face dropped as he held up two halves of the same oar. The pole had done some damage after all. I looked over at Emily, who was putting pressure on Bennie's arm. This was a fight we could not win. My stomach began to churn.

Then we heard it. A motor. We all looked toward a black Zodiac rounding the point and heading directly toward us. A lone silver-haired man was at the rudder. As Solomon came into focus, I could make out the scowl on his face.

"You took my boat out!" he fumed, cutting the engine and throwing a line to Thomas, who tied it to our boat.

"And whose boat is that?" Solomon barked.

"Theirs," Bennie replied, pointing to Ross and the other kids on the shore.

Solomon's eyes caught sight of the sea turtle on the gang-boards of his boat.

"They locked it away in a church!" I blurted as he tried to comprehend what he was seeing.

He jumped aboard and began to examine the sea creature. "A leatherback," he said, running his hand over its shell. He turned his attention to the boys onshore. "What were you doing with it?" he called to the older boys.

"Gonna sell it. It's got to be worth something to someone," Ross called back.

"It's ours, old man," Rounder added with a puffed chest.

"This is no one's turtle!" Solomon shouted toward the shore. "And you could all be charged under the Endangered Species Act!"

"You're just trying to scare us!" Jody Buckle shouted.

"The courts will decide! It will either be juvenile hall on the mainland or a big fine, which I'd imagine your parents would have to pay."

Solomon's words had hit their mark. The older boys fell silent.

"Just give us our boat back!" Ross yelled.

"Untie it," Solomon ordered Thomas.

"Wait," I said. "They have Anna."

Solomon looked at Emily, then at me. "Do you know anything about the missing girl?" he called out.

"Don't know nothing about that," Ross replied.

"He went out with her," Emily said. "He must know something."

"Perhaps a night or two on the island might loosen your memory!" Solomon called out.

"You can't leave us here!" Jody shouted.

But Solomon remained silent as he filled the gas tank of our boat with the jerry can from the Zodiac.

"Ross never went out with her, okay," Rounder shouted. "It's all bullshit."

Solomon stared at Ross the way my father had stared at his dad that day on the water. And just like his father had done, Ross turned away. Solomon untied the line to their boat and tossed it in the water. He took one more look at the sea turtle, its eyes now closed.

"Start pouring buckets of water over its back," Solomon instructed us as he secured a line from our boat to his Zodiac before firing up the motor. "We've got to get it back to the sea."

TWENTY-FOUR

As soon as the island was out of sight, Solomon turned off the engine.

"As good a place as any," he said, jumping down into the after standing room.

"Are we too late?" Emily asked.

We all stared at the sea turtle. We had been pouring water on it, but its eyes were still closed.

"She's not done yet," Solomon said.

"She?" I asked.

"See here," he said. "She has a short tail. Males have much longer ones and a more concave underbelly. This one is a juvenile, still young."

"She's gonna get bigger?" Thomas asked.

"Some leatherbacks can weigh up to two thousand pounds," Solomon said. He took out his knife and began to cut away the pieces of netting around her neck and flippers. We followed his lead.

"Careful now," Solomon instructed.

Once the final piece of netting was removed, we gently lifted her to the gunwales and pushed her over the side. She made a splash when she hit the cold water.

"She's not moving," Bennie said. We all watched the creature float lifelessly beside the boat.

Then Emily gasped, squeezing my arm. "Look!"

The turtle's eyes sprung open. And for the first time, her huge flippers began to move, slowly at first, but it wasn't long before they propelled the majestic creature into the deep.

I looked at Emily, who was bubbling with excitement. I took her hand and kissed her on the lips. I remember the taste of vanilla ChapStick coated with a fine sprinkling of sea salt—sweet and salty at the same time. As I pulled away, Emily smiled at me, then tucked a wisp of hair behind her ear.

Thomas made a retching sound like he was going to puke, while Bennie just grinned at me, having come to terms with the undeniable connection I had with his cousin. Solomon smiled and shook his head. "Kids," he said.

We continued to sail onward to our own island. Thomas regaled Solomon with tales of our journey, about the growlers that almost sent us all to the bottom of the sea, how we'd almost smashed the boat on the rocks of Clayton's Island. He explained everything about our trek through a ghost island in search of a missing girl. And breaking into a church and finding a giant turtle behind the altar. Solomon's eyes were wide, but he didn't say a word.

As we hugged the shoreline heading home, we came upon the iceberg I'd shown Emily the first day we met. I was admiring it when Solomon called out from the stern.

"What's that?" he shouted, pointing to the rocks some three hundred feet away.

I looked in the direction of his outstretched finger. There was a flash of light, much like the kind my father's watch used to give off as he checked it while sailing toward the narrows.

"I'm going in for a look," Solomon said. He steered the boat closer to the jagged coastline. The boat was now parallel to the rocks. My friends and I jumped up on the gangboards to get a better view of whatever was glinting in the sun.

Before Thomas could say anything about fairies, there was another flash of light. As we drifted closer to shore, I spotted the source—a wide, silver cuff bracelet on the wrist of a girl lying face-down on the rocks. Her jet-black hair covered her face. Her blue jeans and jacket were soaked from the ocean spray, and her limbs were splayed, lifeless.

"Oh my god," Emily said, her hand over her mouth.

"Dear child," Solomon said, lowering his head.

I didn't need to see her face to know that it was her. Anna. Anna, who calmly talked me back up the ladder when I was too scared to go out to sea. Anna, who gave me the frowny-face button to tell me it was okay to be sad. Anna, who sat next to me when the iceberg rolled over and showed its belly. Anna, who had had a more profound impact on me in our three short encounters than most people would have for the rest of my life.

I gazed up at the cliff overlooking our iceberg. I knew then exactly what had happened. She'd fallen off the edge.

Ten days. Ten days had passed since Anna Tessler had disappeared. We had found her by accident. But we didn't find her alive.

"I'm so sorry," Emily said, squeezing my hand. Thomas and Bennie moved closer.

I couldn't take my eyes off her.

"We need to get her off those rocks," I told Solomon. Tears were streaming down his face.

Solomon shook his head. "We can't do that."

"We have to," I said.

"Pierce, listen to me. We are going back to get help."

"I won't leave her. If you won't do it, I will." I tried to get past him to the Zodiac we had in tow, but he stopped me and held my arms.

"We'll come back for her, Pierce. And we'll bring her home. I promise."

TWENTY-FIVE

Father Jerome stood in front of the altar as he delivered Anna Tessier's eulogy to a community in mourning. Her body lay in a closed casket in the center aisle of the church. The coffin was draped in a white linen cloth with a thick, red embroidered crucifix running down the middle. Her mother, in a pew on the left, held on tight to Anna's little brother and sister, who were crying as she pulled them close. Her stepfather sat next to the children, his eyes on Father Jerome. Anna's father, who hadn't been back home in months, was seated alone in a pew on the right.

It had been a week since we happened upon Anna's body. An investigation by the authorities quickly confirmed what was obvious—there was no foul play involved in Anna's death. Instead, it was deemed an accident. She'd slipped and had fallen off the cliff. Her sketchbook was found on a ledge a quarter of the way down. It was flipped open to an incomplete drawing of an iceberg.

My friends and I stood at the back of the church. My mother was seated in the last pew just in front of me. It was her first time at church since my father's death. She reached her hand over her shoulder in search of mine. I took it and squeezed.

The sheer body heat from a packed house made the grief feel

even more overwhelming. Mourners fanned themselves with the memorial pamphlets, which had a school photo of Anna on the front, smiling in front of a sky-blue backdrop.

"I like her style. I think we would have been great friends," Emily whispered, looking down at the pamphlet in my hand.

I nodded.

The photo on Dad's memorial pamphlet had featured him standing in the kitchen after my mother had given his hair a trim. He was smiling brightly, looking at something off camera. I knew exactly what he was grinning at. He was grinning at me.

A hand on my shoulder brought me back to the service. Solomon Vickers, clean-shaven, wearing a dark blazer and khaki pants, stood beside us kids.

"Doing okay, young fella?" he asked.

"Yeah," I replied.

After he returned us to the harbor, Solomon went back to those jagged cliffs with Sergeant Trang, Constable Munro, and some seasoned fishermen. Together, they retrieved Anna's broken body from the rocks.

Needless to say, neither the authorities nor our parents were pleased with our unsupervised trip to Clayton's Island aboard a stolen boat, but all was forgiven since the end result was the recovery of Anna's body. As for the matter of the illegal capture and confinement of the leatherback sea turtle, the police left that matter in Solomon's capable hands. A few days after we found Anna's body, Solomon went to speak to the older boys down by the wharf. I don't know what he said to them, but Solomon told us that Ross Coles and the Arseholes would never bother any creature on land or in the sea ever again.

In the church that day, I looked across the aisle to where the

Arseholes were standing. Ross and I made eye contact. He nodded and I nodded back.

We had all come away from the experience relatively unscathed, the one exception being Bennie's wrist, which his own father stitched up for him. Thomas had never seen stitches before and couldn't take his eyes off them.

As Father Jerome delivered his standard sermon, I found myself getting annoyed. Why did the church always make such ceremonies about the institution rather than the people who supported it? Anger swelled inside me at the clergyman's generic words of comfort. He knew nothing about Anna. I felt like marching up there to tell everyone about the real Anna. How she was a great artist. And that she knew so much about the people and things she drew because she could see something in them that no one else could.

But I didn't. I just stood quietly in the back with my friends.

After the service, Anna was laid to rest under a flowering lilac tree in the graveyard behind the church.

Not knowing what else to do, my friends and I went back to the wharf to see if we could make a few dollars cutting out cod tongues. At the very least, it was a distraction. Bennie's busted wrist meant that he would be relegated to the sidelines for a while. He would, however, act as supervisor, offering up helpful tips about how Thomas could cultivate his knife technique and improve his productivity.

"Pack right off, Bennie," Thomas said when he'd had enough of Bennie's advice. He flicked some gurry off his blade in Bennie's direction to drive him away from his perch.

We had fewer and fewer days cutting out tongues after that. Days with no fish turned to weeks, which eventually resulted in a reduction of my mother's shifts at the plant. She tried to compensate by working more hours at the video store on the mainland, but that meant late nights and long commutes for less money. It also meant we didn't see each other as often. Still, she never complained, not once.

Solomon decided to stay and finish his research. He bought a small saltbox from one of the families who were forced to move off the island to find work. I remember the day I called him over to the house. It had been about a month since we'd laid Anna to rest.

"This better be good," he said to me after greeting my mother warmly and helping himself to a date square from a plate on the table.

That's when I told him. "My boat. In the backyard. I want you to have it. We can fix it up together, and you can use it for your research."

Solomon looked to me, then to my mother, who nodded her approval.

"Are you sure?" Solomon asked.

"Yes," I replied.

I could think of no better hands to guide its rudder. Even the old trap skiff was adapting to our changing world.

Emily, Thomas, Bennie, and I spent the rest of that summer in my backyard replacing rotten planks and caulking seams before applying a few coats of paint to the boat under the watchful eye of Solomon Vickers. And on the last Sunday in August, Solomon gave our work a final once-over.

"Did we pass or what?" Thomas asked as all four of us looked on.

"She looks ready," he said, running his hand along the keel. "And she wants to go back into the water. She's wanted that for some time."

"Then what are we waiting for?" Bennie asked.

"Not my call to make," Solomon replied. "That's up to the skipper." He turned and looked at me.

"Well, skipper?" Emily said, smiling at me. "Is she ready for the water?"

I gazed at my father's boat with its freshly painted white planks, bright-green trim, and gray interior. It had never looked better, and the make-and-break engine was ocean-ready, thanks to some help from Thomas's dad.

That afternoon, a bunch of fishermen helped us push my father's boat down the slipway and into the ocean, where it belonged. I will never forget the pride I felt as she gently floated across the water to the cheers of my friends. That evening, Solomon and I took Emily, Thomas, and Bennie out to jig a fish, which we cooked up in the stillness of the cove. Afterward, we drank tea and told stories about the fairies until the sun began to set. It was one of the best days I'd had in a long time. All my anxiety about being out on the ocean had finally melted away.

A couple of other bright spots emerged from the darkness of that summer. Ross and the Arseholes never bothered us again. Perhaps it was because Solomon had threatened them with juvie. Or perhaps it was because he kept their idle hands busy by having them sort and catalog specimens he collected in the hopes that they too would gain some appreciation for the world around them. Or maybe Anna's death had impacted them the way it had us.

The other ray of light was my growing relationship with Emily. We had become even closer, spending time together away from Thomas and Bennie. We were as much boyfriend and girlfriend as two twelve-year-olds knew how to be. There was even some more kissing. And I was grateful to be there for her when she found out that her mother's cancer had returned. Sandra had known a few months prior to her trip back to our island, but she had kept it a secret from her daughter, wanting her to connect with family and not worry about her. They stayed on the island with Bennie and his parents before returning to New York for treatment in September. Fortunately, she would beat it once again. When Emily went home to New York, I was lost for a long time, but I also felt eternally grateful for the time we'd had together.

With the boat no longer in the yard, my mother and I worked the soil in preparation for the spring, when we would plant root vegetables. She was as happy as she'd been since losing her husband. Part of it had to do with us spending time together. The other part had to do with creating life in ground that had lain barren for far too long.

In the fall of that year, my friends and I made the trek on the ferry to our new school on the mainland. It was so much larger than the one back home, with ten times the number of students and two classes for every grade. The big school had many things our school didn't, including a cafeteria, a music room, a library, and a gymnasium. Despite the rumors, we didn't experience much bullying from the older kids. In fact, we became friends with many of them.

Though we stuck together that first year, I could feel a distance growing between Thomas, Bennie, and me as we made new friends and took advantage of the opportunities the bigger school offered, with its after-school clubs and sporting events. And as our school years rolled on, I began to wonder about the world beyond the mainland. My fear of change was like the old, crumbling breakwater on Clayton's Island. It could not withstand the waves of curiosity that were washing over me.

EPILOGUE

Solomon Vickers was right. The cod fishery was in a state of crisis due to extensive overfishing. And in July of 1992, just one year after that fateful summer, the federal government would announce a moratorium that shut down the industry indefinitely. Once again, the stroke of a bureaucratic pen would have a devastating impact on almost every community across the province as fish plants closed down and boats were pulled from the water. Not a single family on our island was immune to the effects of the closure. Fishermen and plant workers lost their livelihoods, which had supported their families for generations. And just as with the resettlement order that would turn Clayton's Island into a ghost town, people left the island in droves, desperate to find work elsewhere. This migration included Anna's family too.

I found this particularly heartbreaking. The Tessiers wouldn't be able to visit their daughter's grave anymore, at least not with any regularity. A part of me couldn't help but feel that Anna had been abandoned, left in the land of the dead while her parents secured a better future elsewhere for her living siblings.

My mother and I—we held out for as long as we could. But it didn't last. Five years later, the summer after my high school graduation, I left the only home I'd ever known. We weren't able to sell our house. No one wanted it. We boarded it up like many others had done before us. Then we moved to St. John's, where I attended university while my mother found work at a grocery store. It was at this point that I lost touch with all of my childhood friends.

Thomas went to trade school for engine repair and then moved to Alberta. Bennie went to medical school in Toronto and became a doctor like his father. Emily and I stayed connected as best we could through letters and phone calls, but eventually we too lost touch. The last I heard, she became an investigative journalist, which I thought was fitting. I'd seen firsthand her investigation skills during that one unforgettable summer. As fate would have it, the only person from that time that I would go on to have a lasting friendship with was the very one I'd once wrongly accused of a heinous crime—Solomon Vickers.

Solomon lit a fire in me that summer, one that would burn even brighter as the years went on. In university, I studied marine biology and returned to the island after the spring semesters to complete my work terms by helping with his research. Using my father's tools, he and I converted my abandoned family home into a summer residence with a small, functional research lab. It took us the better part of six summers, but eventually we found all the missing bones to complete the great auk skeleton. Solomon donated it to the provincial museum in his wife's name.

When I finally graduated from university and accepted my diploma, my mother was on one side and Solomon was on the other. He stood next to me again as the best man at my wedding. And though my work as a marine biologist would take me far from the home that I once knew, I made a point to visit him once a summer, every summer, until he passed away in his sleep in the springtime at the age of eighty-eight.

When summer came round again, I took my eight-year-old son, Luke Jacobs, on his first trip to the island. Over the years, the place had gone through quite a transformation. The old fish plant had been retrofitted to process crab that was harvested just offshore. A tourism industry was flourishing, with thousands of people from all over the world flocking there every year thanks in large part to investments in infrastructure. The picturesque island was now home to a seafood restaurant, an ice cream parlor, several boutique B&Bs, and a number of scenic boat tours. Even the old cottage hospital that served as Solomon's marine lab was now the site of a microbrewery. My fears that this place was destined to become a ghost village like Clayton's Island never came to fruition. Instead, people did what they had done for generations when faced with adversity and hardship. They carried on.

After Luke and I enjoyed some ice cream served in a sculpin-shaped cone, I took him to visit his grandfather's grave in the family plot. We cleaned away the debris before placing some flowers on the flat headstone despite the fact that no body lay below. I reminded Luke about his namesake, that his grandfather had been a fisherman and an incredible dad. "But he was silly and foolish too," I said.

"You mean, like you?" Luke replied.

I pushed the brim of his baseball cap down and turned away so he wouldn't see the tears in my eyes.

On our way out of the cemetery, we stopped at Anna Tessier's grave under the shade of the lilac tree. Her plot was well cared for, with fresh flowers in a vase just below her name on the granite headstone. All these years and she hadn't been forgotten.

"Who is Anna?" Luke asked when I stopped in front of the stone.

"She was my friend, son," I replied.

He ran off to read some of the other names. I pulled from my pocket the small frowny-face button that Anna had given me the very first time we met. I rubbed my thumb across the faded yellow face before placing it atop her headstone.

Afterward, my son and I made our way down to the wharf, where we set out in my father's boat, though there was hardly an original piece of wood left on it given Solomon's meticulous up-keep over the years. Always one for passing knowledge and tradi-tion down from generation to generation, Solomon had willed the boat to my son. He'd also left me his pocket watch.

With my hand over his on the tiller, Luke and I sailed through the narrows before heading out over open water. The *put-put* sound from the old make-and-break engine echoed over the water as we journeyed out to sea. We kept our distance as we steamed past a large, glistening iceberg that towered some two hundred feet above the water. Luke's eyes grew wide as he took in the magnitude of the glacial giant. He had questions, lots of them. I was reminded of the first time Emily laid eyes on an iceberg so many years ago.

My son and I sailed to a familiar grouping of rocks jutting up from the sea—the Saddle. As Luke threw a piece of homemade bread to a squawking gull, I took out a small, silver urn from my knapsack and scattered Solomon Vickers's ashes into the sea.

ACKNOWLEDGMENTS

This book would not have been possible without editor extraordinaire and now internationally bestselling author Nita Pronovost. It only took ten years, but Nita finally convinced me to step outside my comfort zone and write this novel. She has been an incredible mentor to me, and I cannot thank her enough for her patience and guidance throughout this process.

I was most fortunate to have executive editor Janie Yoon agree to bring her incredible talents to the project. Janie's editorial skills and tireless efforts greatly elevated the work, for which I'm beyond grateful.

I'm so appreciative for all the support from Samantha Haywood and her team at Transatlantic Literary Agency.

My incredibly talented partner, Maureen Ennis, read every single word, line, and chapter after every draft written. Your constant support meant the world to me. You are the very best.

A heartfelt thank-you to my mother, Irene Chafe, and to all my family and friends, and to Fogo Island and my hometown of Petty Harbour for serving as inspiration for the setting of this story. Special mention to my grandfather, Pierce Chafe, who will forever hold a very special place in my memory and whose namesake lives on with my nephew.

ABOUT THE AUTHOR

© Maureen Ennis

PERRY CHAFE is a Canadian television writer, showrunner, producer, and songwriter. He is a cofounder and partner in Take the Shot Productions. Perry was the cocreator, showrunner, and head writer for the TV series *Republic of Doyle*, which ran for six seasons on the CBC, and an executive producer and writer for the Netflix/Discovery series *Frontier*, starring Jason Momoa. In addition, he was an executive producer and writer for *Caught*, a CBC limited series based on Lisa Moore's award-winning novel of the same name. He is currently a writer and producer on the hugely successful CBC series *Son of a Critch*. Born and raised in the small fishing community of Petty Harbour, Newfoundland, he now lives in St. John's, Newfoundland. *Closer by Sea* is his debut novel. Connect with him on Twitter and Instagram @PerryChafe and on Facebook @Perry.Chafe.

CLOSER BY SEA

PERRY CHAFE

Reading Group Guide

This reading group guide for Closer by Sea *includes an introduction and discussion questions sparked by this book. The suggested questions are intended to help your reading group find new and interesting angles and topics for your discussion. We hope that these ideas will enrich your conversation and increase your enjoyment of the book.*

INTRODUCTION

On a small, isolated island off the coast of Newfoundland in the nineties, a local girl goes missing. Twelve-year-old Pierce, who lost his father just three years prior, suspects a stranger to the island is involved in her disappearance. He and his friends are determined to find out more about the mysterious man, who is not what he seems. Part coming-of-age story, part literary mystery, and part suspense thriller, *Closer by Sea* is a page-turning and poignant novel about family, friendship, and community; about death, grief, and renewal; about the survival of an industry, a people, and a way of life.

TOPICS & QUESTIONS FOR DISCUSSION

1. The novel is set on Perigo Island, a small island off the coast of Newfoundland. How do the landscape and the surrounding Atlantic Ocean act not only as a setting and backdrop, but almost as characters in the novel? How does place and environment shape the community and the kids? How does it reflect their history and legacy?

2. Twelve-year-old Pierce is deeply marked by the loss of his father. How has his father shaped his character? What lessons does he recall his father imparting to him?

3. Pierce has spoken to Anna only three times, but she left an indelible mark on him. Why does Pierce feel so close to Anna?

4. Pierce, Bennie, and Thomas's friendship is one that is built on adventure, jocular rivalry, and close bonds. How does it strengthen when confronted by Ross and the Arseholes? How does it change with Emily becoming a part of the group?

5. What is the significance of the boat in the backyard? Why is it so important to Pierce to repair it when he is so afraid of the ocean?

6. What does the iceberg symbolize in the novel?

7. What kinds of lessons and values does Pierce's mother impart to him? How does she play a role in easing him out of childhood and into adulthood?

8. How does the collapse of the codfish industry affect the community? In addition to the economic threat, does it also threaten other aspects of people's lives?

9. Pierce, Bennie, Thomas, and Emily are children who are in some ways standing at the threshold of adulthood. In what ways do we see glimpses of their future selves? In what ways are their talents and strengths employed in the story?

10. Why does Solomon take the time to teach the children about ocean life? How does his message echo Pierce's father's talks with his son?

11. In many ways, the novel is a love song to a time, a place, and a way of life. What aspects of 1991 Perigo Island appealed to you? What aspects of the cod fishery appeal to you?

12. The novel is also about childhood friendship. How do these formative relationships not only affect one's childhood, but also carry reverberations into adulthood?